London Irish

London Irish

John Broderick

BARRIE & JENKINS
COMMUNICA · EUROPA

© John Broderick

First published in 1979 by
Barrie & Jenkins Ltd
24 Highbury Crescent London N5 1RX

ISBN 0 214 20649 1

Typeset by Thorneycroft Photosetters, Birmingham
Printed in Great Britain by litho at The Anchor Press Ltd
and bound by Wm Brendon & Son Ltd
both of Tiptree, Essex

To
Adam Lamb

Part One

I

Rosamund Emerson sat waiting for her cousin Michael in her usual place under the Harry Clarke window in Bewley's café. It was one of the busiest places in Dublin, and to secure her seat Rosamund always came early. She did not object to the wait. This was one of the few places in Grafton Street which had not changed since she was a girl, and she found the clatter of cutlery, the rattle of cups and the buzz of voices comforting rather than distracting. When she remembered to buy the morning paper she read it; and when she did not she enjoyed watching the faces around her. She had made many of her best sketches in Bewley's.

This morning she had neither a sketch-book nor a paper, and this she knew from experience always left her open to an approach by people whose faces she knew, but whose names she could not recall. One of them, a rather smart woman of sixty or thereabouts, had in fact pounced a few minutes after she sat down. She informed Rosamund that she knew her mother, remembered herself as a small girl, was now living in London and was so delighted to read of Rosamund's exhibition in the newspapers. All this was poured out with very few pauses for breath, and there was nothing for it but to smile and hope one was not looking as silly as one felt.

At last the woman picked up her bag and prepared to go.

'Have you heard from your uncle lately?' she enquired, peering at her docket with short-sighted eyes. 'My dear, the prices! As bad as London.'

'No. Yes,' murmured Rosamund vaguely. Would the blasted woman never go?

'I'm so glad he's getting married again, aren't you?' A pair of narrowed blue eyes glanced away from the bill and watched Rosamund closely, but the younger woman was listening with but half an ear. If her informant was expecting a reaction which indicated some dismay she was disappointed.

'Oh, yes, of course,' said Rosamund with an automatic smile. 'It was so nice seeing you again.' Michael had appeared in the doorway and had stopped when he saw the stranger at the table. He would go out again if the woman lingered.

'Lovely to see you too, dear. Perhaps we'll see you in London. For the wedding, you know.' And with a flashing crimson smile she went off.

'Who was Miss Thing, or was she Mrs?' said Michael, edging his way on to the banquette beside her.

'I haven't the faintest idea. She lives in London, she says. And do you know, Mike, she's just told me that Nunky is getting married again. I wasn't listening much by that time, but I'm perfectly sure she said that.'

Michael raised his thick black eyebrows and pursed his mouth for a silent whistle.

'Have you heard from him recently?' Rosamund went on looking at her cousin's cat-like profile: the low forehead, the broken nose, the tawny freckled skin. From long habit she had watched him as carefully as another woman might examine her own face for signs of age. He turned round and put out his tongue—something he often did when he caught her looking at him with her speculative artist's eye.

'No, not since Christmas. But that's only two months ago. Unless this has been very sudden he'd surely have known then.'

'Yes, but would he have told us?'

'No, perhaps not,' said Michael in his slow, deep voice.

The waitress came over to take their order. These two were among her favourite people. Miss Emerson with her beautiful ash-blonde hair, her fine skin and her friendly smile; Mr Pollard, so tall and broad-shouldered and masculine-looking, not like the long-

2

haired weirdies that passed for men nowadays. They chatted about the wet morning and how awful it was getting anywhere in this weather. They ordered coffee and buns.

'It's not much dearer than tea now,' said Rosamund. 'And besides, I'm an addict.'

'I hope you don't drink too much of it black, miss,' said the waitress. 'It's not good.'

She went away to get their order. Rosamund clasped her strong hands on the table and studied them for a moment. Then she turned to Michael.

'Well?'

'Well, you,' he replied, stroking his broken nose, smashed in an unexplained brawl in Paris many years before. 'How do we know if it's true?'

'We don't, of course, although it's hardly likely that the woman would make it up. Malice like that needs intimacy. But how do we find out?'

Michael thought for a moment, tapping the table with his fingertips. He had big red hands, remarkable in a man who had never really worked in his life.

'I suppose we could ring up the office and ask Billy. He'd be bound to know, and Nunky does most of his business from Queen's Gate nowadays, doesn't he?'

'Of course. I should have thought of that myself. But the news was so sudden I must have stopped thinking. We can ring from my place. Are you free this morning?' Michael sometimes gave the impression of a man with a great deal of business on his hands, and Rosamund was always careful to preserve appearances when she suggested that he use her telephone on one errand or another.

He nodded. The coffee came. They smiled, made another observation about the weather; and were ready to leave in ten minutes.

'You're in a terrible hurry this morning,' said the waitress, as she gave them their dockets. They always paid separately. 'Easier to keep acounts that way,' as Rosamund put it.

They sloshed across Grafton Street, made their way as quickly as they could into Dawson Street, and turned up into the Automobile

Club where Michael kept his battered little Ford. As they made their way through the steaming rain they were silent, Michael hunched over the wheel and Rosamund wiping the windscreen with a cloth. She lived in a pretty little mews cottage off Morehampton Road, and as they turned out of the hissing traffic into the quiet lane they both breathed sighs of relief.

'God, how I'd hate to have to drive,' exclaimed Rosamund. 'Cheaper than taxis.'

The mews had been purchased and decorated ten years before by an American woman novelist who had settled there on account of the tax-exemption laws for writers. But not even this considerable saving had reconciled her to the Dublin climate, and she had taken off for Ibiza, never to return. Rosamund had got the place on a long lease for a very reasonable rent.

Michael made himself a strong whiskey-and-soda, while Rosamund prepared some more coffee for herself. There was nothing about the living-room to indicate that a painter lived there. Rosamund was a tidy person who kept her work separate from her social life. She worked in a room upstairs, and no one, not even Michael, was invited to inspect it. Before he put through his call to London he paused for a moment under the picture that hung over the fireplace. Blue skies, an apple tree, and an old, red wall; two adolescents sitting on the coarse grass; one fair-haired, wearing a white dress protected from the grass by a rug, in the throes of puppy fat, with a red bow fastened to her breast; the other in flannels and shirt-sleeves rolled above his elbows, crouching over a book, his black curls glistening in the sun, his arms already covered with crisp black hairs.

The summer of 1960, when he had been eighteen and Rosamund a year younger, in the orchard of the house in Kildare which their uncle had taken for his ailing first wife. It all seemed centuries ago now, and it was incredible to him that Rosamund had painted it from old photographs and memory only a few years ago It always gave him a slight jolt when he looked at it. It was not in her usual style. 'My Academy picture,' she had said; and that was exactly what it was like: something out of an earlier, more direct and less

4

fragmented world. Perhaps that is how it had been at the beginning of their passionate friendship, which had waxed and waned but never entirely died out, so that now they were rather like a tolerant married couple, living their own lives, having their own affairs; coming together at moments of confusion and injury. But it had always seemed slightly obscene to Michael, to reconstruct so exact an image of something so fugitive, like a 'doctored', youthful portrait of an ageing woman.

'Oh God,' said Rosamund, coming back with the coffee. 'All right, I'll take it down, but memory is a good deal more precise than paint.' Useless to explain the artist's double vision.

Michael said nothing. He looked at the telephone, then paused before he dialled.

'Suppose it's true, what sort of woman do you think has hooked him?'

Rosamund bit her lower lip and considered.

'About forty-five, rather squat, with dyed black hair and a sharp eye. What had you in mind?'

'About twenty-two, blonde and lubricious.'

'Oh, go on and ring. You're letting your fancies take over.'

Rosamund poured out a scalding cup of black coffee which she drank without sugar. During Michael's conversation with Billy Boyd, who looked after the public side of her uncle's many property interests from a cluttered little office in Maiden Lane, she looked out at the tiny front yard, iron-grey in the rain. Billy was a man of few words. In less than a minute Michael put down the receiver.

'I win, although I'd prefer to have lost. She is in her twenties, blonde, pretty, and she's been his secretary for the past six months. She's also American.' Michael took up his glass and fortified himself.

'My God! An American!' Rosamund gasped with no exaggeration. 'I can just see the headlines in the papers here. "Self-made millionaire to marry blonde secretary." He must be mad.'

'That's a matter of opinion.' Michael sat down, and crossed his legs, encased in long black boots. 'If it does appear in the papers—which I doubt—he'd probably be more upset about the self-made

5

bit. You know how furious he was when he was called that after selling Fortfield'—they both instintively glanced up at the disputed painting—'when Aunt Ita died.'

'Yes, I know. He's so conscious of coming from a well-off family—not that there was all that in it. That's what I can't understand about this. He was always so respectable, and conservative and bourgeois, and now this—' Rosamund threw out her large ringless hands.

'At seventy-two men are apt to behave oddly, especially where pretty blonde secretaries are concerned.'

Rosamund took up her coffee cup again and glanced round the room. When she took the place over the walls had been bright orange, the sofa and chairs upholstered in black and white, and the carpet mauve. There was little she could do with the carpet except cover it with as many decent rugs as possible; and she had repainted the walls grey and covered the sofa with chintz. But there were other improvements she wanted to carry out; she had promised herself a summer in Greece; and there was a little Bourdelle, one of his good small canvases, on which she had paid a deposit out of her last Dublin exhibition to a gallery in Bond Street. She shook her head and left down her cup with an impatient hand. Coffee slopped on to the saucer and splashed her finger.

'And where does all this leave us?' she asked, fumbling in her pocket for a handkerchief. It was the question which had been in the forefront of their thoughts since they had first heard the news; but people rarely express these without some preliminaries.

'Out in the cold, I suppose.' Michael scratched his chin. 'It couldn't have come at a worse time—inflation, bank charges, every bloody thing.'

'Yes, I know.' Rosamund wondered how he was fixed; but Michael did not like to be asked questions. He had his own equivalent of her locked studio in his flat on the north side, into which she had never been invited. Once long ago they had broken down all barriers and found the wind icy; now they were content to be bound together by a couple of closed doors.

'Are you going to London for your exhibition?' he said.

'It's just opened, and there are no reviews yet. If it gets some good ones I had intended to go, yes. There's nothing more depressing than standing about in an unsuccessful showing. But it's a convenient excuse, although we'd go anyway, wouldn't we?' Rosamund never talked about her work; and her selection, with three other Irish artists, for a London exhibition, although important for her, did not tempt her to change her habit of reticence. Besides, she considered it unlucky to talk about it until she was sure of her reception.

'The boat, I suppose?'

'Of course. Plane fares are ridiculous now.' She stood up and looked out. 'You'll stay? I'll make omelettes for lunch. We'll light the fire and draw the curtains on that damned rain.' She went over and touched his hair lightly. 'A nice lazy day. And I've got a couple of steaks for dinner, and wine of course.'

He touched her hand, but with an enquiring look.

'Yes, I know. I'll take down the picture. It's really for the public anyway. A public who'll never see it.'

II

That afternoon the rain ceased in London, but the streets were still wet after the morning's downpour. Andrew Pollard stood at the office window of his house in Queen's Gate Terrace and watched the cars hiss past on their way to the Gloucester Road. The room behind him, large and high, had once been the front dining-room of a prosperous Victorian family. Now, with its off-white walls, yellow curtains, thick blue carpet, leather chairs and big bookcase filled with travel and biography, it had rather the air of the consulting-room of an austere and expensive psychiatrist.

He stood with his hands behind him, holding a newspaper which crackled from time to time as he crushed it between his fingers. He leaned forward as a small brown car turned into Gore Street opposite and parked at a convenient opening. He turned back, sat

7

down at his desk and put the newspaper in front of him. Then he clasped his large bony hands over it and waited, staring straight ahead with fixed, unblinking eyes, as if he were engaged in some sort of meditation.

A bang on the front door, a tattoo of heels on the marble tiles, a sharp knock, and a small, squat, bald man came bustling in, holding a brief-case in front of his groin like a sporran.

'I thought it better to take the car,' he began in his broad Ulster accent, 'since you wanted to see me in such a hurry.' Billy Boyd dumped down in a high-backed chair and put his case on his knees. Like all Ulstermen, he managed to insinuate a note of reproof into his voice whenever he felt called upon to account for his movements. Billy hated to have his routine upset; and this had happened too often recently for his peace of mind.

'Yes, of course,' said Pollard in his deep, slow voice. 'Much more convenient.'

'I wouldn't say that,' replied Billy, sighing deeply.

Pollard knew, and Billy knew that he knew, that the Underground from Covent Garden to Gloucester Road was a great deal quicker than driving a car across London; but a protest had been entered, and that satisfied Billy's conscience. Both of them also knew that he had brought his car because he intended going home to Putney after seeing his partner.

'Have you seen this?' Pollard took up the newspaper, a copy of an evening tabloid.

'Of course I have.' Billy tapped his brief-case impatiently. 'Is that what you wanted to see me about?' The reproving note was very strong now.

'Yes, it was.' Pollard opened the paper where he had folded it at the gossip column. Both of them knew the paragraph by heart. "Self-made Irish millionaire to marry blonde American secretary-socialite." 'Who told them?'

Six months, or even two months ago, Billy would have retorted sharply with a 'How should I know?'. But there was something in his employer's fixed stare, in his tense, still manner, which made the other pause. These two old men had been working together in close

8

co-operation for thirty years, and they knew each other's moods and reactions to the flicker of an eyelid, or a sudden change of mind. But recently Billy, who was an extremely sensitive and intuitive man behind his Northern bluster, had become aware of a change in his old associate. Their business dealings were no less confidential; in that field there were still no reserves; but for some time now there had been a nervous intensity, almost a hysterical note, in Pollard's manner which had alarmed Billy. As a bachelor he had little experience of the effect a sudden passion can have on an elderly man of fixed habits and convictions. The nearest he had come to dealing with such a crisis had been when his father had 'got religion' at the age of sixty, and joined a revivalist sect to the eternal shame of his solid Presbyterian family. He devoutly hoped that Andy Pollard was not going off his rocker.

'I don't know, Andy,' he replied in a conciliatory manner. 'Naturally, I didn't mention it.' The tone was aggrieved now. 'I suppose it's known in the organization—these things get out.'

'But somebody has to put them out.' Pollard's voice was softer, almost apologetic. Of course he knew that Billy would not deceive him; but he also sensed a reserve in him which usually meant that Billy disapproved of something, but did not consider it his business to comment. The last time Pollard had noticed it was two years before, when he had wanted to give a job to an ex-priest. Billy had said nothing; but his silence had been thunderous.

'Of course somebody put it out,' he was saying now in a clipped, hostile voice. 'But I don't know who it was. If I did I'd tell you.'

'Would you, Billy?' Pollard stood up and dropped the paper into a waste-basket. He turned away and looked out of the window. At another time such a question would have provoked an angry 'What the hell d'you mean by that?'; but now there was silence. If Pollard had turned round he would have seen Billy's face, always red and shining, turn several shades deeper, and his small, prim mouth tighten. In the silence that followed, Billy drummed on his brief-case with his short, stubby fingers, and Pollard listened to the passing cars again. Suddenly he turned back and gestured with his hands.

'I'm sorry, Billy. But you know how this publicity business gets under my skin. Have a jar.'

Billy grunted. Pollard went to a cabinet and took out a bottle of Billy's favourite Northern concoction, Bushmills. He collected glasses and a jug of water and poured out a generous libation. Billy took his glass without the usual gleam in his eye.

'How is Gertie?' said Pollard pleasantly.

'She's all right, thanks.'

'And the dogs?'

'The dogs are all right too, thanks.'

It would take a little more than that to thaw Billy out. Pollard knew that he had made a false move; the sort of remark that can endanger even the oldest trust. He was angry with himself, and longed for a gesture of reconciliation from his partner. But his instinct told him that he would have to wait.

As Billy sipped his whiskey, his face set in a frozen mask of grievance, but his thoughts were very different from his appearance. Such a thing to say to him after all these years. Thirty-one to be precise. He had just come out of the army, in his late twenties, and he was nearly sixty now, and had been a partner in the firm for five years. He was grateful to Pollard, but if this sort of thing went on he would settle his affairs and retire. They could always get a bright young man to look after the property; after all, it would come to that some day.

In the midst of these bitter reflections, he had a sudden vision of his father, standing on a soap-box in the lashing rain, shouting that the day of wrath was at hand in his old cracked voice. He blinked and shook his head to banish that black scene. Then he was struck by another thought. That young fellow who had telephoned from Dublin this morning. Andy had been very like him thirty years ago; the same height, the sense of latent physical power, the large straight nose which Michael had had before his injury, the same wide, piercing eyes. Andy was a well-preserved man for his age; his face was ruddy and unlined, and he walked with a firm step. But his eyes had changed. A curious, almost furtive expression now some-times narrowed them. Andy was old; and there were times when he must feel it in his bones. Perhaps that was the real explanation of all this foolishness. They were all getting old, he thought sadly; and no one to come after them.

Billy took a gulp of whiskey. He could not keep this up. It was too painful.

God damn and blast all Yanks; they caused trouble everywhere they went: no common sense. He should have fired the young slut after her first week in the office.

'Elizabeth had a litter the other day,' he mumbled in his glass.

'Isn't that the champion?' responded Pollard quickly. 'How many had she?'

'Four beauties, and by my own dog Quicksand. One of them is a certain champion, and the other three are booked by America. I was told to name my price with that breeding.' Billy gave a shy, embarrassed grin, and Pollard held up the bottle.

'We'll have to drink to that, Billy. Hold it out.'

They talked dogs for some time, always a soothing subject. Billy Boyd had two great recreations in life. Every July he packed his sash, brought his bowler hat out of mothballs, and took off for his native village, Broughshane, in County Antrim, to take part in the Orange procession. On this glorious occasion he regularly got roaring drunk. His other outside interest was breeding Yorkshire terriers. In his house in Putney he had over twenty exquisite little mites, line-bred by himself and shown for him by his sister Gertrude, a spinster who had dedicated her life to him and to the breed.

'And that reminds me, Andy, now before I forget it. Your nephew Michael rang me up from Dublin this morning. He wanted to know if the news was true.'

'And what did you tell him?' Pollard's voice tightened again.

'I told him the truth, Andy, as I usually do when I'm asked a straight question. After all, I wasn't told to deny it.'

'No, no, of course not.' Pollard looked down at his desk and shook his head. 'Well, well, news travels fast, doesn't it?'

'You carry a fair amount of weight, Andy. You can't have it both ways. And after all, he's your own flesh and blood. Why wouldn't he be interested?'

'Yes, yes, of course.' Pollard got up and walked across to the far wall where a framed map of the SW7 district hung. 'I thought Michael would take over from me at one time, as you know. You remember the two years he was with us how successful he was. And then he suddenly lost interest, and has never done a tap since. I suppose the trouble is having enough money of his own to live on.'

'You could have done the same when you came in for *your* uncle's property.' Andy turned his head and peered up at the map.

'Yes, the Cornwall Gardens houses.' Pollard tapped the glass of the map with his knuckle. 'My God, how long ago it all seems now—1931.' At another time, especially when stung by a report that he had started with nothing, Pollard would have recounted the story of how he had really started. His uncle had been a member of a stockbroker's firm and had over the years done well for himself in a modest way. Left a widower, and childless, he had invited his young nephew, then newly qualified as an architect, to come and set up in London. Two years afterwards the older Pollard died suddenly, leaving his fortune of twenty thousand pounds and three houses in Cornwall Gardens to Andrew. Then had followed the purchase of other houses, the borrowing and selling to acquire more; the snapping up of derelict warehouses during the war; the foundation of his own construction company; until, quietly and without even much speculation, he had become a considerable property-owner whose estate appreciated in value with every passing year. He had sold the construction company a few years ago; but Billy still managed the property from the old office in Maiden Lane.

At that moment both of them were thinking of those houses, now set in flats, and of one of them in particular. A shadow still lay between them. Billy, fortified by whiskey, was the first to make the attempt to banish it.

'How is—' he began. Since Nancy Cook had been taken from his office in Maiden Lane by Pollard and appointed his private secretary, Billy had not been quite able to call her either by her Christian name or by her surname.

'Nancy?' Pollard came back to his desk and took up his glass. 'She's taken the afternoon off. She wants to settle things in her flat

12

and do some shopping.'

'Aye,' said Billy, glancing towards the window in the general direction of the young lady's activities. When she came to him Nancy had been sharing a flat with a girl-friend in Earl's Court. Pollard had given her one of the Cornwall Gardens flats which had become vacant at the time.

'I suppose I ought to ring Michael up, or rather Rosamund since he hasn't a phone. Yes, I'll do that. I suppose they've had expectations, what, Billy?' Pollard chuckled, and Billy looked down at his boots.

'I wouldn't know,' he muttered, swirling whiskey in his glass.

'Naturally they had. And of course to listen to them talking you'd think they were starving. In fact Rosamund does very well with her daubs, apart from the nice legacy she inherited from her father. And Michael owns six houses in Dun Laoghaire. If I had them they'd be twenty-four by now, at least.'

'Aye.' Billy did not doubt this for one moment.

'Instead of which he just lives on the rents, and does sweet damn all.'

'Aye.'

'I could never make out what Rosamund thinks of him. I hear he leads his own life, very much so. Still, they're always together.'

'Aye.'

'Oh, well, they'll just have to get used to the idea of not getting everything. It might do them good.'

'Aye.'

'Well, I won't keep you from the pups any longer, Billy.'

'Good,' said Billy standing up and giving the impression that he had just lost a valuable afternoon. Pollard watched him march out, stiff-legged and bristling, and smiled wryly as he took up the telephone and put a call through to Dublin.

III

Two days afterwards Rosamund and Michael made their way up

the Gloucester Road from the Tube station. London roared past them and frowned down from the façades of huge and ugly mansion flats. The weather had turned dry, and as usual the city was warmer than Dublin. Both of them loved London for much the same reasons: its anonymity, its careless and infinite variety, its indifferent tolerance, the illusion it gave of still being the centre of the world.

They had got into Euston that morning exhausted after the usual horrors of the journey; but a few hours wandering about the familiar squares and streets behind the British Museum had restored them. Breakfast in a small and sordid hotel near the station was an old adventure provided one was not hungry: they sat in the gloomy lounge and read the papers. The morning ended, as it always did, with a fairly expensive lunch in a small Italian restaurant near Covent Garden. After a bracing bottle of Chianti and a couple of brandies they took the Underground, timing their arrival carefully for well past lunch-hour.

As they came to the row of shops at the junction of the terrace and Victoria Grove, Rosamund stopped and pointed to the Boot's near the corner.

'I suppose we ought to buy her some sort of a present, don't you?' she said in an uncertain voice. They were both beginning to feel a little nervous as the moment of meeting approached.

'No, I don't,' said Michael firmly. 'We've never met her. I think it would be an odd thing to do.'

'I suppose I should have brought something more presentable with me.' She looked down at her old camel-hair coat and her dusty jeans. Both of them travelled light, bringing only night things with them on the principle that London was a better place for picking up new skirts and blouses, pants and shirts.

'You look perfectly all right, Rosie. What's the matter? I've never seen you so nervous before.'

'I think I am. After all, it is rather a false situation, isn't it? Everybody knows that this isn't a casual visit. We've come to size up, and they'll be doing the same.'

Waiting to cross the street, Rosamund looked up at the massive columned length of the terrace. The bone-white of the façades had darkened with the rain. Here and there in this area the skyline often reflected a Venetian fantasy of embossed pillars and porticoes. She had often sketched those quiet corners and imperial bulges in the past: now she had an idea which made her linger, looking round at the familiar sight.

'Yes, I know what I'll do,' she said to herself. 'I'll paint the walls of all this to represent bone. That's it. These Victorian houses are down to bone everywhere.'

She had missed the crossing, and Michael was waiting for her on the other side.

'I'm sorry,' she said, as she joined him. 'I had an idea.'

'I wish I had,' he said absently.

Yet in spite of her nervousness Rosamund carried the meeting splendidly. Their uncle opened the door himself, and seemed pleased to be kissed heartily on both cheeks by his niece.

'Travelling light, as usual,' he said affably as he shook hands with Michael. 'It's the best way. Come on down.'

As they passed the room behind his office they could hear the sound of a typewriter. She's going to make an entry, thought Rosamund. Well, that will be instructive. Nunky looks older somehow, and slightly feverish. That kind of excitement always looks like an illness at his age.

Pollard lived in the basement, having fixed up a flat there for himself after his wife died. With the exception of three bedrooms on the first floor, all the rest of the enormous house was let out. Pollard liked the thought of everything he had, including his own quarters, paying its way.

Downstairs he had a living-room, a bedroom, a kitchenette and a dining-room—not much used either, since he ate out most days. It was dark and cosy and very quiet in the basement, and Rosamund and Michael had always liked it. The sitting-room was a jumble of furniture, some of it good, and on fine days had a cool, sequestered air from the light in the area. Today the two standard lamps glowed warmly under the low ceiling. Nothing had been changed, Rosamund noticed with approval. Somehow she expected this family upheaval to reflect itself in the furniture.

'I suppose you'll have coffee, Rosie? Will you have a brandy with it, Mike?' Uncle Andrew lifted a bottle. But before they could reply there was a sound of quick footsteps on the stairs, and they all instinctively paused and looked towards the door.

The young woman who stood there did not at first sight appear very different from hundreds of her kind to be seen in the streets. She was dressed in the uniform of the day, tight, worn-looking jeans and a yellow sweater. She had pale blonde hair, large brown eyes, a slightly upturned nose and waxen skin. She looked at Pollard and smiled, and immediately her naïve, almost girlish expression changed. That glowing, faintly pouting face was not made for laughter: it narrowed her eyes and exposed the insides of her lips, giving her a faintly negroid expression.

'Come in, my dear,' said Pollard, holding out his hand. She walked to his side with a quick, lithe step and linked her arm in his. She looked up into his face, and then turned to the visitors. The corners of her mouth quivered slightly, and her eyes flickered with amusement. She looked charming.

She said, 'I'm happy to know you,' to Rosamund, and 'hullo' to Michael, looking into their eyes with a straight, rather blank stare; then took a glass from the tray and held it up to Pollard like a child asking for more.

'I've typed twelve thousand words since lunch and I need something.' Pollard turned to the cabinet and got out a bottle of Martini. Nancy turned and looked directly at Rosamund. 'A long report from one of the architects that has to be copied.' She spoke with an American accent in a small, clear voice. 'Oh, thank you.' She held up the glass which Pollard had given her. 'Well, good luck, cheers, mud in your eyes, bottoms up and everything.'

She sat down on an embroidered stool in front of the fireplace and began to talk quite naturally and with apparent candour. She thought it was wonderful to live in Ireland; she had heard about it all her life. No, she had no Irish blood, she must be one of the few Americans who had not. Her ancestors had been German and English. Her father had been an executive of Gulf Oil, and she had

16

spent most of her childhood with her grandmother in Michigan; summers in France, and boarding-school later in Switzerland. And wasn't Yeats wonderful? She didn't pretend to have read Joyce, but she just adored Wilde.

She looked up at Pollard, who had been following this recital with the half-amused regard of a parent showing off a clever child, and held out her hand to him. He took it lightly and dropped it again with a little embarrassed giggle which Rosamund found curiously touching, but which made Michael look down into his glass with studied attention. It also occurred to her that neither her uncle nor Nancy had heard of her exhibition in London; and somehow she found this comforting. To have come for that reason would have been a little too pat.

'Did you read about us in the paper? Andy was furious. I know he thinks I'm responsible.' Nancy stirred her Martini, and grinned.

'I didn't say that,' protested Pollard, getting red.

'You didn't have to, darling. I know your tiny mind.'

'Was it in the papers over here?' said Rosamund with genuine astonishment. 'We didn't see it.'

'Yes,' went on Nancy playfully. 'The *Evening Standard*.' She raised one shoulder and put on a bored, pouting face, a sudden and quite funny transformation. 'I was described as a socialite.'

'And are you?' said Rosamund.

'Of course not. In school in Switzerland there was an English girl whose father is an earl. She brought me to a few parties when I came to London, and we got photographed with gilded young men.'

Rosamund smiled and Michael sipped his brandy. Pollard studied his clasped hands.

'You're both only children, aren't you?' said Nancy, suddenly serious again.

'Why, yes,' said Rosamund, looking round at Michael. He was still nursing his glass, remote and silent in his seat a little apart from the rest.

'Naturally, I've been wondering what you'd be like. When I heard you were an artist I was all excited. I knew artists in Paris,

17

and do you know what one of them said to me? He said all artists are only children.' She leaned forward and looked at Rosamund earnestly.

'I can see what he meant, yes, it's good. But Michael isn't an artist, and he's always been more of an only child than me.'

Michael grinned and looked up to find Nancy regarding him with a sort of playful intensity. His grin widened as he stared back at her for a moment before raising his glass and finishing it. He did not reply; and aware that he was expected to say or do something, stood up and gestured towards his uncle, who looked slightly ill at ease.

'I'd better check in at the hotel. It's getting on. Is Rosie staying here?' This had always been their practice in their uncle's house. Michael put up at one of the small hotels around the corner in Queen's Gate. It was as if he had deliberately refrained from joining in the polite conversation in order to give special effect to this sudden pounce. Pollard looked fussed, cleared his throat and prepared to speak; but Rosamund got in before him.

'Oh, don't bother about me,' she said quickly. Obviously the girl was living here. 'At this time of year one can get in anywhere.'

For a moment there was a silence, one of those moments in which beams of communication shorten or lengthen. Pollard and Nancy looked at Michael, and Rosamund followed their glance. In the low room he seemed to be looming over all of them, tall, massive and dominant. The older man and the girl sitting on a pouffe at his feet were suddenly reduced in stature; she with her small American hands and feet was a diminutive figure, while Pollard, whose fine physical presence enhanced by years of effortless authority, had always made him formidable, seemed to shrink. Yet it was he who recovered first, falling back on his duty as a host.

'Don't you want to stay here, Rosie?' he asked quietly.

'Of course I do,' she gushed, embarrassed by her own misreading of the situation. 'But I thought you might have let out the spare rooms.'

'Not at all.' Pollard stood up abruptly. The delicate balance of invisible weights and measures which calculates the effect of every human encounter had been upset, and he sensed that it was not in his favour. For a moment the two men looked at each other with naked

18

antagonism, but it was a mere flash which Rosamund in her slightly flustered state did not recognize. 'Your room is ready for you.'

'Yes, and I helped the cleaning woman get it ready this morning,' put in Nancy with her sudden ageing smile.

'That's perfect. And I'm dying for a bath.'

'Of course,' went on Nancy making for the door. 'And I hope you two aren't going out for dinner. I'm fixing it here this evening specially for you. You've simply got to come.'

'We will,' said Rosamund, looking back at Michael. He nodded and put down his empty glass with an air of finality. There was going to be no little chat with Uncle Andrew.

IV

'Well, what do you think, Mike?'

They were sitting in the lounge of Michael's hotel, a dim, rather dingy place where breakfasts were served in the morning. It smelled slightly of cold fat, the aftermath of years of fried bacon. The chairs were covered with worn red repp, and the wall behind some of them was stained by the imprint of oily heads. Rosamund and Michael had cornered the only sofa in the room, and sat facing an official photograph of the Queen, whose mouth was smiling, but whose eyes were not. A family of Spaniards cackled in a corner.

Rosamund had rested for a short while after her bath, and then hurried round to the hotel to have a chat with Michael before dinner. He too had bathed and shaved, and put on a clean shirt.

'What was going on before you left?' he asked in reply.

'She was typing. I went in and said we'd be round about eight. Nunky was with her, holding a sheaf of letters and looking very business-like. By the way, she told me she has a flat in one of the Cornwall Gardens houses, so I very nearly put my foot in it.'

'You mean I did. I got the impression that you weren't going to be asked to stay.'

'So did I. He seemed quite put out when you asked. I thought that was odd.'

'Perhaps it suggests some other arrangement with her,' said Michael thoughtfully. 'I rather think it does.'

'Did he say anything to you after she and I went upstairs?'

An old-fashioned clock in the hall chimed six ponderously, and Michael cocked his head to listen.

'Nothing much. Just a few questions about Dublin, then I came round here to register. Did she say anything?'

'Just hostess talk. But I must say, I don't think she throws her weight around.'

'No. She doesn't have to. Of course, I didn't expect him to drool. He's behaving quite well in the circumstances. By the way, did she give any indication of what religion she might have, if any?' Michael looked down at his tight jeans. He did not seem to notice that the muscles of his thighs were flexing and unflexing, a nervous habit he had when uneasy.

'No, but I doubt if she's a Catholic. Does it matter?'

'It would, I think, ultimately with Nunky. You remember how he was always asking us if we went to Mass and so on.'

'Oh, yes, it was an awful bore. Do you think he might make things more difficult for himself?' Rosamund looked across the lounge to find one of the Spaniards staring at her with an expression of admiration and invitation in his lustrous eyes. She gave him a friendly smile to put him off, which it did.

'I think so. After all, Aunt Ita was a kind of a lay nun, and he was devoted to her. This is one of those elderly infatuations. They want something younger and warmer. Which would be all right if our friend Nancy was a different sort of person.' Michael ran a finger round the collar of his shirt. It was a little too tight for him, and made the veins in his powerful neck swell.

'You mean a little older and more staid?'

'Well, yes.' Michael twisted his neck and puffed out his thick lower lip. 'You see, I'm pretty certain that she's experienced—men, I mean—and I doubt very much if she confines herself to him.'

'Oh, I don't know,' said Rosamund thoughtfully. She found herself inclined to like Nancy. 'She may be quite attached to him. There are girls who prefer old men, and of course his money is an attraction.'

Michael was looking at a youngish woman who came downstairs with her room-key in her hand. She was pretty and carried herself well. Upstairs he had passed her on the corridor and she had returned his searching glance. Long experience had given him almost second sight in these matters.

'Yes, of course there's the money,' he went on as the woman passed out into the street. 'That's certainly a powerful factor. But she may also admire him—a sense of power, you know. And he's still a handsome man. All the same, I have a hunch she's deceiving him.' He pulled at his lip, making a tiny slapping sound.

'And if she is?'

'I don't think he'd take quite as liberal a view on that as we would.' He looked at her with a sort of challenge in his eyes. Rosamund, who had her own sensitivities, felt a slight chill, half excitement, half fear. The meeting at her uncle's had passed off very well, all things considered; they had all behaved well; but she was aware of many things having gone unexpressed, perhaps not even consciously formulated, but still there, deep and instinctive.

'No, of course not.' In most situations Rosamund felt herself to be quite intuitively detached, and therefore unscathed. But in this situation Michael had unexpectedly taken over, even giving notice of having done so. Many people, she knew, regarded him as rather a weak character, because of the apparently aimless life he led. Rosamund thought otherwise. From the very beginning he had resisted everything that might interfere with his passionate desire for privacy; the simple if dangerous privilege of staying unattached in his own room. He rarely allowed himself to become entangled with the ordinary ropes of everyday sailing, cast as they were from a raft that was so often adrift, and aimed at a bollard, a spike, a hand that sometimes were not there.

'Well,' he said, waving a finger at a sad elderly waiter, 'I expect we'll know a little more after dinner. Watch her hands, they are revealing. Let's have a drink before we go back, shall we?'

V

'Well, what do you think, Nancy?'

Nancy pushed back her typewriter and blew out her cheeks as she looked up at Pollard. He was leaning against the desk with his arms crossed, a grave expression on his face. It was a look she was familiar with, and it conveyed an unexpressed need for reassurance.

'She's very elegant, very chic, isn't she?' Her voice was a little lower now, more definite, the American intonation less evident.

'Elegant, chic—Rosie?' Pollard was genuinely surprised. 'In that rig-out?'

'The same as mine, honey, and she wears it much better. She's got that long, supple kind of figure that can wear anything and look good. It's partly the way she carries herself.' Nancy's restless little hands, plump and dimpled and curiously spatulate, formed a figure in the air. 'I've seen it in Paris, women with a blouse and skirt and white gloves who made everyone else look like ten cents. I like her. I think she's honest.'

'I hope so.' Pollard looked up at a painting on the wall behind Nancy's desk, a powerfully dark and menacing portrait of a man leaning forward in the act of lifting a newly born and dead lamb. His hands were bloody, damp hair stuck to his forehead, and perspiration was running down his cheeks. He was a youngish, heavily built man, and under his clinging shirt the muscles rippled in his shoulders. But it was the expression on his face which gave the picture its frightening quality: a mixture of anger, defiance and greed. He had lost something which he could ill afford.

'That's by her,' he went on, pointing to the painting.

'Is it? I never knew. I always thought it was an odd picture for an office, a bit unsettling, but fortunately I always have my back to it. Are all her pictures like that?'

'A good many of them. She does other things now, but she used to be best known for that kind of thing, portraits of dock-labourers and so on, that type. I think she picks them up and does sketches for them. Anyhow, that's what's said in Dublin.' Pollard chuckled to himself.

'Gee, Andy, that's kind of hard to believe. I mean, she looks so refined and everything. I'd expect her to do sort of willowy things like trees and flowers and sunsets. I mean, that's brutal, when you really look at it.'

'Well, painters and artists are odd people, they're rarely what they seem.'

'And what does Michael think of all this?' Nancy went on, pushing back a stray lock of hair which had fallen over her ear. 'I'd say they were pretty close. Of course he's kind of brutal himself. Maybe that's it.' Her voice trailed off, as if she felt she was making a slightly improper suggestion.

'Well, I thought for years that they were going to get married, but they never have. Pity in a way, since they seem to suit each other so well, but I don't suppose they're the marrying kind. What did you think of Michael?' Pollard's voice was light and so casual that Nancy looked up at him. He was still staring at the painting.

'He's the quiet type, it's hard to say. I thought both of them were very nice.' It was a flat statement, and because of that rang true.

'Yes, they are, but don't make any mistake about it, they're here to see how the land lies.' He reached out and tapped her gently under the chin. Nancy stared back at him for a moment before she took his hand and pressed it.

'They must be disappointed,' she said steadily. 'I think you ought to settle something on them, something substantial. They're your own.'

'Do you, Nancy? I'm glad you said that. I think you're right.' He was pleased. They both felt a sense of relief.

'Oh, it's only fair after all. I like them, and I'd hate to think I was the cause of any family trouble.' She patted his hand and drew a deep breath. 'And now this baby is going to have her bath. Everyone seems to be having one except me, that's how hard I work. I won't be long.' She reached up and kissed his chin before running out of the room.

Pollard looked up at the painting again, took up a pen which he had left on the desk, made a few notes on a piece of spare paper, then followed her slowly downstairs. She had already undressed when he got to his bedroom. Her jeans and scanty underwear were thrown on a chair; her shoes and tights on the floor. Next door in the bathroom he could hear her singing tunelessly over the running surge of water.

He sat down on the bed and leaned forward with his hands between his knees. He felt light-hearted and more than usually lucid. Everything had gone off well. He was pleased that Rosamund and Michael had behaved themselves. Everything was going to be all right. Then another less pleasing reflection flashed through his mind. They had said that they had not read the paper in Dublin. He hoped so. When something is set down in print it takes on an added force. His age coupled with hers made him look ridiculous; a silly old fool. He felt anger mounting in him like bile from the stomach. He squeezed his hands between his knees, trying by physical pressure to avoid a development of this galling topic. After a short while, the singing in the bathroom ceased in the sound of splashing water. It diverted his thoughts. Nancy is right; she seems to read my mind. A settlement will not injure her, and will make all the difference to them. But he decided not to tell them yet. It would seem like an insult. Nancy was so sensible. That's what people did not understand about her. She was a real help to him. He calmed down as he went on to consider all the occasions in which her good sense had surprised him.

He got up and went into the other room to pour himself out a finger of brandy. He looked round the room with its tranquil Paul Henry landscapes, and Frank Eggington water-colours of blue Irish mountains and cosy white cottages nestling against them like puppies against their dam. A canvas by Rosamund would have a distinctly upsetting effect here.

When he went back to his room Nancy was coming out of the bath, looking like an urchin in his towel-robe. The sleeves hung down a foot over her hands, and she was clutching a side of it to allow her to walk. The room was filled with the heavy scent of bath essence.

'Oh, this robe,' said Nancy in a little-girl voice. 'I feel like somebody caught under a tent. Come along, Andy, rub me down.' She held out her arms on either side with the sleeves falling over them and turned her back to him. Pollard began to dab the towelling over her shoulders and under her arms. She wriggled under his hands, as slippery as a fish and smelling like a flower. It was a sensation which never failed to excite him. Nancy made a mewing sound like a cat in great contentment. She leaned back against him for a moment, and his fingers tightened over her waist.

Suddenly with a fast, agile flip of her body she slipped out of the robe, leaving Pollard with the dizzy impression of clawing at empty air. The robe fell from his hands and crumpled around his feet on the carpet. Nancy was lying face down on the bed with her head buried in her folded arms; her body was as slight and pink as a child's. Pollard sat down beside her and slowly with care and deliberation began to stroke her thighs, still damp in patches and warm as sun-drenched marble. Her buttocks were small, and quivered beneath his fingers. She sighed deeply and lifted her body under his smoothing hands. He massaged her shoulders gently, and teased the back of her neck between his fingers and thumbs.

'Yes, yes,' she murmured in a stifled voice. 'Oh, it's so good.'

The damp patches on her soft, girlish skin dried out under the feverish pressure of his exploring hands. He was like a blind man touching the contours of a face, moulding it into an image for himself, communicating with his nerves. It was the closest intimacy that Pollard had ever experienced with another being; an intimacy to which Nancy responded with an abandonment that sometimes frightened him. But it always remained a dazzlement to him, imparting an intoxicating sense of power.

Again with a speed and suppleness that always took him by surprise she disengaged herself, reared up before him with a coiling twist of her body and lay back upon the pillow facing him. Her eyes were closed, her thin arms thrown out, the fingers fluttering and coiling like antennae. Gently, as if touching something infinitely delicate, he placed his large, dry hands on her small, cold breasts, feeling them warm and stir under his palms. This was the moment of their greatest communication. A shivering sense of involvement tingled through his arms, firing his old body and giving him the illusion of a total commitment of forces. He was intoxicated.

Nancy stirred and moved her body like someone following the rhythm of a dream, and her voice when she spoke had the drugged note of a medium.

'There. There.' She raised her hands, plump, rosy and avid, and placed them over his, coiling her fingers about his thumbs and guiding them in a slow, gentle exploration of her bud-like nipples; murmuring an incantation.

'Don't stop, don't stop, don't stop.' Her voice was weak and breathless; she lay torpid and trance-like under his touch.

But the pink-tipped hands rose languidly again and fastened themselves about his neck. Gently she drew him down until his mouth closed over the rosy tip of her breast. Pollard allowed himself to drift, conscious of his power to please and pleasure. The blonde arching body swayed under a babbing white head and thin brown hands speckled with liver-spots, the grave-marks of the ancients.

Suddenly, like a snuffed flame, desire died in Pollard. It was a condition of his years, if he had but realized it; since he did not, it made him angry: the abrupt irrational petulance of the aged. He tasted with the soft bud in his mouth something slimy, oyster-sharp and redolent of brackish moss. It filled him with nausea, and his stomach heaved as if he were about to vomit. He pulled himself back roughly from his lickerish feast and rose unsteadily to his feet. For a moment the room swayed and blurred about him. It was an entirely physical reaction, the result of over-excitement; but neither then nor afterwards did he admit this to himself.

'Oh, God,' he moaned, sinking into a chair, and covering his face with his hands. 'Oh, God.'

Nancy's eyes opened as swiftly and mechanically as a doll's and she sat up, smooth and gleaming like an oiled spring.

'I'm sick, sick,' Pollard muttered to himself: an old man in a dim seat accusing himself of sin outside a confessional box. In moments of acute physical sensation the flesh sometimes recalls the echoing silence of the infinite. But Pollard, at odds with his birthright, out of tune with an invisible harmony, could only appeal to the god that was nearest his heart.

'They're all the same, all the same,' he went on swaying from side to side in an agony of abasement. 'The same, the same.'

Nancy sprung from the bed, picked up the bath-robe and slid into it. She knelt down by his side, but did not attempt to touch him.

'Andy, are you ill?' she pleaded softly. 'Can I get you anything!'

'Go away, you're just like the rest of them. They came here to see if their money was safe, and you made a good bargain. Jesus Christ, curse the lot of you.'

Nancy got to her feet and picked up her clothes. In two minutes she was dressed. She went to the door and was closing it behind her when he dragged his hands from his face and looked after her.

'Where are you going?' he demanded in a hoarse voice.

'I'm going home. And not only to Cornwall Gardens, where it would appear I'm kept by you. I'm going home to my Pappy. He won't allow me to be spat on like this.' Her voice was cold and perfectly steady. She might have been a woman giving notice to a landlord.

'Come back,' he croaked, pushing himself to his feet from the arms of his chair. He was deathly pale, and his eyes were yellowish and frightened. 'You can't leave me like this.'

Nancy did not hesitate. She could have prolonged the argument, invested herself with a palpable wrong, made him beg like a chastened dog; but that was not her way. She was not a fighting woman.

'The next time you have a liver attack coming on, tell me,' she said; and after a pause he looked at her with a wintry smile.

'Yes, yes,' he mumbled, 'it was that, wasn't it?' His voice was slightly blurred, and he sat back heavily in his chair, clutching the arms so tightly that the veins swelled in his mottled hands. Nancy was about to say something soothing, and go to his side, when she stopped and clasped her own hands together. For a few moments they both stared at each other wordlessly, marooned in their own thoughts.

Nancy was suddenly transported in time and place, and found

27

herself staring at another old man rigidly gripping his chair. Her father after his first stroke, seated in his dressing-gown before the bedroom fire. She had come back unexpectedly to the rented house in Mougins tired but excited, pleased with herself after a pleasant day's shopping in Nice. Clearly he was waiting for someone else, and was unable to readjust to her sudden appearance. His eyes were bloodshot, staring piteously, wild. He looked insane: a ghastly caricature of the not ignoble wreck he had become since his stroke. A dribble of saliva ran down his unshaven chin. He began to whimper, making animal sounds like a dummy. She had turned and fled, running down the dappled stairs out into the sunlight. It had taken her an hour to pull herself together over a couple of cognacs in the café opposite; from where she had seen the expected visitor call and come away again: the retired British army officer who lived in a room at the back of Cannes and placed her father's bets for him. It was her first direct contact with an obsession.

She shook her head and pulled herself back to the present. Pollard was now looking at her with a little more expression in his glassy eyes.

'Don't look at me like that,' he said petulantly. 'It's bad enough to have to live with my conscience. I'm being punished for my sins.'

'Oh, if that's all it is,' she said lightly, glad of something harmless and neutral as a topic to relieve the tension. Besides, Pollard's senile anger seemed less harrowing than the memories he had just evoked.

'Is that all?' he repeated in a grumbling tone, looking down at his knotted hands. They were like parchment spotted with damp. 'You're a complete pagan.'

'Sure,' she, said brightly, smoothing her hair with cool, plump fingers. 'Sure I am. And that reminds me, are we going ahead with this dinner party?'

He looked up, alert at the prospect of a commitment: an old dog listening to distant guns.

'Of course we are. We don't want to disappoint them, do we?'

'Suit yourself.' Then she reconsidered, frowning and nibbling her lower lip. 'No, of course, you're right. Besides, I'm looking forward to it. They intrigue me.'

'Hhmm,' he snorted, now almost completely recovered as his mind moved into an area in which he felt assured of himself. 'You say that about everyone.'

Making conversation, making conversation, she thought, glancing about the room, checking the slightly rumpled bed-clothes, the bath-robe she had thrown on a chair as she dressed. She picked it up, threw it over her arm, left it down again, straightened the bed, then picked up the robe again and went into the bathroom.

When she came back he had gone out, and she felt suddenly tired and dispirited. It was not the first time he had rebuked himself for his sinfulness; a term she took to mean a sense of waning vitality. She had always been gentle with him, comforting him with her quick, spontaneous sympathy. But this scene had been different. She supposed that the arrival of his relatives had affected him. Other people, her father used to say, make our lives for us. She had a vague sense of something ended, something begun. But this was no time to get morbid. She went out in search of a drink before tackling the dinner.

VI

Rosamund sat down on the piano stool in front of the dressing table and began to polish her nails. She had bathed and dressed and was wondering what she ought to do about breakfast. No mention of it had been made last night when they broke up after dinner, and she had not been able to have a word with Michael.

She sighed, put down the polisher—a singularly useless possession in her case, since her nails were cut like a man's, and were often stained and ragged. She used it mostly to pass the time.

She got up and pulled back the blue velvet curtains. It had rained again during the night, and motor tyres still hissed over the wide black road below. The long line of columns supporting the porches of the houses opposite were now the colour of sour milk. She narrowed her eyes, and they wavered and grew blurred, like a building collapsing in slow motion in a film. So much for representational art, she thought wryly as she turned back into the room. It was one-half of the big first-floor drawing-room, and she wondered, not for the first time, why Aunt Ita had bothered to make so many bedrooms and furnish them. Perhaps even then, when there was no talk of flats, Pollard had encouraged his wife to buy as an investment.

Massive brass bed, green carpet, thick oak chairs that must once have stood in a corridor, mahogany wardrobe and dressing table bought at a hotel auction; reproductions of Paul Henry, and a Murillo Virgin and Child over the mantelpiece. Yet Rosamund had an affection for the room, as she had for every place where she had stayed for more than a few days. This succession of rooms, their furnishing so often deplorable; streets, gardens, mountains, lakes and roadways which form the undusted bric-à-brac of most people's lives, were to her the jumbled colours on a palette out of which she fashioned a design.

Someone knocked at the door, and Rosamund hurried to open it. Nancy stood outside holding a tray. A delicious smell of coffee drifted into the room.

'Oh, but this is too much, Nancy. I can't have you carrying up trays for me.'

'Oh, it's only for the first morning. I thought you might like to sleep on. I've taken a risk, boiling an egg. Perhaps you like it hard-boiled. Toast, honey, brown bread, pepper, salt.' Nancy put down the tray on a table at the end of the bed and counted everything carefully, like a young housewife on her first morning after the honeymoon. 'I don't think I've forgotten anything.' She looked round with a pleased smile.

'You're an angel.' Rosamund pulled over a chair, sat down and held her hands outspread over the tray. 'And I hate hard-boiled eggs.'

'Do you mind if I smoke?' Nancy curled up on the end of the bed and took a packet of cigarettes from the breast pocket of her shirt-blouse, a gesture that reminded Rosamund of an American serviceman.

'I always have one myself with the last cup of coffee. Mmm, heavenly brown bread.' Rosamund sniffed it and wrinkled her nose with pleasure. Nancy put back her lighter in the pocket of her jeans and inhaled deeply.

'Do you mind being watched while you eat?' she said, resting an elbow on the rail of the bed and supporting her chin in her hand.

'Of course not.'

'I guess you know the run of the house. Andy has his breakfast at eight, collects the post if it's in, and is in the office well before nine. I usually make another cup of coffee for myself when I come in, often it's the first if I'm rushed, which is mostly. So if you get down about nine we can get together over a cuppa. I suppose you think I'm a gold-digger.' This was said in exactly the same flat tone as the information which preceded it, and for a moment Rosamund did not take it in.

'I, ah—' she mumbled with her mouth full of brown bread.

'You missed a beat there,' said Nancy with a little gurgle of laughter. Rosamund swallowed hard and sipped some coffee.

'Is that what you say?' she remarked presently, looking up at the girl with a smile. 'No, of course I don't.' She cut a slice of toast and added, 'Well, are you?'

Nancy took the cigarette from her mouth and leaned her two arms on the rail, resting her head on her wrist like a child peering over a gate-post. She waited until Rosamund was well into her breakfast before replying.

'I suppose I am in a way. I mean to say, I don't think I'd marry Andy if he was living on the old-age pension. But then, he wouldn't be the Andy I know, would he?'

'It's a neat definition, my dear,' was all that Rosamund could think of in reply. She felt that this conversation, if it had to take place at all, should happen by tacit arrangement in a public place over cocktails. Two women in a hotel lounge huddled under the potted palms; leaning over garden walls in the afternoon; grouped around a well, or kneeling over the washing by a river-bank; in a gaggle at street corners, their fingers crooked over their mouths;

31

facing each other over a motionless body which they had just laid out on a death bed; with heads together in a sudden bright flash of a passing train: the secret understanding of women; the universal conspiracy of those who bleed. Rosamund saw these images in her mind's eye as she paused to butter another slice of toast. She had a feeling that she was being subtly suborned.

'Yes,' said Nancy, feeling in her pocket, and bringing out a small cardboard disc. 'It's something to think about, isn't it?' She pressed a finger in the middle of the disc, which assumed the shape of a cone.

'What's that?' said Rosamund, glad of a distraction.

'Portable ashtray.' Nancy stubbed out her cigarette half-smoked in demonstration. 'I guess it's the Yank in me. I love things like that. I tackled Andy about you and Michael. Said he should settle something on you both. He agreed.' She crumpled the paper tray in her fist, and held it up with a little, terrier-like shake.

'That was very kind of you,' said Rosamund stiffly, wiping her fingers with a paper napkin. 'But was it necessary?'

'I thought so,' went on Nancy calmly. 'Money is always useful. And if Andy hadn't met me, I suppose you'd get most of his property. And this must have come as a surprise.'

'What makes you think we're interested?' Rosamund was annoyed and confused by this sudden pounce. She took the lid off the coffee-pot and sniffed. As she knew, it was real coffee, freshly ground, as it had been last night. It reminded her of Bewley's; sitting in her usual seat against the wall, watching the door for Michael to appear.

'Maybe you're not. All the same I think I should get some credit for it.' Nancy's face was sullen, the pout of a disappointed child.

'Oh, you mustn't think that. It was very good, and thoughtful of you.' Rosamund was recovering; falling back on serviceable politeness; adapting herself to the other's methods. It was rather like listening to a stranger in a train recounting some intimate family affair.

'My father wouldn't like it at all, if he heard about it,' Nancy went on, sitting up straight and folding her hands over her stomach.

'He always used to say: "Winner takes all". That's what comes of gambling too much.'

'Tell me about your father,' said Rosamund, sensing that sudden changes of direction were habitual to Nancy.

'Oh, he's an invalid now,' said Nancy, after a pause during which Rosamund wondered if she had said the right thing. Nancy, she was beginning to sense, had her own social manner; only the tempo was different. 'He had a stroke two years ago while we were in Cannes. When he came out of hospital we took a small house in a village in the hills behind—Mougins. I stayed with him until he was able to walk again. Then I came back here and got a job with Andy's man in Maiden Lane.' She took out her cigarettes and offered them, staring over Rosamund's head as if she were looking into another life.

'No, thanks. I'll stick to my own.'

'Of course, he has a good pension. The Company are very OK about that. Still, he must miss things, travelling and all that. He's only fifty-six. My Mom's dead.' She flicked her lighter, and the tiny sound seemed to bring her back to actuality in a curious, almost robot-like way. She grinned; an engaging grimace which did not disclose her teeth. Rosamund thought: she knows about her wizened smile; she must have developed this in front of a glass. 'Pop was that sort of a man. We kids adored him, he didn't seem to really care about wives. Mom was killed in a plane crash. But they were divorced long before that.' She looked at her watch, and pointed her forefinger at Rosamund. 'Now, tell me all about yourself. Maybe I sprung this money business too quick at you. I'm like that, you know. I guess we'll come back to it some other time, when you know me better.'

Rosamund got up to look for her own cigarettes. She scrabbled in her bag, and then remembered that she had left a packet on the night-table. She lit up carefully and blew smoke in the direction of the window through which a faint beam of sun was wavering. A man in a white shirt was polishing a window in one of the houses across the road. A second face, pale, long-haired, ambiguous, appeared over his shoulder for a moment; then disappeared.

33

'Well,' said Rosamund slowly, 'I think I always wanted to paint.' But someone knocked at the door, and with a sense of relief she called out, 'Come in.'

'I missed you downstairs,' said Michael, standing in the open doorway and looking at Nancy. 'I didn't want to disturb Nunky, so I came up.'

'We were having a heart-to-heart,' said Nancy, sliding off the bed, and crossing to the fireplace, where she put her cigarette, still alight, on a white delf ashtray. 'But I'd better go back and get something done, or I'll be sacked.' She picked up the breakfast tray, and stood in front of Michael, her face on a level with his chest. 'Are you going to be in to lunch?'

'No, I don't think so. Are you Rosie?'

'No, I don't think so either. You mustn't fuss over us, Nancy.'

'No fuss, it's a pleasure. Just let me know if you want some more coffee before you go out. I drink it all day long.' She went out; and they stood still, looking after her, and listening to the clink of china as she went downstairs. Then Michael closed the door quietly, and Rosamund sat down on a chair by the window.

'What did she want?' It was characteristic of Michael to assume that such an early-morning visit had some purpose behind it. He stood in front of the fireplace, looking slightly grey as he often did in the morning. He had cut himself shaving, and a scrap of newspaper covered the wound on his chin.

'She brought up breakfast, which was nice of her. She told me she had been talking to Nunky about us, told him he ought to settle something on us before he married.' She looked out through the window: the faint sunlight was strenthening, and she could feel it warming her shoulder. She stroked her arm, gently nursing the sun.

'Oh, I see. Was it a deal?'

'I don't know. Perhaps. It's difficult to tell with her.'

'Well, it would be. All the same, I imagine she'd like to see things settled. I thought she was uneasy last night. Oh, very bright and hospitable and all that, but uneasy. And that was a very odd speech Nunky made about religion. Not very tactful if she's non-Catholic.' He tapped the scrap of paper gently with his little finger.

'No, I suppose not. Quite an assault on the liberals. But he was always like that. It's all very odd.' Across the room she could smell the faint tang of Lifebuoy soap with which he always washed. It reminded her of other mornings.

'Yes, odd. I wonder if he suspects that she's deceiving him.'

'You said that before. Have you discovered anything?'

'No, just a feeling I have about her. I caught her watching me while he was going on about Lefèvre. A sidelong look. It may mean nothing, of course, yet she is watchful.'

'Well, she would be with us. That would be natural enough. Perhaps she fancies you.' Rosamund was smiling. It was so like Michael to assume that every woman was on the make. Nancy did not look an innocent to her; but that was irrelevant. There was something else about her which Rosamund had not quite resolved: a kind of childish greed; an impatient grasping of the moment; an inability to defer any pleasure for the sake of a greater reward. It was evident in the way she grasped at the fruit at dinner with her plump little fingers, and swallowed her food almost without tasting it. Perhaps her sudden announcement of financial arrangements for the visitors was shrewder than it appeared; but Rosamund did not think so. However, she was prepared to wait. She looked out. The man in the window was sucking a knuckle.

Michael had turned round, and taken the ashtray off the mantel. He looked at it with a slightly disgusted expression. Nancy's cigarette had burned down almost to the tip. He threw it into the fireplace without putting it out.

'She doesn't seem to think of the price of cigarettes much,' he remarked.

But Rosamund's attention was divided. His appearance in her room had unsettled her. Nancy could wait. Other London mornings mingled with and blurred this one. Their first visit together. In those days they had stayed in Brown's Hotel, in adjoining rooms. Long, narrow, twisting corridors, low ceilings, bright coal fires in the lounge. From her window a glimpse of Albemarle Street: tweed jackets and military trousers in Gieves across the road; Michael sitting on her bed reading the morning papers. She turned back from the window as she had turned back then; but now he was frowning; looking at her with impatience.

He was well aware of these elegiac moods of hers. At the moment he was in no temper for a game of 'do you remember?'. The past was coiled about them: shafts of sunlight illuminating a dusty road through a line of darkening trees; the sort of memories that a middle-aged married couple, no longer physically involved, might share. But at the moment there was work to be done.

'What are you doing this morning?' he went on briskly.

'Looking around, shopping. I must get a few new things. And I want to make sketches of Victoria Grove.'

'I want to go up-town. No lunch, just a snack. Shall we meet for dinner? I suppose we'll have to bring Nancy out some evening. But in the meantime, no deals. I may be all wrong, of course, and if everything fails, we may have to think about her offer.'

What a cold, calculating bastard he was, thought Rosamund, getting up and looking round for her purse.

'Where shall we meet?'

'In the York Minster. If I'm not there at half-eight, it means I'm on to something.'

'Nancy made off with my tray, I wasn't finished.'

'So I noticed' he said, as he went out.

VII

Billy Boyd stood at the window of his office and looked down at the street. It was a habit he had when he wanted time to think. He was famous for his Ulster poker face which never in any circumstances betrayed anything. Only Billy himself—and occasionally his sister—knew of the difficulty he had at times in controlling a nervous system which was all the more troublesome for being buried deep below his granite-like exterior. And at the moment he had to take a decision which involved the last thirty years of his working life.

An old woman, poorly dressed and clutching an empty shopping bag, came slowly up out of the Roman Catholic church down the street. She paused for a moment, looked around vaguely, then turned and limped towards the Strand. A tall Negro in well-cut English tweeds was looking into the window of the publishers opposite. He turned away and padded on, graceful, loose-limbed, arrogant. At the church entrance he stopped, kicked a finely shod toe against his heel; then took off his hat and went in. Billy turned round.

Michael was sitting in one of the two circular café chairs which were kept in the office for visitors. He was sitting up straight, his hands on his knees, his boots planted firmly on the dusty brown carpet, as if he were holding himself ready for a quick departure.

Billy sat down heavily in his chair behind the wide leather-topped desk he used for interviews. Most of his real work was done at a roll-top bureau wedged between a line of green filing cabinets at the back of the small, flaking room.

The two men glanced at each other for a moment without expression. It was not necessary. Both knew what was in the other's mind. It was a situation Billy had often found himself in with sub-contractors, suppliers, trade-union officials and workers; on occasion also with other employers. It was a game with very high stakes, and the players were all experts. But there had been nothing personal involved. Now there was.

'I really don't know,' said Billy quietly, picking up a letter-opener—a gift from the Isle of Man—and tapping the leather of the desk gently. 'There is of course the pub across the road.' He glanced at the window and back again to the inkstand on the desk.

'Yes, of course,' said Michael patiently. He had already been in the Peacock before coming on to see Billy; and the bartender had no recollection, no recollection at all, of anybody answering Michael's description of Nancy.

'I sometimes go across there myself,' went on Billy carelessly, 'usually for a beer in the summer.'

They had chatted amiably of this and that since Michael put in an appearance twenty minutes before, having come straight to

Maiden Lane after leaving Rosamund. Eventually he had remarked that he had been more surprised than he could express at the news of his uncle's engagement; and Billy had replied that yes, it had been a surprise.

'Do you like her, Billy?' he had asked suddenly, with a frank smile.

'Not much,' replied Billy bluntly. An expert at sticking to the truth while giving nothing away, he could afford to admit that. 'She was good enough at her work. Quite competent. But she had an unsettling effect on the others. Griffin was always standing over her desk, and Miss Brooke was put off her stroke.' He smiled faintly, and rubbed a finger over his mouth as if to erase it.

Michael thought of Miss Brooke, soft-faced, white-haired and smiling in the outer office for over twenty years; deceptively fluttery: a paragon of efficiency and loyalty. And Mr Griffin—did he have a Christian name, Michael wondered?—fiftyish, sapless, with a nervous tic in his cheek; genteel, soft-spoken; rather like a perpetual curate; but a compulsive worker; hardly raising his head when anyone came into the office. When Mr Griffin took to lingering over a young lady's desk, no wonder that routine was upset. Michael had noticed, coming in, that the new typist was thin and lank-haired and sported a moustache. She was not likely to take anyone's mind off their work.

'Yes, I can well imagine that Miss Brooke did not approve. Curious thing about Nancy—we had dinner with her last night—she doesn't appear to have any friends.' It was then that he asked the question which prompted Billy to go over to the window. 'I've often wondered about Miss Brooke and old Griffin. Is there any pub that they drop into for a drink on the way home?' It seemed a simple enquiry; the sort of remark anyone might make in connection with two such pillars of rectitude. But Billy, experienced in such apparently aimless queries, on which the fate of an important deal might depend, sensed that Michael's question was rather more loaded than was apparent. At the window, looking down at the old woman with the limp and the elegant African, he thought he understood what lay behind it. Nancy had not mentioned friends. What more likely than a friendly get-together of the office staff at a pub which they were accustomed to frequent on their way home? Griffin would have been more than eager to buy a drink for the attractive young American; and Miss Brooke, Michael had heard his uncle say, was not averse to a glass of sherry from time to time. In the early days, before Pollard had indicated his interest, before Griffin had taken to lingering at Nancy's desk, such a little party was more probable than otherwise. It was also possible, if less probable, that Nancy, if she had a friend, might have let it be known that the pub was a good place to meet her after the office closed. Friends of young, unattached girls often met them in this way, especially on the friends' day off.

It was a long shot; but Billy recognized it for what it was. It was the ability to pounce on such seemingly harmless remarks, often casually thrown out during a session of hard bargaining, that had made him a rich man in his own right; and transformed his partner into a millionaire.

'I never keep drink in the office,' Billy went on, holding the paper-opener between two outstretched fingers. During his pause by the window he had carefully analysed and thought out the implications of Michael's question; but he had not yet decided to act.

'Some people, I know, have an idea that the best way to do business is over a working lunch, or with a round of drinks in a pub. Well, it isn't.' He looked at Michael searchingly for a moment. The man might be wasting his life in Billy's estimation; but he was no fool. And after all, if what he suspected was true, perhaps he ought to be given a chance to prove it.

'No, of course not,' agreed Michael. 'I've heard Nunky say the same thing.'

They talked of business methods in England, and Ireland; the inflationary spiral in house prices; the downward trend in bank rates; the remarkable success in business of the Irish community in London. The way led gradually back to Pollard and his standing in the community.

'I wonder what they think about this Nancy business,' said Michael. 'Especially as she isn't a Catholic. Or is she?' It was strange that she had mentioned no religious connection; but that did not mean there was none. Michael felt suddenly uneasy. Perhaps she was, after all. In which case the Irish community would close ranks; the priests would see to that: marriage was sacred.

'No,' said Billy, shaking his head. 'She's not. But then neither am I, and it has never done me any harm with Andy. Money has no religion.'

They both laughed; but Michael was sure that Billy understood exactly what was behind that question also. He knew immediately he had mentioned the pub that Billy recognized the query for what it was. Yet he had not dismissed him. Michael was well aware that his father's partner was not a man to waste time in polite chit-chat, even with Pollard's nephew. He waited, finding that he was rather enjoying this subtle and hard-headed game.

'Yes,' Billy was saying, 'your uncle is well liked by the Irish here—in so far as anyone who has made a success of his life ever is with them. He has helped a lot of them with jobs, and money. Some were worth it, others not.' He paused and glanced at the window. 'Talking about pubs, there's one at the back of Wellington Barracks—have you seen the new barracks in Knightsbridge?—well, there's a fellow called Daly, from Andy's own part of the country. Came over here as a labourer, hardly able to write his name. Andy gave him a job on a site in Islington. Ended up as foreman, never drank, married a girl from his own place with a farm, and ten years ago he was able to buy a pub just off Petty France, in Palmer Street. It's become a great meeting-place for the Irish, the sensible ones. Fellows with tweed caps, and they have more money in the bank than I have. Och aye. Friday is their great night there, and Sunday. You see, it's not far from their cathedral. And the strange thing is that when the soldiers were in Wellington Barracks, not one of them came into Daly's, they had another pub round the corner. Aye. But what I really wanted to tell you is that Larry Daly sends me a case of Bushmills every Christmas, and a case of champagne to Andy. Decent fellow, Daly.'

Michael listened attentively with a polite smile. He wondered if Billy would have more to say about the Irish in London; but he had not. He inquired after Rosamund; spoke of his dogs; mentioned with pride a nephew in Antrim who had just qualified as a doctor; and having exhausted all possible topics between them, indicated by an upward inflexion of the voice and a pause that the interview was at an end.

As he came away Michael wondered, not for the first time, at the man's incredible alertness; the extraordinary finesse with which he gave information which might or might not be important; the way in which he had avoided involving himself. Perhaps it was because of the subtlety and agility of mind which they applied to their business undertakings that successful men so often made a mess of their private lives. Billy had avoided even this snare by having no private life at all.

VIII

'Why don't you do a drawing of Nancy?' Michael asked that evening during their dinner at Bianchi's. Rosamund had as usual been looking round at the other diners in the small inner room with its plain furnishing and sometimes exotic clientele. She had just remarked on the expression of a young girl sitting at a table by the window with a young man of striking and etiolated beauty. 'Too like an inferior El Greco, not really interesting after a first glance. But she's very like Nancy, don't you think? I suppose there's an American type.'

'And yet everybody's different,' Michael said. 'Why don't you do a drawing of Nancy?'

'It is a good idea, and yes, I'd like to draw Nancy. I'll ask her tomorrow. She has a very mobile face, and then there's that ageing smile.' Rosamund nursed her brandy and glanced again at the girl by the window. She was laughing now, and her expression was quite different from Nancy's; this girl was young, and when she smiled she looked younger still.

41

After dinner they walked down Shaftesbury Avenue to the Tube; Rosamund taking Michael's arm as they strolled through the slow, watchful crowd in Piccadilly. It had been a pleasant evening. He had turned up earlier than she expected at the York Minster and the dinner at Bianchi's had been more than usually good. Or was it that she had been in better form, falling in with Michael's mood? There were times when she deliberately took him at face value rather than spoil the moment. When he was in good humour he was a delightful companion; recapturing all the indolent charm of his youth: a great big purring cat warming himself at the fire of life. It might have been their first visit to London; in some ways it was even better; they knew each other more intimately now; the old longing had abated, even if in her case it still flared up inconveniently from time to time; but not on a comfortable, relaxed evening like this. She looked at the passing faces: curious, blank, hungry, searching—a multitude aimlessly drifting in search of nothing really important—and found none of them to compare with him. It was after all not a small thing to have him still by her side, amiable, thoughtful, surely fond, and attached in a way he would never now be with another: that at least she was sure of. She pressed his arm and laughed with pure pleasure when he returned the pressure, looking round at her with a grin and a wink. It was an old joke, but a shared one.

She mentioned the drawing to Nancy next afternoon. Pollard had gone out to an Irish funeral; Michael had gone 'up-town' again; and the two women found themselves alone.

'Oh, I'd love it,' exclaimed Nancy, clapping her hands in excitement. 'I've always wanted someone to do it, although I'm sure the result will be just terrifying. Could you do me two—one telling the real truth, and the other a nice chocolate-boxy thing that I can send to Pop? You know, he had quite a collection of modern paintings, but none of the artists ever volunteered to do me. It's real nice of you, Rosamund.'

She was curled up on the sofa in the living-room, and with one of the standard lamps behind her she looked very young and vulnerable. In the short time that she had known her Rosamund had come to the conclusion that in spite of a native shrewdness, which made her wary of giving much information about herself, the impression she gave of being somewhat less than calculating was not very far from the truth. Probably the spontaneity and artlessness that she displayed in day-to-day matters did not extend to the secret places within her; but it was not assumed.

'Right,' said Rosamund. 'I'll just go up for my sketching block. Be back in a minute.' She put down the cup of tea which she had been sharing with Nancy after they had both agreed to have a lazy afternoon sitting around. 'What's the good of marrying the boss if you can't take a few hours off?' Nancy had declared when she called Rosamund down from her room where she had been arranging her drawings of the Regency houses in Victoria Grove. It was raining, and there was no prospect of working outside that afternoon.

Left alone, Nancy sprang from the sofa, snatched up her bag and went over to the big mirror over the fireplace. She frowned at her reflection; then smiled broadly, frowned again and shook her head. She twisted her face into various clownish masks, and finally stuck out her tongue at herself, before hurrying from the room. A few minutes later she was back with the light lipstick she wore gone, and her face freshly scrubbed, her pale, smooth skin glowing from contact with a rough towel. She pinched her cheeks, pursed up her lips and arranged herself carefully on the sofa, lying full length with one dimpled hand hanging over the edge of the arm.

Rosamund laughed as she came back with the tools of her trade.

'Do you want me to draw you as a sort of pop Madame Récamier?'

'It mightn't be such a bad idea. Perhaps I'll open a salon when I'm a married lady.' Nancy raised her head, stretched her neck and struck an attitude. 'Have you been to Nancy Pollard's afternoon, darling? It's such fun, really amusing people, and she's so witty, I wish I could think of half the things she said. I mean, you just haven't lived, if you haven't been.'

'Yes,' laughed Rosamund, switching on the centre light, and

walking back and forward in front of Nancy, head cocked, eyes narrowed. 'But somehow I don't think Nunky would take to that, do you?'

'No, he wouldn't.' Nancy heaved a theatrical sigh. 'I'm terribly frustrated. I know I was born to be a nursemaid of genius, and I'm going mad with all my talents wasted. Do you want me to talk while you're at it?'

'Not too much. I'll tell you when to shut up if I'm working on an expression.'

'Well then, you say something. I'll burst if I have to lie here while you're plumbing my soul. Oh, and that reminds me, I want to ask you a few things about religion. I'm an awful pagan, but when I hear Andy talking, like he did the other night . . .' Nancy sat up, abandoning her pose; with a concentrated frown, she looked absurdly young. 'I mean, it's all so profound and everything. I feel like a savage sometimes.'

'Stay like that,' Rosamund commanded, sitting down and flicking her sketch-book open. She was a fast worker; and although she had done few portraits, the human face fascinated her; there were nearly always people in her canvases, amalgams of various expressions she had caught in hotel lounges, bars, trains, beaches and outside old cottages in the Irish countryside; an eye, a nose, a mouth, an ear: she would spend days arranging them, forming a sort of chemical combination. Everybody was different; but in a strange way one person was also everyone.

That afternoon she drew Nancy in more than a dozen expressions, ranging from tiny thumb-nail sketches to full-page outlines, leaving the details to be filled in later from other sketches. As she worked she felt herself curiously excited, and increasingly baffled. The faces she had studied and learned to love hitherto had mostly been those of peasants and working men and women in the city. They had all revealed, as she drew and erased and drew again, getting nearer and nearer to the bone, a sort of common humanity; an indication of primitive depths; an infinitely complex design of tissue and sinews shielding something implacable and inexplicable: rather like a darkened tunnel carved with ancient and unyielding images, leading to a great shadowy gate, locked and inaccessible.

But as she drew on she became aware of a certain numbness in her fingers, as if her body sensed that below the planes and shadows and smooth surfaces of Nancy's face there was a bone structure that supported the youthful flesh, and yielded nothing more. Rosamund felt slightly shocked; yet intrigued. Could it be that lying below the commonplace disposition of supporting frames she would, if she burrowed deep enough with her pencil and her imagination, come upon a place that was empty and wind-blown; a sanctuary long ago despoiled of its ancient altar and treasury? She would have been less surprised, and a great deal less baffled if her pencil had told her that her subject was cool, calculating and full of hidden menace.

'Break-time,' said Nancy, springing up, as Rosamund leaned back and closed her eyes for a moment. 'I'm going to have a drink, aren't you?' She wagged a finger and grinned. 'And I'm not even going to take the littlest peek at the drawings until you're finished. Or are you? Even if you are we'll still take a break. I need something to fix me up before I look at them. Gee, it's awful being a great beauty, always worried in case your public will spot a flaw.'

'No, I'm not quite finished yet,' said Rosamund, feeling refreshed after a sip of Martini.

'Boy, I must be interesting.' Nancy curled up with her drink and wriggled her shoulders cosily. Above the tang of the cocktail Rosamund could detect a slight odour of sweat mingled with the verbena which Nancy used as scent. Then as her concentration relaxed Rosamund found that she herself was sweating; and she looked around, moving uneasily in her chair. The low-ceilinged room was still with heat; the radiators were turned up full; and it was not difficult to imagine the lamps and pictures slightly blurred as in a miasma of drifting summer air; cigarette smoke coiled heavily around them under the low ceiling.

'You are,' said Rosamund with a rueful smile.

'So are you. You know, I've been meaning to ask you, but some-how I didn't seem to have the courage. I mean about your people. You're obviously Andy's sister's child, and Michael must be his brother's, but what was the family like? I love hearing the lowdown about families.'

'Hasn't Nunky told you?'

'Not really.' Nancy pouted over her glass. 'He talks about this uncle who did so well in London, and sometimes he mentions friends and relations in Ireland. But he's never really told me anything.'

Rosamund was afterwards to wonder if there was anything significant in her uncle's silence; but at the moment she was relieved to lapse into family lore. She was aware of a certain tension; and thought perhaps she had read too much into her own drawings.

'Well,' she began, settling herself comfortably, 'we all come from peasant stock. My grandfather was born on a small farm in Roscommon. He got a job in a pub in Roscommon town, married the daughter of another shopkeeper and set up in a pub of his own—there's always room for one more in Ireland. His brother went in for the Church, got himself educated, but left before ordination, came to London and ended up on the Stock Exchange. Grandfather had four children; one went as a nun to Australia and died out there. The old man was determined to give them a good education, so Michael's father qualified as a solicitor, married the daughter of another lawyer, and died at the age of forty. His wife lived only about eight years after him. She had some money of her own, and she trailed round France and Italy with Michael, got diptheria in San Remo, and died there. A curious thing happened. There was no one there except Mike, who was only sixteen; and in the confusion they buried her out there in San Remo. The family were furious, of course—Irish people lay great store by burying the dead with their own, as if it mattered—but Mike very properly refused to have her dug up. Awful, wasn't it?'

She looked thoughtfully at her glass, and Nancy got up and replenished their drinks. Then she sat down, leaned her elbow on her knee and went on listening intently.

'My mother got a job in the Bank of Ireland, and married my father. His family had a hardware shop in Dun Laoghaire, and he was in it. He died when I was seventeen, and my mother was killed in a motor accident a year afterwards—'

'Just like mine,' exclaimed Nancy. 'Isn't it funny? Accidents run

46

in families.'

'Yes. So I went to the School of Art in Dublin, and here I am.' Rosamund looked down at the sketches she had made, and knew they were unsatisfactory; but they were all good likenesses; and that would no doubt please Nancy.

'I think that's all terribly interesting. Families fascinate me. I love novels about them. Go on, I'm riveted.' She paused and looked at Rosamund with round, inquisitive eyes, like a child about to ask for a sweet. 'How did you meet Michael?'

'Oh, that.' Rosamund smiled, and stared across the room. 'We were both orphaned about the same time. I had an aunt in Dublin and so had he. Then Uncle Andy took a house in Ireland, and we spent a lot of time there.'

'So you've been together all that time,' breathed Nancy incredulously. It was not very tactful; but it showed a considerable understanding of the situation. People always instinctively talked of Rosamund and her cousin as a couple.

'Yes, all that time.' Rosamund lingered on the words, finding pleasure in them, as if she were sipping a rare wine. 'We're almost like an old married couple now.'

'Why didn't you . . . get married, I mean?'

'Well, neither of us really wanted to.' Rosamund sounded very definite; all the more so since it was not true. But she had over the years fashioned a careful and well-constructed past for herself in relation to Michael; as women so often do with men they love, and have not succeeded in holding in the way they would wish. Conversations like this were very agreeable. She looked at Nancy with soft, slightly condescending approbation; an older woman, secure in her love; wise, slightly sentimental, a little maternal. The fact that this was a pose that she had perfected over the years did not in the least spoil the pleasure she took in her part. It is a part that women play more often than they are prepared to admit.

'You see,' she went on earnestly, 'we both value our freedom. I mean, there's not much point in fooling one another. We've never tried to do that. And it's worked out. For us.' She raised her hands and shrugged. There was enough truth in it to make it convincing even to herself.

'I think you're very wise,' said Nancy slowly. 'I'm sure a lot of women must envy you. I mean, Michael's so good-looking and everything.' She frowned into her glass, and was silent for a moment. Then she raised her head and shook it slowly. 'But Andy wouldn't approve.'

'I'm sure he wouldn't, dear.' Rosamund sounded slightly smug: a married woman counselling an erring one. There were times when she felt like that also. 'Now, shall I do a bit more scribbling?'

'Yes, of course. But—' Nancy bit her lip, and looked from under her lashes. 'I'm dying to know, and I've never dared ask anyone. But somehow I feel I can say it to you. What kind was Andy's first wife? Sort of perfect, I guess?'

'Well, yes, in a way. I don't think she was exactly enthusiastic about certain intimate aspects of marriage. But she was what is known as a good woman. And so she was, according to her own lights. Very kind, very patient, very generous, and of course deeply religious. I always said she should have been a nun.'

'Yeah,' said Nancy, twisting up the corner of her mouth ruefully. 'That's what I figured. He must think me an awful savage, especially about religion. I know it's terribly important to him.'

'Perhaps he likes you the way you are.' Rosamund was anxious to get away from this subject.

'You could be right. All the same ... Oh, well, I must tell you about my folks some time. Weird, some of them were.'

Rosamund left down her glass and took up her pencil. Nancy tilted her face towards the light and struck a pose. The artist worked on, dully aware that there was something slightly false about this sitting.

IX

As he passed the back railings of Wellington Barracks Michael remembered walking this way before during his rambles round London. Then there had been the homely smell of horse manure from the regimental stables, transforming Petty France into a main street in a country town. Now the horses were gone. All the Queen's horses and all the Queen's men, he hummed to himself as he turned into Palmer Street.

It had been easy to pick up two of Rosamund's drawings. It had not been a satisfactory sitting, and she had left the disregarded sketches lying on a table in her room, and he had nipped up, while the two women were drinking coffee in the basement room. He had selected a full-face and a three-quarter from the heap of drawings. Rosamund would not miss them; she rarely bothered about preliminary work. They all seemed very good likenesses to him; and Nancy had been delighted with the completed sketches which had been given to her. Her pleasure had been as eager and unselfconscious as a child's; and there were moments when Michael had half hoped that his mission might be unsuccessful. Yet he had a strong feeling that it would not.

As he turned into Daly's he was thinking that it was lucky that Rosamund had an exhibition in London; and the first reviews had been very favourable. There was a possibility that the paintings might be brought on tour with the work of half a dozen other artists. It meant that both of them had a reasonable excuse for staying on in Queen's Gate. Pollard had no great interest in art; but he appreciated a success. And Nancy had taken to Rosamund with what seemed genuine enthusiasm. Michael felt quite pleased with himself.

There was nothing to indicate anything specifically Irish about Larry Daly's house; but Michael had barely time to record a fleeting impression of red-papered walls and prints of 'Spy' cartoons on the walls when he felt that sense of being watched, sized up and priced, which he had always experienced on entering a pub in Dublin, and even more down the country.

The barman, a tall, lanky fellow with a long, pale, clerical face and a mop of black curly hair, gave him a quick, piercing look and then nodded amiably. There were two customers at the counter,

49

both unmistakably Irish. They turned back to their drinks as Michael came up to the bar.

'Long over here?' said the barman in a light, husky voice as he put down Michael's glass of Powers.

'Since Monday.' He dug some coins out of his pocket. Irish silver was always a problem in London.

'Yes, it's all right,' said the barman, looking at it. 'The bank takes it. It's the same metal. Thanks a lot.'

Eight men were sitting in twos and threes at the tables. They were all middle-aged, soberly dressed in dark suits, and white or striped shirts. They were speaking in low voices; and it seemed to Michael that they became lower still. They were all certainly Irish; but the atmosphere was very different from any of the Dublin pubs which Michael frequented; more like one of the business places in the City. Gradually, as he sipped his drink and kept his eyes guarded, he began to understand what may—for he was by no means sure yet—have been behind Billy's casual reference to Daly's.

He had once found himself taking shelter from the rain in a pub off Kingsway. He had struck up a conversation with a friendly Australian; and as time went on he began to realize that most of the other customers were Australian also. As a friendly alien his acquaintance had given him a few useful tips. London had a series of unofficial parliaments: Jews in Willesden and Stepney; Italians in Islington; Greeks in Camden Town; Africans in Notting Hill; Scots off Knightsbridge.

'And the Irish?' Michael had asked.

'They're the biggest group of all. Camden Town, of course, Hammersmith, Kilburn, Finsbury Park and I've heard there are a few places near the centre, but they're very close about it, like the Jews.'

Michael gathered that these meeting-places—mostly pubs—were used by elders of the various communities to keep in touch with matters which might affect the well-being of their co-religionists or fellow-countrymen. In the case of the Australians in Kingsway it was mostly a social club where they could talk about themselves; but the Irish elders were reputed to have considerable influence socially and politically. It was from such gathering places that the word had been passed to the IRA that their London bombing campaign had no support from the Irish community. Jobs were discussed, and suitable people told of them; scandals were hushed up; and decisions taken as to who should be supported in County Council and general elections. Newcomers to the scene were put in touch with addresses of employers and landladies who might be useful to them; and those who got into trouble were spirited back home, if they applied for help before the police got on to them. Above all, they were centres of information. As in the home country, everybody knew everybody else. If a friendly journalist wanted to know who had attacked an Irish labourer in a dark alley off Aldgate, he knew where to apply. And of course the doings of famous compatriots were closely followed. A celebrated novelist had taken a new mistress; a popular television personality was rapidly becoming an alcoholic; a great actor was no longer able to memorize his lines; a chain of suburban restaurants was being taken over by Irish interests. If they had no serious business to discuss the elders could always enjoy a good gossip, just like the old men sitting on a stone wall in Connemara comparing the generations.

Michael sat down on a stool, and wondered what he was going to do next. None of the men beside him had given him a second glance; and the barman had moved to the end of the counter, where he was reading an evening paper. He was just about to order a second drink when a man came through a door at the side, raised the counter-flap and came behind the bar.

'Good evening, men.' He spoke in an unmistakable Irish mid-western accent, hardly touched by an English intonation.

'Good evening, Larry,' the men at the counter responded; while the customers behind raised their hands in salute.

'Good evening, sir.'

'Good evening.' Michael found himself looking at a tall grey-haired man of distinguished appearance; large straight nose, a fine forehead, short upper lip and a well-shaped mouth. The eyes were grey and friendly. 'You never lost the blas.'

'I hope not,' smiled Daly, leaning his elbows on the counter and clasping his hands; they were large and strong, but well-shaped and well-manicured. Larry Daly was not the first Irish labourer to bear himself with formidable dignity. Billy had said that the habitués of Daly's were apt to wear tweed caps; but he must have been indulging in a rare outburst of Orange partisanship. Perhaps they were in evidence in the public bar; here in the saloon a cap would have seemed as out of place as a bikini in church. Michael could see Larry Daly in a well-tailored blue-striped suit, setting off for Mass in the cathedral.

'Not far from Roscommon, I'd say, Mr Daly.'

'No, indeed. A place called Fuerty, near Frenchpark, if you've ever heard of it.' Daly was smiling, sure of himself. An Irishman gives his home address only when he is seen to be a success.

'I know it well. My family came from a few miles nearer Roscommon.' Michael smiled, not without some stirring of emotion. The soft accent, the evocative names, the memory of green fields flowing into low purple hills; the gentle recollections of holidays with a grandmother in childhood. That more than anything else was what Roscommon meant to him.

Daly looked at him searchingly, the grey eyes suddenly shrewd and penetrating. Then his expression relaxed; and the friendliness returned.

'Don't tell me,' he said in a low voice, leaning forward and tapping Michael gently on the wrist; a gesture which could be interpreted as a warning, or as near as the Irish ever come to an embrace. 'I can usually tell. Yes, I think I know. You're very like your uncle.'

Michael chuckled and shook his head. The bar was well heated, and the atmosphere was one of solid, quiet comfort. But now he felt a surge of warmth within him. A traveller coming home on a black frosty road seeing the yellow light of his kitchen across the fields.

'Would you care to meet some of the men?' Daly went on in a lower voice still. He was leaning across the bar like a priest straining his ear to catch the confession of a mumbler.

'Well, I came hoping to see you.'

'Ah.' Daly nodded his head, lifted the flap and looked back, signalling to Michael to follow him. Beyond was a narrow corridor with a door at the end. As he followed his host Michael thought of how smoothly the whole thing had been carried out. No names had been mentioned; the men in the bar would be told nothing; and most important of all Daly had not committed himself publicly.

The room into which he led his guest was small and furnished with a desk in front of a curtained window, a couple of leather arm-chairs, and a large bookcase inside the door. Daly pointed to one of the chairs, and opened a cabinet in the niche by the fireplace. Michael looked around at the large, framed coloured photographs on the walls.

'Ah,' he said, pointing to a water-colour over the fireplace. 'Lough Key.'

'Yes,' said Daly, putting a bottle and two glasses on the desk. 'My mother came from outside Boyle. I've always thought it the most beautiful place in Ireland.'

'It is.' Michael looked at the photographs of Boyle and Roscommon Abbeys. Prominently displayed on the desk were two photographs in silver frames, one of Cardinal Heenan with an inscription which Michael could not make out; the other of a young man in a Roman collar.

'That's my son Tommy,' said Daly quietly. 'He's a curate in Salford. And these are his books. All the Irish writers, even the modern novelists. He's very broad-minded. Now say when.'

The whiskey was smooth and glowing, with a faint tang of turf smoke. Daly always kept a small store of it for special occasions. As he raised his glass Michael felt the cold eye of the Cardinal staring at him. Clearly the photograph served a double purpose: loyalty, and an indication that there were certain matters about which one did not come to Larry Daly: abortions, divorces, and the consequences of the more exotic sexual fancies were not likely ever to be discussed here. But the Cardinal might be expected to approve of most business arrangements.

'Yes,' said Daly following Michael's eye, 'he was a great friend, God rest him.' He sat down and lifted the fire-guard to one side. 'Slainte. Well I'm glad to see you. Make yourself comfortable. Of course I've heard about you. How is Miss Emerson? I see she's had a success with her pictures. The wife bought one. Very powerful.'

'She's staying with Uncle Andy.'

'That's nice. Fine place he has in Queen's Gate. Although I could never understand why he didn't buy a house in the country. Something with a nice garden, near a church.'

'I think it was Aunt Ita. She was in poor health for so long. And then they took the house in Ireland.'

'Yes, I suppose that was it.' Daly's voice became even softer, and he tapped his fingers against his breast; a gesture which Michael had noticed him making when he spoke of the Cardinal and of his son. It was not until several days later that it occurred to Michael that he had observed the same movement made by old men in the country when he was a boy. 'Oh, they're touching their scapulars,' his grandmother had explained. Daly had come a long way from Fuerty; but he had brought his household gods with him.

They chatted easily and amiably for some time; and Michael got the impression that over and above the remarks they made, there was a great deal that was left unsaid. It was rather like knocking on a plywood wall that concealed an empty and echoing space. The taps made sense in the accepted code of communication; the reverberations beyond indicated other things. He had a curious vision of ghosts listening, their fingers upon their bloodless lips. Faces from long ago; his mother, his grandmother, Aunt Ita; all the people that Daly knew of and respected for the only things that were ever really admired in their native countryside: kindness, friendliness and virtue. And beyond that a host of other things they knew with their bones: white-robed figures in the cloisters of the abbeys; fingers moving slowly across jewelled manuscripts; green graves in lonely abandoned churchyards; bugles over a hundred battlefields; and the banners of Fontenoy. In that warm room Michael sensed all this without the benefit of words. It did not for a moment occur to him that the errand he was on was neither virtuous nor romantic.

Daly talked on about the first job Pollard had given him; his employer's well-known contributions to charity; his approachability; his little eccentricities; and the autocratic gestures he was capable of as a paternalistic and sometimes ruthless figure: all now remembered in the ease of success and the passing of time. Then Daly paused. After all, business was business. The hospitable preliminaries were over.

'I wonder if you could do something for me,' Michael began.

'If I can.' Daly tapped his chest again.

'I'm trying to trace somebody. This girl.' Michael took the two drawings from his wallet and smoothed them out. 'She was living at one time in Earl's Court.' He caught Daly's eye, slightly puzzled now. Michael felt sure that he had recognized the face.

'Has she disappeared?'

'No.' He paused, finished his whiskey. 'But a friend of hers has. Two in fact, another girl and a man. They used to go out for a drink in the usual way in the evening.'

'Where?'

'Well, Earl's Court, of course. But they did move around a lot. It could be almost anywhere, but it would be in the centre of London.' Michael paused and stroked his lips. 'There can't be many foreign barmen in London.'

'Some. May I have this——' He made a gesture with his hand.

Michael gave him the drawings; and for a moment was aware of a sudden tension. He was almost certain that Daly knew what he was about. At length the older man raised his head, chewing his lower lip.

'I'll try. It may take some time, and of course I can't guarantee anything. Now I'm always here from six on in the evenings.' He put down the sketches on the desk under the Cardinal's eye, took an envelope from his pocket and wrote down a number. 'Ring that, and it'll get me. Give me a week. Now, do you want to go back through the bar?'

Michael shook his head. Daly led the way back to the corridor, opened a door on to a narrow alleyway, and bade him a gentle and courteous good-night. Michael noticed that he did not ask to be remembered to Pollard.

Part Two

X

In early March the daffodils were out in the parks all over London; and a flowering cherry under the shelter of the Mall was already shedding its blossoms in St James's Park. The weather turned mild; window-boxes blazed; and the hardier Londoners left off their winter coats, but not their underwear. People lingered by walls in private gardens, hoarding the yellow light in their open palms; flags fluttered bravely in the brisk wind; and hopeful publicans put iron tables out on the pavements.

Michael waited for a week, trying hard to forget his impatience. He went for long walks; up the Broad Walk in Kensington Gardens, stopping to admire the vista across the Round Pond, a great swath cut through the trees down which he almost expected to see a mounted procession advancing. It was, like so much else in London parks, a magnificent illusion, especially at that time of year when the beeches were barely touched with green. He strode on, a tall, long-legged figure, not unaware of some of the glances he invited but did not return; preoccupied, and uneasy; as nervous and hungry as a big cat in a clearing making for the trees and the kill. Back by the Ride and the Serpentine and into Knightsbridge. He fell into the habit of dropping into a pub on the Brompton Road, where the Irish barmen reminded him of others coming together in the off hours, looking at a couple of pencil drawings, shaking their heads and giving names of other colleagues.

One evening he rang up a number he had, and made an appointment in a block of flats near Holland Park. The girl was slim and blonde, and looked rather like a debutante of the twenties; she matched his urgency with the sort of pliable depravity which his mood demanded. At another time he might have been tempted to return; but his need was purely prophylactic; he felt no pleasure in her simulated masochism; the prey he pursued was more than fleshy. But he felt agreeably numb; had another drink on his way home, and fell into bed with a drowsy mind.

Rosamund busied herself with the marketing side of her exhibition. She dined with a director of the gallery, an exquisite young man of fifty who had the mannerisms of an eccentric nun, and the mind of a pedlar. Pale, shy, withdrawn, he would make sudden jerky movements as though his bones had never felt the sap of a tumescent warmth; then he would expound at some length on the awful price of dog biscuits. Rosamund, fully aware of her worth on the strength of several more good notices, held out for double the percentage he was offering for her next exhibition; and earned his grudging admiration at the end of two hours of haggling in the Savoy grill.

'Why is it,' she said that evening as she sat with Pollard and Nancy after dinner in her uncle's sitting-room, 'why is it that rich people always haggle in the most expensive places?' She dropped a lump of sugar into her black coffee. The aroma was comforting; somehow one never discussed anything really harrowing over coffee.

'I never did,' said Pollard good-humouredly. He was sitting on the other side of the fireplace, while Nancy curled up on the sofa with a heap of cushions at her back. 'I remember being invited to working lunches, as they call them, at the beginning, but I soon got fed up with them. It's just a tax thing, and there are other ways of saving on that. Besides, you're saving their tax, not your own. No, I always preferred to do business in an office, my own office. I always felt better on my own ground.'

'My man says you've got to be seen,' went on Rosamund.

'Perhaps in your line,' said her uncle, 'it may be thought

necessary. But surely it's more necessary for him than for you. No doubt he is seen by people at a place like the Savoy who might buy from him.'

'My father always says that the biggest money people are always invisible,' put in Nancy thoughtfully. For the past few days she had been very quiet; friendly as always, but a little remote. Rosamund wondered if she was bored; she seemed not to be much interested in quiet evenings of desultory chatter. The day before she had complained of a headache, and had gone back to her flat to go to bed.

'Yes, that's true,' nodded Pollard without much interest. Rosamund had a feeling that they were all going to nod off. Nancy uncoiled herself and put down her cup on the table. She stood up and stretched herself.

'Where's Michael?' she said, stifling a yawn.

'He's having dinner with some Dublin friends he met in a pub the other day. Strange how you run into people in London, isn't it?' Rosamund stirred her coffee and wondered if Michael had been telling her the truth.

'What percentage did you get out of this fellow?' said Pollard. 'The art man.'

'Not what I asked, of course. We split the difference. I think he was rather surprised at the way I held out. After all, this is the first time I've been shown in London.'

'Have you been waiting?' said Nancy, sitting down again. 'I mean, had you always had your eye on the West End?'

'I suppose so, in a way. Not at the beginning, of course. I was damned glad to have an exhibition in Dublin. But later on, yes, I did think of it, especially after I had got as far as I'd ever get at home.'

'I'd never have that sort of patience,' said Nancy earnestly. 'Working and waiting.' She hunched her shoulders and shivered. 'It must have been awful.'

'No, not while you're working. You forget things then. It's when you're not working that you get impatient and ambitious.'

'No, I don't think you would,' said Pollard, disregarding Rosamund's remark, and looking at Nancy with an indulgent smile.

Rosamund wondered, not for the first time, if he knew his wife-to-be a great deal better than she and Michael had supposed.

'Michael is the same,' the old man went on, putting down his cup and clasping his hands comfortably over his stomach. He gazed into the artificial flames of the electric fire for a moment, twirling his thumbs, like a pensioner recalling the memory of old neighbours. 'He wants a quick kill. His father was the same. If he brought off a big case in the courts he'd sit at home for the next month reading detective stories.'

'That hardly satisfied him,' said Nancy. She was showing more interest now. They all were.

'Of course not. He was never really satisfied. He'd go on to the next bit of business, and he'd live with it night and day until he had it cracked. Then he'd curl up until the next time.'

'Well, you're not like that, Andy.' Nancy rubbed her nose and peered at him from under her lashes. Rosamund realized with something of a shock that she was not wearing an engagement ring. Perhaps Pollard considered it silly, and was waiting until she was an acknowledged wife to give her jewels.

'No,' he said, pressing his thumbs together. 'I'm like Rosamund. We're the waiting kind. We don't give up easily. And what she says about work is very true. You don't really think of the end result while you're going about your business, except in a general way. Billy's like that too.' He shook his head and smiled to himself. He looked the picture of contentment: an elderly man who had made a success of his life, and could afford to look back on it with indulgence.

They all sat for a few moments staring into the fire. This is what it would be like, thought Rosamund, if Aunt Ita were alive: cosy chat after dinner about friends and relations; except that the dead lady would have put in a word for her brother-in-law, Michael's father. 'Oh, but he was such a good man, Andy.' She saw good in everyone. Perhaps that was what the religious sense meant, although Rosamund had her doubts. The real saints were pretty rugged characters.

'Oh, by the way,' said Pollard, 'do you know that woman who

has the hall flat in Cornwall Gardens? Mrs Reid.'

Rosamund, who was beginning to feel sleepy after the dinner, the wine and the coffee, found herself listening more attentively than she had been.

'Oh, Mrs Reid,' said Nancy after a pause. It was this slight hesitation which made Rosamund look up. Was it imagination or had Nancy suddenly tensed herself? She had been stroking the handle of the coffee-pot; now the plump fingers were still, and she was looking at Pollard with more interest than she had displayed all evening. 'Yes, I know her to see, and her name's on the bell. I never bothered to put mine up.' She paused again and crooked her finger round the ebony handle. 'What about her?'

'Well, she rang up the other day, and gave me a month's notice. I was surprised, especially since I gave her the flat at a reduced rate. She looks after the hall, and keeps an eye on things. She's a widow with one married son. I gather she's had a pretty hard time. A decent woman.'

'Maybe she's getting married again,' said Nancy with a sudden gurgling laugh. She clasped her hands together and pressed the fingers against her mouth.

Pollard frowned and pursed his mouth. Nancy's remark was not in the best of taste. 'I just wondered if there was anything wrong. Did she say anything to you?'

'No, of course not.' Nancy shook her head and threw out her hands. One of them caught the top of the coffee-pot and knocked it over. 'Oh, Christ!' she exclaimed, jumping up and setting it back again. Nothing had been spilled; but Nancy acted as if she had broken something precious. She fussed and fretted over the tray, and then stood over it looking helplessly at Pollard.

'What, say we have more?' she asked. 'And what about a little Kümmel? It's divine after dinner.'

'Not for me, thanks,' said Pollard. 'A drop of port, perhaps.'

Nancy picked up the tray and bustled off. Rosamund felt slightly uneasy—she did not know why. Perhaps Nancy and her uncle were not yet used to quiet evenings together. It was all going to be pretty dull for the younger woman.

61

Pollard went on talking about Mrs Reid, and Rosamund listened politely. An Offaly woman, married a drunk, widowed, got a job in London, cashier in a restaurant in the city, somewhere behind the Royal Exchange. It was the sort of talk she had heard a thousand times before.

Nancy came back with the tray and two liqueur glasses. She brought the two bottles from the cabinet, holding them up like a boxer with his gloves, smiling broadly, showing too many large teeth.

'Let's have a celebration,' she declared loudly. 'It doesn't have to be about anything. I had a friend who declared a birthday whenever he felt like celebrating. Who was born on the third of March? Must be lots of people we'd like to honour. Come on, folks, I feel good.'

Going up to bed that night, Rosamund wondered how her uncle was going to adapt himself to such lightning changes of mood. She hoped he was going to enjoy them.

XI

'Hello, is that Mr Daly?'
'Ah, Michael, is that you? How are you?'
'Fine, and yourself?'
'Can't complain. Well, I think I've been able to trace the missing person. The night before last she was in the Pickwick in Cosmo Place. That's a narrow street between Southampton Row and Queen Square—do you know that part of London?—down from Russell Square. You do. Good. Well, she often goes there with a friend. The barman knows him well, although he doesn't know the girl's name.' There was a pause, which Michael took to mean that neither Daly nor his informant wanted to know about her. 'The man is a regular by the name of Hansen, he's a Dane, about thirty, fair-haired. He used to go there a lot with another regular called

Armstrong. Well, the Dane was telling our man some time ago that Armstrong had gone off to visit relations in Australia, and that he was keeping the flat warm for him. It's a big, old-fashioned block off Russell Square in Guilford Street, near the children's hospital. I'm sure you'll be able to trace her through that.'

'I'm sure I will. It's wonderful, Mr Daly. I can't thank you enough. I can hardly believe it.'

'It's nothing, nothing. We all know one another in one way or another. A bit like back home. How is your uncle keeping?'

'Oh, very well, very well. I haven't seen him looking so well for a long time.'

'I'm glad to hear that. And Miss Emerson, is she keeping well?'

'Oh, yes, very busy with her exhibition. It's going on tour.'

'I must tell the wife that, it'll give her something to crow about. Well, now, any time you feel like having a chat, drop into Palmer Street.'

'I will indeed, Mr Daly. You've been awfully kind.'

'Oh, it's nothing, nothing. Well, God bless now.'

'God bless, and thanks again.'

Michael stepped out of the phone booth in Knightsbridge Green, and stood for a moment staring at the Friday evening traffic rolling along the Brompton Road. His impulse was to go up-town, have a look at the Pickwick and make up his mind there as to what he was going to do. It was cold with a slight drizzle. He turned back and went into Tattersall's. The horsy, military atmosphere was agreeable to him, since he had little interest in either way of life.

While he was standing over his whiskey at the counter he surveyed the lie of the land. He had dropped in at Queen's Gate Terrace at six. Nancy had gone back to her flat, but was returning at eight to prepare supper for Pollard and herself. Rosamund, he knew already, was having dinner with another of the gallery people to meet the man in Manchester who was hanging her exhibition. 'It's going to be an awful bore, darling, just like selling fish.' It was quite likely that Hansen would look in at his local that evening. Michael took out his pocket diary and consulted the Underground map. He could get straight from Knightsbridge to Russell Square. He finished his drink in a gulp, colliding with the elbow of an elderly man standing next to him.

'Can I bind up your wounds?' he said in a flirtatious manner when Michael apologized.

'Are you a surgeon?' was all he could think of saying as he made for the door. He was thinking how very easy it was to get into conversation in a London pub if one felt in the mood. Perhaps the Dane might say something similar.

On the Underground to Russell Square he turned over several plans in his mind, and rejected most of them. It was always better when one was not absolutely sure of one's way ahead to trust to the ear.

The Pickwick made little concessions to mid-Victorianism beyond a few oak tables and chair at the end of the bar; a mullioned window behind them; and a series of drawings of the great man himself, Jingle, Buzfuz, Tracy Tupman, Dodson, Stiggins and Tony Weller and all the rest of the merry company. Michael ordered a drink and looked around at the drawings, or as many of them as he could see between the shoulders of the customers. There were two barmen, and one barmaid. The man who served Michael had a very English accent; there was nothing for it but to bide time until he could re-order from the other. He was middle-aged, bald, ruddy, and sported a set of false teeth which were a prominent reminder of the British health service. His voice when he spoke might have seemed Cockney to a foreigner; but Michael recognized the kernel. He had to wait for nearly an hour before he had an opportunity to speak to him; during one of those lulls which suddenly descend on crowded pubs: most of the company have been served, a few have moved out, replacements have not yet arrived.

'Pretty busy tonight.'

'Yes, sir. I've seen it busier.' The barman was leaning an elbow on the counter, resting his feet, looking into space. His red forehead was shining with perspiration. He looked suddenly elderly and dispirited. Michael thought it best to capture his attention, if he was to hold him between drinks.

'I've never been here before. Larry Daly told me about it.'

The man shot him a quick, searching look under bushy, raised eyebrows.

'Excuse me, sir.' He went off to attend to a middle-aged woman who blew him a kiss. 'Mick, darling, fill me up again.' It was very likely that most of the customers here were regulars. The barman stayed away slightly longer than might have seemed necessary; but he did come back.

'Decent fella, Larry. Got on well. He was always lucky. Me and him came over the same time. I remember him on the buildings. MacAlpine's first, and then Pollard's.'

'He told me it was Pollard's first.'

'Maybe it was. I was never on the buildings myself. The wife wants me to open a pub of my own. But what would I be killing myself for? The kids are all done for. One a doctor, two in the civil service here, another girl married a fella that owns a hotel in Sheffield. You tell me why I should kill myself.'

'That's great,' said Michael, who knew the form. 'That's what I always say about England, they give you your due. I mean, it's on merit.'

'You can bet your uppers on that. Excuse me, sir.'

The crowd moved and merged, swaying a little in the smoky air; faces bobbed up and down like corks on a stream; young, smooth, expressionless; old, strained, watchful, clutching their glasses tighter with bony fingers, as if the drinks represented the life they were holding on to faster and closer as the years went by. All over London they were preparing for the week-end billet, poised between two engagements, one known, used up, already evacuated; the other lined up, part of a dim, serried mass; detaching themselves, taking up positions, getting ready to be mown down or to penetrate another few feet into enemy territory. The beers, ales, whiskies and wines made it easier to forget that next week and all the weeks to follow would always find replacements. Mr Pickwick with jovial vast waistcoat and beaming countenance had taken up his position behind the lines; the immortal peace-maker; sure of his warm, impregnable hearth. Perhaps the throng below him were paying unconscious tribute to a tactician who had outwitted the invading hordes.

'The same again? Sure. Are you over here yourself?'

'Just for a few weeks. My name is Pollard. I'm staying with my uncle. Strange that you should mention him.'

The barman shot him another look; this time harder, and a great deal more interested. He was weighing up.

'Actually I'm looking for a girl. That's why I asked Larry Daly. He told me she often came in here with a man called Hansen.'

'So you're old Andy's nephew? Well, well. I was expecting someone to turn up, but they didn't tell me it was you. Now that I look at you, you're a bit like him.' He gave a friendly flash of his elaborate teeth, and went off to serve four Guinnesses. When he came back he leaned forwards a little and lowered his voice. 'Yes, I recognized her at once.'

'You mean from the drawings?'

The barman nodded. That enquiry had completely cured his suspicions. And what had he to lose? There were no witnesses; and something to gain if he did the Pollards and Daly a good turn.

'Yes, sure. She's been coming in here with him for about a year. American, isn't she? Well, it's like this. Excuse me. Now where was I? Oh, yes. Well this Hansen is a regular for a couple of years. Used to come in with a man called Armstrong.'

'He's gone to Australia, hasn't he?'

'Yes. I thought they were a couple of queers, to tell you the truth, although you can't be sure nowadays, the way the men are dolling themselves up. You see, this girl was coming in with both of them before Armstrong left, then she was coming in with Hansen. They were here two nights ago.'

'Really? What's this Hansen like?'

'Good-looking fellow, about thirty I'd say. Tall, nearly your height, fair hair, you'd think it was dyed, but maybe it isn't, as he's a Dane. Always very tanned, and that'd make you think. Nice fella, though, I must say, civil and all that. Cashed a cheque a few times, but it was OK. Says he's a journalist for a Danish paper. Anyway, he's living in Armstrong's place around the corner.' The barman sighed, as if he had a secret sorrow; but then, as Michael had

66

observed, most of them thought they had. It probably came from listening to customers' life-stories.

'Is this girl living with him?' said Michael casually.

'Now, that I wouldn't know. I wouldn't have said he was a lady's man myself, but there you are. I've seen her stroking his hair, and kissing his nose and the like. In my day that was thought disgusting in a pub, but now they're all at it. Just goes to show you, don't it? Excuse me.' He came back frowning and busy, and clearly giving Michael to understand that the interview was at an end. A moment later Michael understood why.

'Ah, good evening, Mr Hansen,' said the barman heartily.

'Good evening, Pascal. Set me up the first one.'

His hair was certainly a startling golden colour, cut short, and worn brushed forward over his forehead. The Caesar style beloved of thinning young men. The voice had an unmistakable Scandinavian lilt, and plump, rounded r's. He was dressed in jeans, high-collared denim jacket, and blue turtle-necked pullover. Michael found himself looking into a pair of large, pale blue, quizzical eyes, with dark shadows underneath. They held his gaze for a little longer than is customary between strangers; his long lashes fluttered, and he turned slowly with a half-smile to Pascal, who was laying out his change on the counter. They chatted for a few moments; and then Hansen leaned forward, put a foot on the step surrounding the counter, and looked straight ahead at his reflection in the mirror behind the cash register. It was a pose Michael had often fallen into himself in Irish bars when he wanted to drink alone; but he was aware that it was also adopted by men who had no intention of remaining alone. Hansen made all the classic moves: he lit a cigarette and glanced quickly at Michael over his lighter; he arranged the packet and lighter neatly on the counter; he blew smoke thoughtfully into the air; he rested his chin on his fist and gazed into the mirror; his reflected eyes caught Michael's and held them for an expressive moment; he gave a ghost of a smile; he leaned away with exaggerated deference as two men jostled his elbow in their eagerness to replenish their glasses. He looked at Michael, made a pouting grimace and nodded, taking him into his confidence as a fellow-sufferer from the rudeness of the surrounding world.

Michael waited, a little tense, not quite sure of how he was going to cope with this: it was not something he had anticipated. He felt a sudden childish panic; an urge to get out and hurry back to Rosamund; he had been foolish to tackle this thing alone in the first place.

'You like Dickens?' Hansen's light voice was concerned: a teacher trying to gain the confidence of a new pupil. If not Dickens, why not Stevenson, Conrad, Bennett, Ballantyne, Collins: his range was wide.

'I used to,' said Michael seriously. After all, he had more or less asked for this; if Hansen had not come in so conveniently he would probably have had to come back here night after night and make an opening himself. 'I don't read him much now.'

'Oh, but you should. He hasn't dated a bit. All those people'—he waved his hand to indicate the pictures on the walls—'they're more alive than most of the rest of us here.'

'Perhaps.'

Gently, with quiet finesse, Hansen slid on to the next stool; there was now only one dividing the two men.

'Oh, but you should read him again, you really should. I have three first editions. It makes one seem so close to him.'

'I suppose so.' During those periods of retreat which were part of his passionately guarded privacy, Michael's friends and acquaintances assumed that he was involved in something mysterious and thoroughly disreputable: he was in fact often sitting at home quietly reading. Only a year ago he had re-read most of Dickens. It was curious, he thought now, how things often prepare themselves beforehand, if one only had the time to work it all out; to find the connection.

'Very crowded here, tonight,' went on Hansen. 'It's a nice pub. I didn't really intend to come out, but—' He passed his hand over his cigarettes like a benediction. 'I live just round the corner. I'm a journalist. I like to meet people. Are you waiting for someone?'

'Not really.' Michael shook his head and smiled; this encounter

68

had its funny side. 'Well, no, not now.'

Hansen paused and looked at him; and Michael, realizing that he had committed himself, smiled back. He knew what he was going to do now.

'First editions,' he said, raising his eyebrows. 'I've never seen one.'

'Then you must.' Hansen smiled happily, and chuckled. 'Have another drink. I've got some really good whiskey at home.'

'I'd like to, I really would.' Michael frowned thoughtfully. 'But I've got to go. It's a pity.'

'Oh, dear. Now I suppose I'll never see you again.'

'I think you will.' Michael looked at him steadily, and Hansen's blue eyes widened. He took his wallet from his hip pocket, and extracted a card. 'That's me. I'm always in at six every evening. Can you make it then?'

Michael took the card and read it carefully, before putting it in his own wallet. Then he slid from his stool.

'Yes,' he said slowly, 'I'll make it all right.'

XII

'What a curious story.' Rosamund looked down at the path below. They were sitting in the Iranian café at the corner of Gloucester Road and Victoria Grove. Across the street Queen's Gate Terrace stretched, its heavily boned pillars bathed in bright yellow sunlight. Below her an old lady passed by with a pale red Saluki on a lead. This had always been a great place for dogs. In the time she and Michael had been sitting over coffee in the café window, raised a few steps over the pavement, she had observed two pugs, a clutch of scurrying Chihuahuas, a waddling bulldog, a dignified standard poodle, and one exquisite little Yorkshire who might well have been of Billy's breeding.

'Perhaps he's a relation,' she went on, taking up an éclair and looking at it as if it were bone china. 'Americans often have all kinds of European cousins. Perhaps her mother was of Danish extraction.' She looked at Michael. He had bought himself a wool-lined sheep-skin jacket which made him look bulky and top-heavy. He thrust out his lower lip and considered what she had said.

'It could be, of course. But if so, why has she never mentioned it?'

'Well, from what you tell me, he's hardly the type to impress Nunky, is he?'

'I suppose not. All the same, I don't think it's a family thing.'

'It's hard to think of it as anything else. Oh, yes, I know, I know, it does happen.' She cut the éclair carefully and sampled the cream filling with the tip of her finger. 'Are you going to see him again?'

'I think so. I may find out something. If there is anything between them, I have a feeling that he's likely to boast about it.'

'But, darling, aren't you going to tell him who you are?' Rosamund, less devious than Michael, always believed in tackling things head on. 'If there's nothing in it, you'll look such a fool.'

'I thing there's something going on,' he said stubbornly. 'She was in this bar with him the night she said she was going home with a headache.'

'Yes.' Rosamund frowned. An incident flashed through her mind. While dining at the Savoy she had noticed an old lady of distinguished appearance, dressed in black with her white hair piled high. She was dining with a young man, strikingly handsome, and beautifully dressed. Her gallery friend had told her the old lady's name; a famous title; and that the young man was her lover. It hardly seemed possible; and yet—

'You always thought that Nancy had someone else,' she went on.

'Yes. I could be wrong, of course, but somehow I don't think I am. You don't?'

'Everything's possible, of course, but no, I haven't that feeling about Nancy. There's something odd about her. I can't quite understand what it is.' She looked out the window, up the road to her uncle's house. 'How does Nunky fit into all this? I mean, what are you going to say to him?'

'Tell him the truth, I suppose,' said Michael slowly. It was something that had occurred to him also. How to go about it?

'He won't thank you for it, you know. People never forgive the bearer of bad news, especially when it makes them look ridiculous.'

'I know. But quite apart from our position, surely he should know before it's too late?'

'I suppose so. It depends on what way he thinks about her. He may very well want to fool himself.'

'You don't really think that about Nunky, do you?' said Michael impatiently. Rosamund, whose presence he had wanted so urgently last night in the Pickwick, was not being very helpful. He felt aggrieved; and cheated.

'Well, no, I don't.' She wiped her fingers in the paper napkin, and looked out the window with vague, troubled eyes. Then she turned back and looked at him. He was holding a hand up for the bill. 'Do you find her attractive, Mick?'

'Oh, for God's sake,' he burst out. 'Of course I do. I find most pretty young girls attractive. That doesn't mean I'm planning to go to bed with them.'

Rosamund waited until he had accepted his bill, put a coin under the plate for the waitress, and began to button his jacket and look round for his gloves.

'In that case the best thing to do, surely, is to find out whether or not she's having an affair with this Dane, and then go to her.' Rosamund had a feeling that the situation was not going to be a simple case of relations smoothing the way to an inheritance. Pollard, no matter what happened, was going to have his emotions bruised; and a man of his age, a prey to sexual jealousy, was apt to behave oddly, if not dangerously. Suddenly Rosamund, while glancing down at a superb, red-gold Chow led by an ornate young man, had an idea. It was a moment she was to remember for the rest of her life: the massive yellow-white façade of the terrace; an old woman leaning heavily on a stick, coming out of the Gloucester opposite; the marvellously coated leonine dog; and Michael watching her as he paused in the act of pulling on a glove.

'No, Mick. We'd better keep as far out of this as we can. It

71

would be much, oh, much, much better to get a third person to tell Nunky, if all this is true, and she really is deceiving him. Of course, you'll have to be very careful with this Dane. Now, don't grin, I don't mean that, but he may be very clever.'

She waited for him outside, looking around at the shops and banks that clustered about the crossroads: one of the villages that flourish about a mile from one another along London's bigger thoroughfares. Rosamund was much attached to this one, and would have been quite content to settle down near by, if Michael could be persuaded to leave Dublin. She thought of the money and property that almost certainly would come to them if Pollard died unmarried; and felt a sudden surge of resentment against Nancy.

Yes, there was everything here in this Gloucester Road settlement: a newsagent, dry cleaners, two book-shops, Boot's, three good restaurants, a shoe shop, a supermarket, a greengrocer, an off-licence, even a pet-shop up the road; and the local across the way, a pleasant pub.

It was time she moved on. Dublin was apt to become a bit stultifying as one grew older. But it was still cheaper than here, especially as she had bought out her place. That would bring in a tidy sum now. She wondered just how Michael was fixed. He rarely talked about his finances; but property was a certain liability also, in spite of its increasing value. She decided to have it out with him some day soon. In the end he usually came round to discussing business with her.

There was a brisk wind, and she shivered as a piercing gust blew round the corner. She watched him come out of the cake-shop attached to the café, counting his change; and another more intimate chill ran through her body. Was it a presentiment, she afterwards wondered.

'Oh, Mike, do be careful,' she said anxiously, as they walked down the street. He stopped outside the book-shop and looked at her. She had put a restraining hand on his arm, and now kept it there.

'Of course I'll be careful, Rosie, you idiot. And that's a very good idea about getting somebody else to break the news. That is, if there is any news.'

'Yes, you do have to find out that first. I suppose the Dane is the best way.' She looked into the window: all the popular titles; all peddling information of some kind. Facts, that's what people wanted now. It made them feel better able to face the withering of personal relations. 'How about Billy?' she said, her spirits reviving with the hope that this idea gave. 'He's the obvious person, isn't he? But would he do it?'

'Perhaps.' Ten days ago Michael would have returned a flat denial to this question. Now he was not so sure. 'It's worth trying, when we know more. By the way, what's Nancy doing tonight? She can't have a headache every time she wants an evening off.' He punched his gloved hands together, and flexed his shoulders inside the warm jacket.

'The more I think of it, the better I like it. I mean, this business of getting somebody else to tell him, it's absolutely essential that we stay out of it. If we don't, God knows what will happen. How about one of the priests?'

Michael looked down sideways, smiling at her eager face. It was amusing to watch how scruples, even carefulness, vanished with the advent of a really good idea. He remembered a line he had once read in an old play which had stuck in his mind. 'What's integrity to an opportunity?' Rosamund was so enthusiastic now at the prospect of success that she had not answered his question.

'Yes, that might be an idea, but I'll sound out old Billy first. Well, do you know what Nancy is doing this evening?'

'She usually doesn't say until about six. I have a notion that she mentioned meeting her old flat-mate for dinner. A girl-friend, of course.'

'I'll look in after six. I'll tell you what, let's go to the National Gallery. It's years since I've been there.'

'Oh, Mike, what a good idea.'

XIII

Everything had gone well. On Sunday morning Nancy announced

her intention of driving down to Brighton with Pollard to see an old friend of his, an elderly priest who was living in a home there. At half-five Michael was walking round the small, pleasant garden in the middle of Russell Square. A few old men—those London monuments, scattered about in every public green place—were sitting hunched like Maillol figures on the benches. A party of early Americans was fanning out in front of the Russell Hotel, looking anxiously at the sky, darkening now with the promise of rain as the lights faded and the neon signs grew stronger.

As the time approached for his interview with Hansen, Michael would have given a lot to avoid it. What a pity that no other person could be trusted to do the dirty work! He had no moral objections to Nancy having a lover, and no doubt she would be discreet if she married Pollard. But she could not be allowed to get away with it: there was too much at stake. All his life, even in Aunt Ita's time, Michael had assumed that he would inherit at least some of his uncle's property eventually. He was not a great spender; he had no hobbies that might run away with his money; the women he had did not cost him a great deal; and he was not attracted to small girls or any of the other vices which the law condemned (thus putting up their prices in a complacent society). His interest in his uncle's property was pure, in so far as any ambition can be said to be free of complications. The last few years of galloping inflation had brought home to him the prospect of less and less independence on a more or less fixed income; and he was uneasy. The time might very well come when he found himself an ageing *rentier* cautiously living off capital.

That was what he told himself, as he walked on the sanded path, past the muffled old men and the pie-soft pigeons. Money gave peace of mind: it was something precious and concealed, like a miraculous limb in a golden reliquary. He stood at the back, like an Italian male at Mass, arms folded, gazing at the kneeling worshippers with a certain indulgence. He had not yet been forced to bow the knee; but he recognized the power of the icon; to repudiate it was as foolish as a refusal to take precautions against the evil eye.

He did not realize that what he imagined to be his greatest strength, something as elemental in his make-up as breathing and sleeping, had become over the years his great weakness. He guarded his independence; but quietly, unobtrusively, unknown to his conscious mind, self-interest had become self-indulgence. More and more now he sought the weakness in others, imagining that his self-sufficiency was still a source of strength. Those he exploited were to him a tribute to his will-power; it never occurred to him that the weak feed upon their own kind. In Rosamund's fond eyes, so piercing when directed at others, he was still the strong young man she had first loved; and he saw that image reflected in her gaze. Nor did he quite understand the horror he felt as he looked at the shapeless, bundled, hopeless figures of the old men on the benches.

Six o'clock; shadows under the trees; lights dotted above in the cliff-like facade of the hotel; an old man coughing; branches rustling in the evening breeze. Time to go.

The buzzer had Armstrong's name on the card beside it. Winchester Mansions was written in dark gold letters on the fanlight above the door. The building was large and solid and ugly; compared with the faded houses opposite it had a menacing air: a successful presence among paupers. He pressed the button.

'Yes?'

'Mike.' He swallowed hard. The whole thing was in the domain of music-hall comedy. 'Come and look at my etchings.'

'Mike, is that your name?' The voice was unmistakable through the static: hard, clear and penetrating. 'This is wonderful. Come up, please. Second floor, last on the right.' The door clicked, and Michael went in. A large, panelled hall, an old-fashioned lift in a cage. He felt a sudden panic, a violent urge to turn and bolt. After all, he was not really in desperate need; the large expenses involved in repairing his property was an investment: he would get it back in time.

At that moment an elderly woman of large and respectable appearance came in and joined him at the lift.

'I'm fourth,' she said pleasantly, as he held the door open for her. There was nothing to do but join her.

'Thank you so much,' she said as the lift halted, and he prepared to get out. After all he could always escape down the stairs. But the door of Hansen's flat was already open, and his face was peering round the side of it.

'Come in, my dear, come in. I've just been soaking myself, so I put on this to receive you.'

Michael supposed that he meant the brief red slip which barely covered his loins; otherwise he was naked. A blur of brown glistening skin, a flash of white teeth, a gleam of yellow hair; and an enveloping current of warm air.

'Yes, I can't stand cold. Don't ever believe that Scandinavians are hardier than everybody else. I'll take that.' His hands were already plucking at the shoulders of Michael's jacket. He took it and hung it on a hat-rack which stood beside a large painting of a white horse galloping across sands; the two objects dominated the tiny hall.

'This way.' Hansen opened a door on to a large room completely lined with books. A desk in front of the window proclaimed the occupant's profession: a typewriter, and a confusion of yellow sheets and newsapers. 'Sit down, sit down. What will you drink? Whiskey, yes? I noticed that in the pub.'

Michael lowered himself into a leather armchair, pressed his knees together like a coy girl and stared down at a Bukhara rug. There was a curious smell of pine-wood which he found soothing.

'Now.' Hansen brought a tray with a decanter of whiskey, water and glasses. 'Help yourself. I've fixed myself up.' While Michael was attending to himself, his host sat down in another chair, a handsome, brocaded winged library chair: it made his nakedness even more incongruous.

'Cheers. You are so reserved. I noticed it at once. But we Danes are not ashamed of the body. Besides, I have a good one, have I not?' He glanced down at his brown chest and belly, his long, surprisingly muscular legs. 'It's nothing to boast about, one has or one hasn't.'

'It's getting cold out, isn't it?' said Michael carefully.

Hansen threw back his head, twisted it against the back of the chair and burst into laughter.

'Oh, my dear, you're so funny. You're thinking of two things only; how you are going to get out of this and save your face. Or—' he lowered his head and looked at Michael with narrowed eyes—'you're wondering how you're going to rob me.'

Michael shook his head and pressed his lips together. He was certainly wondering about the first accusation; and in a way he had come to rob this curious stranger.

'Good. All the same, I'd better warn you that I take precautions. I'll tell you about them later. Well, now, what have you come for?' The brilliant blue eyes were wide open now, but still as searching.

'The first editions, of course.' Michael knew that he sounded very uncomfortable. It seemed a very silly reason now.

'I have *Oliver Twist*, the monthly numbers, Bentley's 1848, or the first volume edition, published by John Murray. There are others, of course, but that's the first I have.' He spoke casually, and indicated the book-shelf behind him with a vague wave of his hand.

'Yes, that would be interesting,' said Michael with a little more confidence. 'I've never seen a Dickens first edition.'

'That, my dear, is painfully obvious. The numbers ran in Bentley's in 1838 to '39, and it was published not by Murray, but Chapman and Hall. Of course, you might still be interested, it's a rare object.' Hansen spoke slowly and distinctly, like a patient teacher dealing with a backward child.

Michael felt himself reddening. This interview was not going as easily as thought; not that he had really planned anything.

'You asked me,' he replied truculently. He put down his glass sulkily. 'I'll go if you like.'

'No, no, you mustn't do that. It would be a shame, just when I'm getting to know you, eh?' He pointed with his glass at Michael's hands. 'I noticed them the other night. They are not the hands of a workman, no? And I noticed the way you carried yourself when you left the bar, and of course the way you came in here. You are a little shy with people you don't know, you have good manners, you bear yourself easily, you are not lacking in self-confidence, yes?' Hansen leaned forward and smiled. 'And you are a woman's man;

your ears, your hands, your eyes, so steady and bull-like, and of course that little bend at the knees, they all tell me something. Oh, yes, I find you very, very interesting.'

Michael did not quite know what to say to this; women had gone on in this fashion with him more than once, but never a man before. He grinned, and felt foolish: was this what Romans felt in the presence of the defeated Asians? Gruff, soldierly men suddenly at a loss before the smooth, the delicate, the infinitely complex. The standards were raised above the victorious legions, the chariots were glittering in the sun; but in still, cool halls there was an echo of mocking laughter; an inflexion of irony in the high, silvery voices.

'My name is Gunnar,' went on Hansen abruptly. 'But everybody calls me Johnny. I regret it in a way. Gunnar is such a camp sound in English, eh?' He chuckled, a surprisingly deep, earthy sound. 'And you are Mike. It suits you, it was one of the names I gave you when I was left in the bar with my own reflection, and Sam Weller looking over my shoulder, like a dream one has after too much plum pudding. Yes, Mike was one, Brian another—there is something Celtic about you, I hope you are not violent in drink. Alan was another, and John, not Johnny, oh no, good, solid political names, my dear. So you see how my fancy roves—and what good English I have.'

'Yes, that is good.' Somehow Michael felt that Hansen had the scales in his hands, and was tipping them in his own favour.

'And you expected me to gaze at your handsome face, and admirable physique, didn't you?' Again the deep chuckle, and a cube tinkling against the glass. 'Well, I am gazing, those broad shoulders, that deep and no doubt massively hirsute chest, and that adorable broken nose—did you have it done with surgery? No, you didn't. But you find yourself at a disadvantage. Oh, my dear, you are so used to dominating other people, aren't you? In a nice way, of course, quietly without raising your voice, almost without their noticing. You wonder how I know all this?' Hansen slipped from his chair, left his glass on the rug, and sat back on his hunkers at Michael's feet, looking up at him with his head inclined to one side. 'Give me your hand,' he commanded, holding out his own and

78

wriggling his fingers. 'Now, don't be silly, I am a man of the world, I'm not a silly old queen, I want to read your palm. Now relax, please, not one other movement will I make, and you are longing to know, eh?'

Michael found his hand supported by long, dry fingers, cool and steady, and quite the reverse of what he might have expected. He found himself relaxing exactly as the other had commanded. The warmth of the room, the sense of privacy induced by the long shelves of books, the fine old whiskey, and Hansen's lilting, incisive voice: he could not deny that he was enjoying himself in an edgy sort of way.

'Yes, just as I thought, not really passionate, sensual when there is no risk, but fiercely independent. There is perhaps one person—a woman?—in your life. Yes, there always will be someone like that, eh? Not creative, no, a little slothful, but oh, how you relish power! Oh, my dear, strong, silent Mike, be careful.'

He relinquished Michael's hand, and looked up at him with a grave, steady gaze. Slowly he raised his hand and placed it over his chest as if he felt threatened in some way.

'Beware of the water,' he murmured with his eyes half closed. He rose to his feet with the suppleness of a dancer, and then allowed his shoulders to slump, and his whole body to sag. He looked preoccupied and vaguely dispirited. Michael glanced up at him, expecting to see a flash of bravado after his performance; but Hansen, if anything, appeared slightly shrunken and dejected.

'Am I supposed to believe all that?' said Michael jauntily.

'Yes.' Hansen turned away and stepped across the room, moving heavily, even awkwardly. Following him with his eyes, Michael felt for the first time a vague sympathy with him; something restless and uneasy in himself had disappeared, and he felt more comfortable than at any time since he began this adventure. Hansen disappeared through a door at the end of the room; and Michael refilled his glass and gulped half of it, feeling the whiskey burning his windpipe: it was not made for drinking like that. He looked round at the room with curiosity. Elaborate stereo equipment, records stored in the bottom shelf of one of the bookcases; heavy yellow silk curtains; an

79

oil painting of a handsome man in eighteenth-century dress over the fireplace; a collection of silver snuff-boxes on a Sheraton table in a corner; some photographs in silver frames on another. He leaned forward and studied them: perhaps there might be some trace of Nancy here. At that moment Hansen came back wearing a black kimono with scarlet lining. He held the red trunks in one hand, and with a flick of the wrist landed them on one of the book-shelves.

'I hate restrictions. Since I mustn't shock you I've got into this. At least it's comfortable. I see you're looking at the photographs. Only one of them is mine. This flat doesn't belong to me, you know. I'm just keeping it warm. I used to live in Earl's Court, so much more convenient, so full of the right kind of *boîtes*.' He had recovered some of his almost aggressive panache; but there was still something depressed and vulnerable about him as if the fortune-telling had exhausted his nerves. 'This is rather a pretty picture. The boy was my lover, of course, an Australian—so handsome, don't you think?' He held out the photograph: Hansen himself, a tall, broad-shouldered young man with an unmistakable Australian nose, and two pretty girls, neither of them Nancy.

Michael handed it back and Hansen studied it again.

'Poor Eric, back in the bush, living with a ranger, I hear. But all that is gall and wormwood to you, eh? You'll want to know about the girls.' He put the photograph back and sat down in his chair, picking up his glass and arranging his kimono modestly over his lap. Michael, feeling easier now, smiled.

'What a charming smile, Mike, it must have ravished many a maiden's heart. I see you are getting used to me. People do, you know. Well, these two girls may have been many a thing, but maidens they were not. A couple of Irish trollops in journalism over here, and the dirtiest pair of sluts I ever met. Eric liked his women that way, his men straight from a shower, his girls filthy.'

'And what way do you like your women?' said Michael with a wider smile.

'Don't overdo it, dear,' said Hansen, wagging a finger at him. 'Your half-smile is better, really charming. Grinning like that makes you wolfish. Well, my women.' He sighed and sipped his whiskey. 'I was married, you know. At twenty. A nice girl; we still meet when I go home. She remarried of course, a businessman, very rich and very stupid. I wasn't stupid enough for her, otherwise we might have made a go of it.' He leaned forward and fixed Michael with his glinting eyes. 'You're not married, I think. No, I thought so, you haven't that look.' He sighed again and held out his glass. 'Fill me up, please. Oh, how I am bored by all this. Do you like girls, are you married, what category do you belong to? You know, it isn't the sex thing that terrifies people about—well, people like me. It's the shaman in us; that androgynous quality that makes us capable of identifying with both sexes. We know too much, it frightens the men even more than the women. See, my dear, how I terrify you.' He chuckled again, and Michael began to wonder if all this time he had been assisting at a highly polished conjuring act. He had an uneasy feeling that Hansen was laughing at him; rejoicing in the confusion which he induced so expertly.

'It's something I know very little about,' he said in an effort to restore the balance which he felt was beginning to tip him up again. He looked at Hansen with a kind of baffled respect; and realized at once that his host probably sensed that also: a sort of benign attention was apparent in the expression of his eyes. Time to move in; silence the ironic voice with a show of rude vigour. 'Certainly I don't understand the women angle. What sort of women are they?'

'You think they must be somehow different too?'

'Are they?' For the first time Michael felt that he had scored. Not a direct hit, perhaps; but something had gone home. The legions were murmuring outside; a cold wind was rising like a wraith among the sands; too much polite talk, and no booty.

'Of course not. They were all depressingly normal, in the usual vague sense of the word. But then, what does that mean? I have a girl-friend just now, nothing could be more normal, and yet, she isn't. Sexually she's completely passive, just your cup of tea, my dear, it would bring out the rapist in you. Now, now, don't frown, you know you like to dominate, possess, destroy, brand as yours. I'm a disappointment to you, eh? How you would have enjoyed to see me grovelling! I think you'd be quite nice about it, but it would have been a pleasure of the subtlest kind.'

Michael shook his head, and made a negative sound in his throat; the very picture of a man out of his honest depth in Oriental mysteries.

'Do you live with this girl?' he said looking towards the door at the end of the room.

'Oh, my dear, you are too naïve, really, so much so that I'm beginning to wonder—ah, well, Rome wasn't built in a day. No, of course I don't live with her. The poor child is engaged to be married to a man old enough to be her grandfather. And you know, she rather likes it. Especially since she still has good old Johnny to fall back on. So like a woman, eh?'

'Not like any of the women I know,' said Michael stolidly. He stared into his whiskey; perhaps with luck Hansen might attribute his uneasiness to ignorance.

'Perhaps not. How very boring for you. You see, her grand-father is very rich, and is not capable of making the ultimate demand upon her.'

'And you are?' Michael was able to look him straight in the face for this thrust. Suddenly they were no longer strangers: the harem had been opened; conqueror and conquered were at last speaking the same language.

'But of course. However, that is not what she requires of me— the first woman, I must admit, who didn't; their demands are ferocious. No, she has a terror of rude male penetration, if you follow me. Something happened when she was a young girl, the usual, I suppose, but she won't talk about it except in portentous little hints. Naturally, she adores all that mystery. But she demands her pleasure, all the same. Fortunately, I'm devoted to her, she's a sweet girl, great fun and very affectionate. It's frustrating, of course. Naturally I want to have her, I get all worked up, very excited. Perhaps one day, if I'm very, very gentle—in the meantime, I must admit I have become very, very fond of her. And in time she will be rich. Then we will travel, all the places I've always wanted to see. Travel lengthens time, you know.'

'And what about her old man?' Michael had no difficulty in

82

injecting a note of disapproval into his voice. This was even worse than he had expected; much more confusing.

'But, my dear, of course he won't know. She will be good to him, look after him, keep him company, make him feel young. At present, of course, we have to be a little careful. She can only get away once or twice a week. But after she is married, it will be different, of course.' He was talking quietly now with no peacock flourishes; there was a note of sincerity in his voice. 'And she understands me so well. She is not jealous of other men, only women. That is so sensible, eh?'

'So you have it all arranged?'

'But of course. What a savage you are.' Hansen threw up an arm, and the wide sleeve slipped back to his elbow. 'It's a very civilized arrangement. It is a good thing for both of us to have a centre in our lives. Without me she'd be just a boring little cock-teaser.'

Michael drained his glass and stood up.

'I think it's disgusting,' he said bitterly, looking down at Hansen as if he would like to knock him out.

'Odd,' said the other, leaving down his glass and standing up also. 'But then moral indignation always is.'

But Michael was not listening to him. He had a sudden appalling vision of Nancy naked with Hansen, abandoned to their lewd, unspeakable mysteries. He felt the blood rushing to his head, and with it an overpowering desire to fling himself upon his host, pummel him, kick him, feel his hands tightening about his neck.

Hansen smiled and took a step nearer. Michael was aware of a gleaming chest, and brown arms framed in scarlet. The next moment he was lifted straight off his feet, whirled in the air and found himself landed on his back on the sofa.

Hansen leaned over him and smiled.

'That's one of my secret weapons, dearie. I could have kicked you in the balls, but that would be a waste of good material, wouldn't it? But you were feeling violent, weren't you? We can't have that sort of thing going on, eh?'

Michael sat up and shook his head.

'You fucking bastard,' he muttered.

'Now, now, language will get you nowhere. Would you like a drink before you go?'

'No.' Michael got slowly to his feet. Hansen was modestly adjusting his dressing-gown, which had opened in the action. But he kept an eye on his visitor. Michael ignored him and headed for the hall to retrieve his jacket.

'No hard feelings, I hope,' Hansen sang out. 'Come again any time, when you're feeling more civilized. Remember, I haven't shown you my first editions yet.'

Michael opened the door and went out fast. Having gained the safety of the street, he hurried towards Russell Square and hailed a taxi to drive him straight home. It had been a most disturbing evening.

XIV

'I can't understand it.' Michael was lounging in the low chair in his uncle's sitting-room, his body slack and listless, his face dark and irritable.

Rosamund looked at him. She had often seen him in this mood: depressed, baffled, edgy. It was a good thing he was not a hard-drinking man, otherwise these fits of sulkiness would lead straight to a week's drunkenness.

'It's not so surprising, after all.' She was sitting on a hassock in front of the fire, her legs pressed together, her strong brown hands twisted on her lap. 'I don't really know what anyone could do in the circumstances, especially Billy.'

It was Tuesday afternoon. They had had the morning to themselves. Pollard had gone to a funeral, something he did at least once a week; Nancy had not shown up, and they had lunched together at the Italian restaurant around the corner.

They had been over the ground again and again. Yesterday Michael had made an appointment to see Billy in a pub in St

Martin's Lane, since he did not want to be seen near the office just at this time. He told him his story, naturally excluding Hansen's skill at ju-jitsu. And Billy had flatly refused to tell Pollard anything about it. 'It's none of my business,' he had said gruffly. 'No, man, it certainly is not.' But what had really upset Michael was Billy's whole attitude. After the tip-off about Daly's, he had expected Boyd to be at least sympathetic; instead of which he had been cool, almost rude. And before he left after one drink he had given Michael a very curious look, scornful, almost contemptuous in its long, hard scrutiny. Michael had not told Rosamund of this; but it had disturbed him more than anything that had happened during the past few days. He had felt like a small boy caught in some shameful act by a respected elder.

Rosamund got up and made herself another drink. She turned round and looked at the window in the area. That morning she had come down and found herself alone in the unlighted room. It was rather like being on the bottom of an aquarium tank. A greenish-grey light filtered through the window, and the furniture and objects in the room appeared ghostly and slightly wavering in the feeble glow. Then she had switched on the lights and sat down to think. For some days now she had been haunted by an image of bone-white pillars receding into a chaos of swirling colour. She had thought of various titles for it: Empire Day, the End of the Line, Recessional. But she knew that quite soon she would have to start work on it; and when Michael came in and began to tell her of his meeting with Billy, and all the complications which now faced them, she was unable to give him more than half her mind. But she knew the attraction that a Byzantine maze of plots and counter-plots held for Michael. It seemed to her that he was reading too much into this curious story of Nancy and her Danish boy-friend; but what had she, Rosamund, to offer in the way of a solution?

Now, bracing herself, she tried again.

'I suppose the only person who might make something out of this would be somebody who didn't wholly understand. I mean about Hansen being like that. The very fact that Nancy was visiting him would be enough.'

'But where are we going to find somebody like that nowadays?' said Michael irritably. He frowned and dug his fingers into his thighs; a curious, cat-like habit which always accompanied a frustrated mood.

Rosamund shrugged her shoulders. Privately she thought they ought to make a settlement with Nancy; but it was useless to suggest that to Michael in his present mood. The episode with Billy had hurt him deeply, she knew.

'By the way,' she said, struck by a sudden thought, 'did the Dane say anything about her staying the night?'

'No, but I suppose it was assumed, by the way he talked.'

'One can't always believe men of that sort when they talk about women. Nevertheless, if she is in the habit of spending the night with him——' Rosamund raised her glass, peered through it with one eye, then sipped it thoughtfully.

'I suppose one could find out that,' said Michael slowly. He did not relish the idea of another visit to Hansen; but it might be necessary.

'If she hasn't, I don't really see what can be made of it. After all, she must have had some friends before she met Uncle Andy, and if one of them is a fairly well-known homosexual, well, that's that, in my opinion.'

'I know she's up to something,' burst out Michael, beating his knees with his clenched fists.

Rosamund looked at him closely, but said nothing. She had a feeling that he was getting himself into deep waters; that his emotions were aroused; that he would not rest until he had worked them off on something—or somebody. She had seen him like this before; in the middle of an unsatisfactory affair; at the beginning of another: the signs were the same. She suddenly thought of Nancy, and wondered about her.

As if in answer to her thoughts they heard the front door bang in the hall above, and quick tapping steps across the tiled floor. Michael looked towards the door, and transferred his hands from his knees to the arms of his chair. A moment later Nancy came in, wearing a blue belted raincoat over her jeans. Her face was flushed and her mouth was open, as if she had been hurrying. She crossed to the cabinet from which Rosamund moved away, and poured herself a stiff brandy.

'Well, hello, you two,' she said breathlessly, after she had shaken her head and puffed out her cheeks from a too-generous mouthful of brandy. 'I'm very late to-day, aren't I?' She fiddled with her belt, but made no attempt to take off her coat.

'Late for the morning, yes,' said Rosamund with a smile. 'But OK for the afternoon.'

'Well, Andy's gone to a funeral, he told me he wouldn't be back until late. Having lunch with the relatives. All those funerals. Sometimes two a week. Christ Almighty!'

Rosamund realized with a shock that Nancy was slightly tipsy; and felt uneasy. She moved away still farther and sat down in her uncle's armchair. Michael was looking at Nancy with a curious set expression, his lips drawn tightly together, his eyes slightly narrowed, while his fingers moved slowly over the arms of his seat. Rosamund realized with a sudden jolt that this attitude was familiar also. She glanced up at Nancy and found her staring down at her glass. But the next moment she had lifted her head, and thrust out her small pointed chin.

'I've just had lunch with a friend of mine,' she said sharply. 'A fellow called Johnny Hansen.' She pressed the brandy glass against her breast and looked at Michael. 'Were you with him on Sunday night?'

She's nervous, thought Rosamund unhappily; and she's worried. Perhaps after all there is more in this affair than one thinks.

'So that's who he is,' said Michael, in that low, slightly menacing voice he used when he also was nervous. 'Yes, I met him in a pub, and he asked me to look him up. Odd sort of a fellow.'

'Odd sort of coincidence too, wasn't it?' Nancy's voice was aggressive, and her colour had deepened.

'I suppose so, but these things happen.'

'Sure, but not as neatly as that.' She paused and helped herself to another mouthful of brandy. 'No, sir. You wouldn't by any chance be following me, would you?'

'No, I wouldn't,' replied Michael in the same low tone. 'Not by any chance.'

Suddenly Nancy crumpled. She raised her thin shoulders and shivered. Putting her glass down on the cabinet, she groped behind her for a chair by the wall and sank on to it, rubbing one hand against the back of another. Rosamund could hear her quick, uncertain breathing; it was like the low sobbing of a child. Not for the first time she felt a wave of sympathy for this girl, who did not seem to have many elements of a cold-blooded opportunist; and found herself in so many false positions. Although Michael had not told her of Hansen's description of their intimacies, she had from the first sensed something unfulfilled about Nancy. He had merely said that they 'necked a little' in such an embarrassed voice that Rosamund had guessed a great deal more.

Suddenly Nancy stood up again, so abruptly that she had to grasp the top of the cabinet for support.

'Listen,' she began tonelessly, 'why don't you two and me make some sort of a deal? This kind of thing just kills me, honest it does. There's plenty in it for everybody. I know what Andy has. I'm no grabber. A house here, a house there, he won't notice it. But for Chrissake quit tailing me.' She wiped her forehead with the back of her hand and picked up her glass again.

Rosamund was about to answer when they heard the front door open again, a sound of feet, a murmur of voices, and then Pollard's voice at the top of the stairs.

'Rosie, are you down there?'

Thankful for any interruption, Rosamund got up quickly, and went out of the room to the bottom of the stairs.

'Yes, I'm here.'

'Is Mike there?' Pollard's voice sounded genial, almost excited. As a result of the tension she was feeling, Rosamund had expected that it would be accusing.

'Yes, he is.'

'Tell him to come up too. I want you to meet someone.'

Rosamund turned round, but Michael was already coming through the door. He looked pale, and he looked at his cousin questioningly. An intense mood is difficult to change; when an interruption comes it is always assumed to have a connection with what one is feeling so emphatically at the time. They both went upstairs with some misgivings.

Pollard was standing in the hall, smiling broadly and looking handsome in his blue suit, grey silk tie and white shirt. At his side was a small, rather dumpy woman in a dark blue-grey tweed costume, white blouse, a single string of pearls, sensible brown walking shoes, and a small, tam-like hat on top of her brown, greying hair. She was carrying an umbrella and a plastic raincoat on one arm, and was holding a black leather bag in her hand.

'I want you to meet Mrs Reid. Only for her I wouldn't have known about poor Paddy Meehan. He had no one left belonging to him, and it wasn't in the papers. I wouldn't have missed his funeral for anything, God rest him.'

'Well, it was the least I could do,' said Mrs Reid, with a smile, 'after giving you notice, and everything.' She had a soft, low voice, a little tinged by an English inflexion, but not more than pleasantly so.

As Pollard made the introductions she held out a small gloved hand and grasped theirs firmly and quickly, with another smile and a quick little jab of her head. Rosamund noticed the gloves, grey and quite expensive: she was to remember them later. And she was also to remember feeling relieved that she had bought a plain jersey dress for herself in Barkers, and could thus meet Mrs Reid on more or less equal grounds. Why should she feel awkward in jeans with this woman? It was ridiculous; and yet she felt she would have been.

'Mrs Reid knew your mother, Rosie,' said Pollard jovially.

'No, no,' said Mrs Reid quickly. 'I had an aunt who lived near Roscommon, and she knew her.' She turned to Michael. 'Also your father, Mr Pollard.'

Michael muttered something polite, and managed to summon a smile.

'You will wait for tea, won't you?' said Pollard, turning to his guest.

'I'm afraid not. I have a lot of things to do, and we've been at the funeral all morning.'

'Yes, I know. But it was a lovely funeral, wasn't it? So many turning up after all those years. It just goes to show you.' Pollard shook his head approvingly.

'I was telling your uncle,' said Mrs Reid, looking at Rosamund, 'how I heard about it. Poor Paddy hadn't been to his duties for years, but he made his peace in the hospital only the day before he died. Wasn't it wonderful? The chaplain to the hospital happens to be a friend of mine—he's from home—and he told me. Thank God.' She nodded her head, and shifted her bag nearer to the crook of her arm.

While she was speaking Rosamund inspected her. Her face was nondescript, but she had bright blue eyes and a small mouth which although thin-lipped was not unpleasant; her skin was rough, and there were furrows in her brow, and wrinkles at the corners of her eyes. She seemed about fifty, but Rosamund knew that she could well have been a few years younger. She wore no make-up; and looked what presumably she was: a respectable middle-aged Irish-woman dressed for a church service; brisk, well-mannered, and essentially tough. Yet in spite of her decent appearance and guileless conversation Rosamund still felt uneasy.

They chatted for a few minutes longer, and then Mrs Reid turned to go. Pollard went with her, insisting that he had brought her out of her way to meet his niece and nephew, and that he must drive her home. As the door closed behind them Nancy came up from the basement. She looked hot and slightly dishevelled.

'Madam Reid,' she said loudly. 'That one is the biggest bitch I have ever met in my whole life, so help me God.' She passed quickly, and a trifle unsteadily, into her office.

Michael and Rosamund looked at each other blankly for a moment, and then made an arrangement to have dinner at Bianchi's that evening.

XV

A great city is like an ocean. The surface is sometimes calm, reflecting an empty and indifferent sky; at times turbulent and heaving, as if the clouds above and the mysterious depths below were moving dangerously and arbitrarily in concert. Upon the surface myriads of citizens like tiny diatoms move to and fro in the rhythm of a familiar swell; the daily tides of law, habit, custom and emotion which govern their lives. These creatures, all convinced of their own absolute uniqueness, swirl and spin, and rise and fall, many-coloured and ever-changing in obedience to the play of light and current on their collective spate. Occasionally they look up to see some of their own kind flashing through the air like flying squid; then the current swirls them on again over the unknown.

At night this multitude has a phosphorescent glow, like the face of the sea under the pale reflection of the stars. It is then that they are joined by larger, more shadowy creatures that during the waking hours are sensed rather than seen; but in the evening drift up, moving and twining, jostling for sustenance among the uncounted multitude. For all these creatures prey upon one another; while in the depths great lurking monsters move, like half-feared and half-forgotten tribal memories, among the plumed sea-horses and the bleached bones.

A vague sense of this ebb and flow with its curious, inexplicable and interlocking relationships struck both Rosamund and Michael that evening as they made their way up Shaftesbury Avenue to the York Minster for a drink before dinner.

Michael stopped dead on the pavement outside the Queen's Theatre, and punched a fist against his open palm. It was a gesture which always set Rosamund's teeth on edge.

'God, why didn't I think of it before! It's so obvious. That little woman Nunky introduced us to this afternoon?'

'Mrs Reid.'

'Didn't you tell me that he was talking about her a few nights ago? Something about giving notice, and having a flat in the same

91

house as Nancy?' Two young men, blank-eyed, gum-chewing, walked between them like somnambulists, but they hardly noticed them.

'Yes. He spoke about her. He said he gave her a flat and that she looks after the hall, which was why he was surprised when she gave notice.'

'Well, she looks a nice old thing, doesn't she? And if she looks after the hall she must have noticed things. I bet she knows all about Nancy.' Both of them had turned round and were walking back again towards Piccadilly.

'And Nancy doesn't like her. Yes. There may be something.' She looked at Michael. 'Are you going there now?'

'Yes, I think I ought, don't you?'

'I suppose so.' Rosamund was thoughtful. She too had a sense of connecting links stretching interminably away into the depths. Mrs Reid was another link; perhaps the final one.

'Half-seven.' Michael looked at his watch. 'Will you ring up and cancel at Bianchi's, or do you want to go there yourself?'

'No, I'll have something at that Persian place opposite the terrace. Then I can see you there afterwards.'

XVI

Whatever gleams of daylight lingered were blotted out by the huge bulk of the houses in Cornwall Gardens. They rose up, two storeys taller than most London terraces, like gigantic flats at the back of a stage. Michael had always liked the place because of its slightly shabby gentility; and its two small gardens, a little overgrown and crowded under the plane trees, filled in summer with people in deck-chairs or lying open-armed on rugs. They might have been gardens attached to houses lived in by elderly spinsters in reduced circumstances. Now beyond the street lights they were as dark and furry as sleeping cats behind their railings.

He went up the steps of Pollard's house and examined the bells.

Nancy's name was not among the cards; but then she had moved in quite recently, and probably had not bothered. Whatever visitors she had no doubt knew which bell to ring. He saw Mrs Reid's name at the bottom, and pressed the bell, thinking ruefully that much of his time these days seemed to be taken up with the ringing of strangers' door-bells. Instead of an enquiry through the intercom he heard steps in the hall, and a moment later the door was opened a few inches, and the woman he had met that afternoon peered out.

'Well, Mr Pollard,' she said, raising her heavy eyebrows, and opening the door wide, 'what brings you here?' Suddenly she frowned, and glanced up at him sharply. 'Is your uncle all right?'

'Indeed he is, Mrs Reid, and I'm sure he sends his best wishes. But'—he paused and smiled; a smile that was warm, carefree and inviting and that never failed of its effect on middle-aged ladies and young children—'I wonder if I might have a few words with you?'

It had its effect on Mrs Reid also. She smiled back pleasantly, showing small, rather uneven teeth, and two incongruous dimples on either cheek. She looks rather like an old-fashioned nun, Michael found himself thinking.

If she was in charge of the hall it did her credit. Everything was neat, polished and in order, and a painting which hung over the table had obviously had its gilt frame newly glossed. It was ruined as a result, but it undoubtedly looked more alive.

He followed her into a room which faced the front. It had a slightly fusty smell, and was obviously used only for visitors. The furniture was cheap, the few pictures on the bright painted walls looked like calendars, and the pieces of china, with the exception of a hideous Belleek vase on the mantelpiece, looked as if they had come straight from a sale in a hardware shop; but they all shone, and were innocent of dust. A sewing-machine was set in front of the window.

'Sit down, please,' said his hostess, stooping to light the gas-fire. 'It's still very chilly in the evenings.' She straightened up as red as a beetroot, and looked at him with a smile, opening and closing the box of matches between her stubby fingers. Her hands were small, but rough and flaring red. Suddenly she glanced down at them, turned quickly and put the matches back behind one of the china figures, then sat down on a hard leather-covered dining-room chair, covering one hand with the other. Michael concluded that Mrs Reid, in spite of her homely appearance, had her little vanities.

He sat down carefully in an armchair and clasped his hands between his knees. His hostess said nothing, but was looking at him with an enquiring air.

'I hope I'm not disturbing you, Mrs Reid,' he said with another warm smile. It was not really calculated, since he had always found the company of middle-aged women relaxing; and if they displayed an obvious admiration, that was quite pleasant also.

'Ah, not at all, Mr Pollard, sure I have very little to do at the moment. I won't be going to my new job for three weeks, and I have plenty of time to do my bit of packing. No, indeed you're not.' She gave a little start, and held up her reddened hands. 'You'll have a little drop of something, won't you? I have a nice bottle of sherry, and a bottle of Powers in the press. I think, maybe, you'd prefer the Powers.' She smiled as her visitor nodded, went to a cabinet inside the door, and busied herself with glasses and a bottle for a few minutes.

'Are you having nothing yourself, Mrs Reid?' said Michael as she handed him a more than adequately filled glass.

She shook her head, sat down again, folded her hands, palms uppermost on top of one another, and looked at him with lively interest. He noticed that she had changed her funeral suit for a dark tweed skirt and a grey twin-set, and was wearing house-shoes rather like men's slippers. Although he had assumed that she was quite old when he first met her, he could now see that she was not; she appeared plump and pleasant, and her small blue eyes could twinkle.

After praising the whiskey, which was excellent and very strong, talking about the weather and the awfulness of Northern Ireland, there was a pause and Michael realized that he was required to state his case. A fashionable young man of means did not call on a middle-aged widow just to talk about the weather.

'I hope you won't mind me talking to you frankly, Mrs Reid,' he began, 'but I'm sure you will understand. I suppose you know that my uncle is marrying again.'

Mrs Reid nodded and rubbed her hands slowly together.

'Yes, I heard it after Mass one day. It was in some paper, wasn't it?'

'Yes. Uncle was very vexed about that. He hates publicity, as you can imagine.'

'Yes, of course. It's not very nice seeing one's private business in the newspapers. Of course Mr Pollard wouldn't like that sort of thing.'

In the area below the window something rustled, rattled, and scurried away. Michael, who loathed rats, started and looked round.

'It's that cat from next door, an awful thief. I once had a grand piece of whiting for my dinner, and when I turned my back, it was gone with that cat out the window.' She nodded, and Michael, after another sip of whiskey, went on:

'I suppose you know who the girl is, I mean—' He broke off and looked at Mrs Reid with raised eyebrows.

'Yes,' said Mrs Reid flatly, 'I know her.' She frowned slightly, and began to twiddle her thumbs.

'She has a flat here. Well, to tell you the truth, we're all a bit worried, that's to say my cousin and I, and also Mr Boyd, my uncle's partner. The difference in age is—' He broke off again. He had a feeling that one did not have to spell things out with Mrs Reid, nor would she have welcomed such blunt tactics. There was something quiet and assured about her; apart from the restless little red hands which were an incongruous feature.

'Yes, she is a great deal younger.' She twisted her hands again, and clasped them over her stomach. 'What exactly are you worried about, Mr Pollard? Her religion, I suppose. She isn't a Catholic, so far as I know, but perhaps she's taking instruction?'

'Well, that, of course. And no, I don't think she's taking instruction.' He paused as an idea struck him. 'I suppose if she were, you'd know about it, wouldn't you?'

Mrs Reid slowly pushed her hands up under the sleeves of her cardigan and looked at him thoughtfully for a moment.

'If she was going to any of the churches near here, I might, yes.

But surely your uncle would know?'

Michael was taken aback. It would not do to let her know that his uncle had never discussed Nancy with him, in any kind of context, religious or otherwise.

'Yes, of course. Well, I don't think she is.' He knew that if Nancy were taking this course she would be almost certain to tell Rosamund. Besides, there was Hansen. 'No, it's just that we're, well, worried that she might be a bit flighty for a man of my uncle's years.'

Mrs Reid looked at him, frowning and pursing her small mouth. It made her look suddenly rather grim and formidable.

'I see. Have you any reason to suspect this?' It was a blunt question, and seemed to demand a blunt answer.

'Well, yes, we have. We think there was, and probably still is, another man in her life.' He paused and coughed lightly; then he looked her straight in the eye. 'Would you, Mrs Reid, living here and being in and out, know anything about that?'

There was a silence. Mrs Reid's expression changed again. A look came into her eyes which Michael recognized with something of a shock. Vague, fluid, wandering, it was the sort of expression he had noticed in the eyes of country women haggling over eggs in a market, and nuns when someone had said something indiscreet. Mrs Reid was either shocked or was keeping whatever information she had to herself.

'Well,' she began quietly, 'as you know, your uncle gave me this flat at a very low rent—otherwise I couldn't afford it—on the understanding that I would keep the hall tidy, and keep an eye on the tenants. No wild parties and that kind of thing. I feel guilty to be giving him notice now, but it is a long way from my work, and besides'—she broke off and raised her shoulders, as if she were in a draught—'I'm going to another job. I'm going to a priest in North London, oh, a very nice elderly man. He's from Tipperary, a Father Kiely, comes from a very good family.' She sighed and raised her eyes ceilingward. 'To tell you the truth, I couldn't stand the language in the place I'm in any longer. Not only the staff, and some of them are foreign, but the few words they did pick up—'

Michael was left to imagine an Italian waiter going about repeating four-letter words to himself, under the impression that they were peculiarly British. He raised his glass and lowered his face over it. 'And some of the customers too. Most of them young clerks from the banks and insurance companies. You wouldn't believe it, Mr Pollard.' Mrs Reid's glance had come down again and was fixing him, brightly and indignantly.

'Terrible,' he murmured, shaking his head, and feeling like a fool.

'So, of course I'll have to leave here when I go to keep house for Father Kiely.'

'Yes, of course. My uncle will be upset about it.'

'I suppose so. But he was very friendly the other day when I rung him up to tell him about poor Paddy Meehan. He worked for your uncle at one time, you know, and I knew Mr Pollard wouldn't have missed his funeral for anything. A fine one it was too, thank God. And Mr Pollard insisted in bringing me in his car, and leaving me back here afterwards, as you know.' She withdrew one of her hands, covered her mouth and coughed politely. 'I told him about Father Kiely, of course. He knows him. Everybody knows the Kielys of Tipperary.'

Michael was beginning to feel a bit bemused. How to get the conversation back to Nancy? While he was racking his brains, Mrs Reid helped him out.

'You said, ah, that you, ah, knew this man?' she said quietly.

'Yes, we do,' replied Michael impulsively, glad to have his work done for him. Immediately afterwards he felt sorry. He had forgotten how to bargain for eggs; or treat with polite, devious nuns in waxen parlours.

'I see.' She sighed, returned her hand to its nest, and inclined her head to one side. She looked the picture of sympathy.

'So that's why I came to you, Mrs Reid,' he hurried on, hoping to retrieve his over-playing. 'I thought—we thought—that you might know of him too. Perhaps visiting here—' He trailed off.

Mrs Reid opened her mouth and raised her eyebrows as high as they would go. She now looked the very picture of astonishment.

'Well, in the name of God, Mr Pollard, what would I know

about it? Goings on like that. If there are any. Besides I don't know Miss Cook very well. Just to pass the time of day with in the hall, now and again. She was never noisy. And then, of course, I knew she was employed by your uncle, so naturally, I took it for granted that she was respectable.' Mrs Reid paused and looked at him with bright, fixed eyes. 'Of course, if anything like that happened I would have reported it to Mr Pollard at once. Oh, yes, indeed I would.'

'But nothing has?' said Michael flatly. He was feeling particularly frustrated by this interview: no nearer to anything; and yet the sense that he was very near, if he could only find the right words. He was given no opportunity, for Mrs Reid embarked on a long monologue about his family, his father, his aunt, and the fair reputation of his grandparents. But mostly she spoke of Pollard; the good employer he had always been; his interest in all his employees; and all he had done for them.

'There isn't a finer man in the whole of England,' she declared roundly. 'Ah, but blood will tell, a little bit of breeding always comes out.' She nodded her head gravely.

'It's a pity he's making such a fool of himself, at his age,' retorted Michael sharply, finishing his drink and leaving it down with the finality of departure.

'Well, I'm sure I wish him all the luck in the world,' said Mrs Reid, rising, and going to the door.

Michael followed her out trying desperately to think of something to say which would break the impasse. But all he could think of as she held the door open for him was:

'If you do hear or see anything, Mrs Reid, I hope you'll let us know. You see, we're pretty sure something is going on that my uncle doesn't know about. And it isn't right, it isn't fair to him.' He felt that he had said the right thing at last. But just as she was about to reply, something dark and furry flashed by his legs and into the hall.

'Oh, that cat!' she exclaimed loudly. 'Thanks be to God, I haven't anything laid out for my tea yet. She's gone straight into the room, the villain!'

'Well, good-bye, Mrs Reid, and thank you so much. You will

remember what I've said, won't you?'

'I will indeed, Mr Pollard. It was grand meeting you. Good-bye now, and God bless you.'

XVII

Mrs Reid went back slowly into her kitchen, after ejecting the cat.

It was very different from the front room, which she had furnished on the hire purchase, recently completed—one of the reasons she had kept her job in the City café so long. She would be receiving a much smaller salary from Father Kiely; but she would have her keep, and be spared the long journey by Tube every morning and evening. Besides, she delighted in clerical company, was deeply versed in all the rules and regulations, traditions and devotions of her Church, and was quite happy to spend hours discussing them with congenial souls.

After putting on the kettle she stood for a moment in the middle of the floor, biting her lip and frowning. Then she went to the dresser and opened one of the drawers. She took out an old tin box, opened it and began to scrabble among the tangle of scapulars, broken rosary beads, medals, hairpins, buttons, spools of thread and bits of sealing-wax, eventually taking out a small piece of rolled-up paper which had been pushed into a corner. She opened it, fetched her spectacles from their case on the window ledge, and sat down to read. It was written in pencil in her own large, rather childish handwriting. Hansen, 837 9087. She looked up, staring at the kettle and brushing the scrap of paper against her stomach. She made tea, three large spoonfuls, and poured it straight into a cup without benefit of a pot, as her father had always done. Then, smacking her lips, she sat down again to consider the position.

Michael had told her a great deal more than she had told him. Cautious by nature, the experience of her hard-working and not altogether happy life had taught her to redouble it. Never tell one's

99

mind to anybody. On the whole it had worked well for her. It had not taken her long to size up Michael Pollard; a nice, well-mannered young man—not so young, she knew his age—what might be called a gentleman; but soft, and without guile. He had had everything too easy; never having had to work for his living; and leading, so far as she knew, a completely useless life. No doubt he looked after his property, and drew up agreements with his tenants, perhaps did a bit of business on the stock market; but in Mrs Reid's opinion all that was no work for a man. Although she found herself liking him for his courtesy and good humour, he was certainly not the sort of person she would open her mind to.

What he had told her was interesting. She had been wondering during the past few days whether she ought to do something herself; and it was partly on account of this that she had rung up Pollard about Paddy Meehan's funeral. The outcome had been encouraging. Hitherto she had regarded Pollard with a certain amount of awe; a very rich man, a landlord, a great employer in his time. After their journey to church and graveyard today her admiration for him had increased, but a great deal of the awe had fallen away.

She stirred her cup, savouring the rich, thick smell of strong tea, and looked about her kitchen. Green linoleum, shining with polish; a gas cooker; a strong deal table to eat upon; and four good kitchen chairs to sit on. Mrs Reid had been used to hard chairs all her life; and when she relaxed in her kitchen she did so on a bentwood chair with a cushion made by herself. She had been unable to find a decent Irish kitchen dresser in England, so she made do with a Welsh one on which her small collection of delf and china was tastefully and neatly arranged. Blue bawneen curtains run up on the sewing-machine; a small fridge; a cuckoo clock that had belonged to her mother. The sink unit and wall cupboards came with the flat.

The small possessions she had managed to bring with her from Ireland were almost the story of her life. The oleograph of the Sacred Heart over the range had been given to her as a wedding present by the girls she had worked with in Williams's shop in Tullamore. The photograph of herself and her husband on their wedding-day in 1952; she rarely looked at it; it was a signpost upon a road

100

she had left behind. She glanced at the large, obsolete prayer-book in a corner of the dresser. It was filled with memorial cards of dead friends and relatives; and there also her husband was commemorated. Died August, 9th, 1957. 'O Immense Passion! O Profound Wounds! O Profusion of Blood! O Sweetness above all Sweetness! O Most Bitter Death! Grant him eternal rest.' She knew the prayer by heart. Killed on a bicycle at the age of thirty-two. Drunk. Mrs Reid did not dwell much on the memory of her marriage; there had been many others like it in Ireland, she knew. But she prayed for the dead.

A small green post-office saving box which she had given to her son, John, on his tenth birthday. It was the only memento she had kept of him. After her husband's death she had come to England, bringing her two-year old son with her. She had got a job in Sheffield in a large dairy and confectionery shop where in time she had become manageress. John went to good Catholic schools and seemed set fair for a fine, educated career, until at the age of twenty-one he had married an English girl two years older than himself and apparently of no religious belief. Mrs Reid had never met his wife; attendance at a marriage in a registry office was out of the question. She had stayed on in Sheffield long enough to learn that her son had given up his religion, and spent all of his time with his wife's family and friends.

After this Mrs Reid came south. She looked at the pretty bone china tea-set which the girls in the shop had given her as a farewell gift; and on the wall opposite the print of the lakes of Killarney— where she had never been—which the directors had given her. Over the unused range hung the Papal Blessing brought for her from Rome by a priest friend; the same man who had advised her to apply to Pollard for a flat.

Mrs Reid considered herself lucky. She was not given to complaining; and although she prayed for her son at Mass every morning, she did not worry overmuch about him. God would answer her prayers in His own good time. And in the meantime she had some money in the bank.

At the moment she had more immediate things to think about. It

101

had not escaped her notice that a tall, fair-haired young man some-times visited Nancy; and on more than one occasion stayed very late. Then came the news of Pollard's engagement; and Mrs Reid recollected that for some time before, and certainly since, there had been no sign of the young man. She assumed that Nancy had given him up. But now, after hearing what Michael had to say, she was not so sure. She looked at the piece of paper again.

A few months before she had met Nancy in the hall. Apart from bidding her the time of day Mrs Reid had not spoken to her; but on this occasion Nancy stopped and addressed her by her name.

'Oh, Mrs Reid, it's lucky I ran into you. I'm in a terrible hurry. Would you do something for me?'

'It depends on what it is,' replied Mrs Reid coldly. She did not approve of young female secretaries who entertained men in their rooms until the small hours of the morning.

'Oh, nothing illegal,' laughed Nancy. 'It's just that I'm supposed to meet a few people this evening, and now I can't. Would you be an angel and telephone this number'—she indicated the coin-box in the hall, which was rarely used by anyone except Mrs Reid herself; most of the tenants had their own telephones. 'Tell whoever answers that I can't make it tonight. You will do that, won't you, please?' Mrs Reid nodded. She was not an unfriendly woman, and this seemed a very harmless request. Nancy had gone off and Mrs Reid had dialled the number. Although she could not be absolutely sure, she thought the voice that answered was that of Nancy's visitor. In the short time before she carried out her commission the older woman had had time to think. 'A few people,' Nancy had said. It was worthwhile checking on that.

'She also told me to ask you to tell the others,' she said when the voice had finished thanking her.

'What others?' it had enquired.

'Oh, I don't know. That's what she said.' Mrs Reid put down the telephone. She had assumed at the time that Nancy told lies like most other young women nowadays; but in the light of later events she had often asked herself why Nancy had lied to her. Once she had thought of dropping a hint to Pollard; but after all there was very little to go on—until now.

As she sat drinking her tea she decided on her course of action. Then she took down her purse from the ledge over the range, took out her rosary beads and began to say her evening prayers.

Mrs Reid always went to six-thirty Mass in the morning, unless it was raining too heavily, when she waited for a later one. Her job in the City restaurant left her free in the mornings until half-ten when she took the Tube from Gloucester Road to Holborn, and changed trains there for Bank station, which brought her within a few minutes' walk of her employment in Old Broad Street. She had always been an early riser, and she rather looked forward to her morning journey through empty thoroughfares to the Carmelite church in Kensington Church Street. She could have gone to Mass in a convent near Cornwall Gardens, as some other local Catholics did; but it was half an hour later than the Carmelites, and was frequented by a small group of English Catholics, all of whom struck Mrs Reid as altogether too stuck up and condescending. Besides, she preferred the Carmelites because of the two statues of the Child of Prague and the Little Flower on either side of the entrance door. To these she always lighted candles every morning of her life; and another one before the Sacred Heart altar. These three offerings, she firmly believed, had brought her good health, safe jobs and a reasonable prospect for the future.

So next morning she let herself out the front door, warmly clad and equipped with plastic mac and umbrella. It was not a great distance; round the corner into Victoria Road and on to Kensington High Street: in her youth she had walked three miles to Mass through the lonely, flat Offaly bogland.

As often happened, she met Maggie Harrington going in the front door. Maggie was also an early-morning regular, and had been during the thirty years she had spent in London as a telephone operator in the Post Office.

'I want to have a word with you, Maggie,' whispered Mrs Reid, as they dipped their fingers in the holy-water font, and blessed themselves. 'After Mass.'

Maggie looked at her questioningly. They always had a word after Mass, walking down the hill to the corner of St Mary Abbots; about which Maggie had once passed a memorable remark. 'They have their nerve, calling their church after a Catholic saint, seeing that they have none of their own. Who's this St Mary Abbots anyway?'

After Mass Maggie was waiting for her.

'Well,' she said, 'what's the big mystery?'

'Would you ever look up this number, Maggie, and let me know who it belongs to, and what's the address?' She handed over a copy of the slip of paper with Hansen's name and number on it. Maggie looked at her curiously, but Mrs Reid's face was blank. Maggie got the message: if she delivered the goods she would hear the story. She put the paper into her purse, and nodded agreement. Then they began to talk about Father Gregory's lovely way of saying Mass, and how gorgeous Father Thomas was in confession.

XVIII

It had been a delightful funeral, and everybody was thrilled with the arrangements. Nothing like the number of cars which would have followed a man like Peter Leech in Ireland on his last journey; but very satisfactory in London.

Mrs Reid sat in a corner of the lounge of the Wimbledon hotel where the quieter sort of mourner had gathered after the burial; the others had gone to a pub down the road to celebrate. The dead man's two middle-aged daughters, both nuns, were sitting in a corner drinking tea with several women friends. Another little knot of women were clustered around a table near by having a discreet round of vodkas and sherries. At the top of the room the men were gathered about the opening of the dispense bar drinking whiskey; nephews, cousins, friends of the deceased; all elderly, over-weight and ponderous in their movements. The dead man had been ninety-three; in earlier days they too would have joined the revellers in the public-house; but they were nearly all in their seventies and eighties and strictly forbidden most of the things that they liked to eat and drink. Besides, there were the wives down the room keeping a sharp eye on them.

Andrew Pollard moved among the men shaking hands, smiling, putting his arm through those of his acquaintances who were older than himself. He was a head taller than most of them, and looked younger than all of them; well preserved, straight; quietly and expensively dressed.

Mrs Reid found herself cut off from the two main groups, in a little islet of silence by herself. Pollard had shown her to a table, ordered coffee for both of them, and sat with her for a few minutes before he got up to join the men. By then the party had divided itself into the inevitable two camps; and she was left alone to watch over the plate of biscuits and Pollard's cooling coffee. Although he had introduced her to many of the other guests, his presence by her side in the church and graveyard, and then for a few minutes at their own table, had assured her by way of inflexible Irish politeness of a degree of solitude. For this at the moment she was grateful.

She had passed four strenuous and worrying days since Maggie had informed her that the number belonged to an R. P. K. Armstrong with an address in Guilford Street, off Russell Square. It was difficult to know what to do; and her first instinct was to watch. Seated at her sewing-machine in the evenings, she missed little of the comings and goings through the front door. She would have much preferred to work in the kitchen; it would have saved gas, and was a great deal more comfortable; but she felt an obligation to keep an eye on things on account of her arrangement with Pollard. It would have come as a considerable surprise to her to learn that the other tenants, including Nancy, were very much aware of her presence in the window and in the hall, where during her tidying operations she subjected every visitor to a sharp-eyed scrutiny. 'Nosey old cat' was how one tenant on the same floor described her to Nancy. 'I can't stand her,' Nancy had replied. 'She gives me the creeps.' Mrs Reid thought she was being both discreet

105

and unobtrusive; and when the tenants replied coldly to her morning or evening greeting, put it down to English reserve. That any of them might have been suffering from frustration or a certain degree of guilt never occurred to her; her standards were so totally different from theirs.

The first evening after Maggie's rather puzzling piece of information, Nancy had come back to her flat at nine and remained there; and on the following night she had been very late, so that Mrs Reid had been half asleep when she heard the rap of her heels on the steps, and the sound of a male voice. Thanking God that she had put out the light in her room, Mrs Reid peered out to discover Michael Pollard saying goodnight on the pavement and walking swiftly away: a puzzling occurrence. But on the following evening Nancy had returned about six, and went out again in about half an hour. Mrs Reid felt instinctively that this was the time to put her plan into effect. At midnight Nancy had not returned; so Mrs Reid went to the telephone in the hall and dialled Armstrong's number, which was answered by a male voice; she was almost sure that it was the same voice she had heard when she had rung up Hansen.

'Could I speak to Miss Cook, please? She told me she'd be there until late.' It was one of the most nerve-racking experiences of Mrs Reid's life; and she had no talent for disguising her voice.

'What a time to call. She's just having a bath. I'll go and tell her if you hold on.'

Mrs Reid put down the receiver quietly, and went back to her flat with a grim look on her face. She did not wait up for Nancy to come back; what she had heard was quite bad enough. Nevertheless, it was not a conclusive proof. Next day she took the Tube to Russell Square and walked behind the big hotel into Guilford Street. Winchester Mansions presented a problem; there was no place near by where she could sit down and watch the door on the chance that Hansen would come out. But she was a determined woman; there was nothing for it but direct action. She pressed a bell marked enquiries, hoping that it would summon a porter. After a few minutes' delay, it did. The door was opened by an aged man with a livid face and a hoarse voice.

'Weel, and what do you want?'

Mrs Reid was disappointed to hear that he had a Scottish burr instead of an Irish one; but that could not be helped now.

'I'm looking for Mr Armstrong,' she said in a pleading tone. No use taking a high hand with a crusty old man like this.

'Gone awa, leddy. Ye didn noo tha?'

'Oh, no. He never told me. And it's urgent.'

'Weel, he'd hardly be lookin' for a hoosekeeper. Or are ye a freend?'

'A friend of a friend.'

'Ah. Weel, Mr Armstrong is a gennelmon, but he kept some verra low company.' He inspected Mrs Reid up and down with his rheumy eyes.

'I hope you're not referring to me,' said Mrs Reid indignantly.

'Aw, noo, noo, wummin. He wurrna like that. I used to knoo him when I was workin' in the Baths round the corner. They're doon now. But if he only knew the way that fella he left in his flat is behavin', it's disgraceful, that's what it is. Wummin! Mr Armstrong niver laid out for that.'

'Women?' Mrs Reid raised her eyebrows in genuine astonishment.

'Weel, only one, but that's more dangerous than a crowd. Mr Armstrong is a fine mon, a decent mon, and generous, but he should never ha' taken up with a foreigner, that has taste in wummin.'

'Oh, it must be that American girl,' said Mrs Reid, feeling her heart beat uncomfortably fast. 'A young, fair-haired girl.'

'Are you a freend o' hers?' he growled, peering closer.

'No. Well, I suppose I'd better write, if Mr Armstrong is not at home. Thank you.' She had walked quickly away; she had heard enough to be going on with.

She was now determined to get in touch with Pollard, and drop him a broad hint. It never occurred to her that he might not care to hear it: surely no man likes being deceived, especially by a girl young enough to be his granddaughter. After what Michael had told her it seemed to her that her duty was plain. She had none of his relation's scruples as to his possible reaction; she was quite

107

simply anxious not to see him make a fool of himself. But she had difficulty in making up her mind as to the best way in which to approach him discreetly. If she telephoned Nancy might answer; if she rang up in the evening his niece and nephew might be with him. She had almost decided to write, asking him to call on her, in spite of the risk of Nancy opening his mail, when the death of Peter Leech came like an answer from heaven. Maggie, who followed Irish news in London with the eye of a hawk and the ear of a dog, told her about it. Pollard, as she expected, was at the funeral, and had offered her a lift back as they came out of the graveyard. Surely the good Lord had heard her prayers.

She thought of this again as she looked around at the company. A tall, fat priest passed her with a friendly nod and joined the nuns. This was as it should be: priests were expected to go from one group to another. It reminded her of decent wakes long ago at home, with the women lined along one side of the corpse, facing the men on the other side, all answering the rosary; all with their eyes fixed on the pale, lifeless face on the white pillow, correctly robed in a Third Order habit, and clasping a crucifix in its rigid hands. The rejoicing mingled with the grief: life goes on, and in the meantime another soul had fled into the infinite to intercede for them all. Mrs Reid sighed with content, and sipped her coffee daintily.

'It's an awful pity poor Peter didn't live until St Patrick's day. Last year he drank a mug of poteen and never as much as blinked an eye.' A small, fat, purple-faced man was talking to Pollard at the edge of the group of men.

'Yes, indeed, and so it is,' Pollard replied, shaking his head, 'but we can't have everything, and he had a good life.'

'Indeeden he had, and a happy death, God rest him for a dacent man.'

Pollard sat down beside her, flushed and bright-eyed, and quite evidently in his element. Mrs Reid could not help wondering as she observed his appearance of well-being how exactly he stood with the priests if he intended to marry a pagan. She could be nothing else. Mrs Reid had come away from her interview with the porter at Winchester Mansions with a sense of orgies. She frowned as she

108

thrust the idea from her mind. Far better to remember the straggling line of men, four deep along a country road, their boots thudding on the uneven surface; the low hum of cars creeping along at five miles an hour; the rattle of traps in the old days; the silence of the fields; the surplices, the purple stole, the low murmur of prayer; and the rain pit-patting on the coffin before it began its last descent into the boggy earth that bore it. People could not keep up such a tradition in all its ritual glory in a city like London; but they could try.

'You know, I think you ought to have a sherry,' said Pollard, looking at her with a smile. He was holding a glass of whiskey himself; not the first, as Mrs Reid had observed. 'It was terrible cold in that cemetery.'

She felt very much like a sherry, remembering how the funerals at home always left people with a great thirst, and often a great hunger too. But she decided against it; it might encourage her companion to have another, and she did not want him tipsy on this important occasion. She shook her head smilingly.

'You're right, of course,' he said earnestly. 'I'm supposed to take very little, but I couldn't send off poor Peter without a toast.'

'Of course not,' said Mrs Reid firmly. 'Wasn't it a lovely funeral?'

'Grand. And fourteen priests at the High Mass. You know, of course, that he donated the high altar to the parish church.'

'Yes, I heard that. And look at the long life he had as a reward. Ah, well, he knows all the answers now.'

'Yes.' He put down his glass unfinished and tapped on the table with his fingers. 'I wish I did.'

'Oh, no, Mr Pollard, you mustn't wish that, it's very unlucky.' She was genuinely concerned.

He looked at her silently for a few moments, then took up his glass and drained it: to leave it unfinished would be very bad manners, and no compliment to the dead. He turned to her with a decisive air.

'That's enough. I think we ought to be going. From now on a lot of this is going to be artificial.'

He got up to shake hands with the chief mourners; and Mrs Reid followed suit after a decent interval. They brought their parts in the ritual to a graceful and dignified conclusion.

XIX

During the intervals of silence on the way home, while Pollard was negotiating some heavy blocks of traffic, she rehearsed the little speech she was going to make when he dropped her at her front door.

In the event it proved unnecessary. As he stopped the car outside the house he turned and said:

'I suppose you wouldn't consider giving me a cup of strong tea?'

'Well, indeeden I would. And as for my tea, it's always strong. Come in, and welcome.'

He went round the corner to park the car, and Mrs Reid waited for him outside the open door as one does for an honoured guest. After all, the house was his.

She led the way into her kitchen, instinctively feeling that he would enjoy the atmosphere there better than the cold formality of the front room. She motioned him to the chair with the cushion, and busied herself with the kettle and the tea-pot.

'You have everything lovely in here,' he said, looking around gravely, and nodding his head.

'Ah, indeed my few old things are not much furniture. But it's a grand warm room, thank God. I'll be sorry to be leaving it, it's a grand place entirely.'

'I'm sorry too.'

'Do you know what I have?' She looked at him, holding the tea-pot in her two hands as she tilted it from side to side so that the hot water would warm it thoroughly. 'A barm brack. My old aunt Kate sends me one every year for St Patrick's day, well in advance, for she doesn't trust the post. Would you like a cut?'

'A brack!' Pollard's eyes opened with delight. 'I haven't tasted a real one for years. They can't make them over here.'

'Indeed en they can't. Do you like a bit of butter on it? Of course you do. Well, we'll have that, and a bit of fruit cake.'

The barm brack was a bit of luck; but it did not materially alter the plan she had made of approaching the delicate issue when he was well primed with strong tea. At length, over the crumbs, when she had shaken her skirt and thrown the tea leaves into the container in the sink, and sat down opposite him, planting her feet solidly on the linoleum and clasping her hands on her lap, she lifted her chin and tackled him, in much the same manner as a tenant speaking to a landlord on the subject of a leaking roof.

'To tell you the truth, Mr Pollard, if you hadn't given me a lift today, and come in as you have, I'd have asked to see you privately. I hope you won't take offence.'

'Well, that depends, Mrs Reid,' he replied with a smile, sitting very upright in his chair, his hands resting peacefully on his knees.

'I suppose if I wasn't leaving this flat, I might think twice about what I have to say to you. After all, you might throw me out. But the funeral today gave me a sort of extra courage.' She drew a deep breath and plunged in. 'It's about Miss Cook.'

'Nancy?' His bushy eyebrows shot up, and his fingers moved a little on his knees. 'I hope she hasn't had a row with you, or something? Or has she bought a dog? She mentioned that a few times.' Clearly Pollard thought there had been some sort of women's squabble; but his bluffness did not conceal a certain wariness in the eyes.

Mrs Reid took another deep breath, and ploughed on.

'Did she ever speak to you about a man called Hansen, a foreigner, I think?' She looked him fixedly in the eye as if the still points might steady her nerves.

'Hansen?' Pollard raised his hand and rubbed his chin. 'No, I don't think so. Although, of course, I come up against a lot of names, in the houses, you understand. One thing I won't have is coloureds, though.'.

'Of course not,' said Mrs Reid firmly. 'No, he isn't a Black, very fair in fact. He lives near Russell Square.'

Pollard shook his head, and looked at his hostess enquiringly, clasping his chin between his fingers.

'Well, he used to spend a lot of his time with her here, but not recently. However, she still goes to see him. And stays very late.'

Pollard remained silent, his fingers held stiffly on his chin. Mrs Reid shifted uneasily in her chair, and longed for another cup of tea.

'I have his telephone number,' she hurried on. 'She gave it to me some months ago, and asked me to leave a message because she was in a hurry. So I rang up the other night when she went out. I left it very late. And she was there.' She felt she had said all she could reasonably be expected to say; impossible to bring herself to tell him of her encounter with the porter.

Pollard thrust out his lower lip and looked down at his feet, comfortably shod in fine Italian shoes. The silence dragged, until Mrs Reid began to wonder if he intended to answer at all. When he did raise his head he looked stern; withdrawn and very determined. Although she did not know it, this was the expression he used with fighting his way out of a difficult business deal; the sort of situation which sometimes provided him with a brilliant last-minute line of defence. When he knew he was beaten he chuckled and shook his head; these setbacks were usually of a temporary nature, as his colleagues well knew.

'I think I know what's behind it, Mrs Reid. Nancy's father was a gambler—still is, in so far as he's able—he lost his job with an oil company on the head of it. But he got into worse trouble than that, because he married three times, and Nancy has a step-brother here in London, who's no better than his father, and is a constant drain on her. She didn't tell me this, but I found out.'

Mrs Reid was taken aback. She knew Americans had very tangled family backgrounds, and were always getting divorced; yet she was not satisfied. Recovering from the shock, she mustered her forces.

'But if he's her father's son, Mr Pollard, surely he'd have the same name?'

'No. Apparently his mother married again very quickly after a bad row, and brought him up under her new husband's name. At least, that's what I was given to understand.' Pollard was becoming

112

more fluent, his gaze more earnest, his whole demeanour confident and forceful. If Mrs Reid had ever tried to argue with him over the small print in a contract she would have recognized the pose, which by now had become almost second nature.

'I see.' All Mrs Reid's instincts told her that Hansen's connection with Nancy was quite otherwise; but she had no proof.

'Has anyone spoken to you about this—ah, Hansen, Mrs Reid?' went on Pollard lightly, brushing a crumb from his knee, and apparently giving great attention to the operation.

'Oh, no. I don't know anything about him, except that I saw him come in and out of here. At one time I was going to report it to you, and then—' Her voice trailed off. 'And then Nancy became engaged.'

'Well, you did very well, Mrs Reid, and I'm extremely grateful to you. I suppose this fellow is pestering Nancy for money, and she won't admit it.' He paused and his face hardened; narrowed eyes, mouth set, peaked nose: an expression rarely seen except by those who had attempted to get the better of him. 'I'll deal with him.' He relaxed and smiled in his usual genial fashion—a handsome old man, expensively dressed, at peace with the world. 'Do you know something, Mrs Reid, I'd give a lot for a sup of whiskey, if you have it.'

Relieved of tension, she sprang up, and in doing so uttered a muffled cry and grasped her hip.

'Is there anything wrong?' he said anxiously.

'Oh, no, no. It's just that I get a pain in my hip now and again when I move too quickly.' She laughed and shook her head ruefully. 'Old age, I suppose.' She went out, walking somewhat carefully. But Pollard did not notice her. Left alone he allowed himself to crumple; sagging shoulders, chin outspread on this chest, hands flaccid in his lap; like an old actor in the wings after a strenuous performance. He remained like this for a few minutes when the clink of glass warned him of her return, when he straightened himself with an effort, his nostrils flaring, his chin thrust out.

'To tell you the truth,' said Mrs Reid as she poured out his glass, 'that's the real reason I'm leaving my present job. There's always a

113

draught sitting in the cash-desk, and I'd be terrified of getting rheumatism.' She paused with the glass in her hand and looked over his head with a troubled look in her eye. 'It would be dreadful if I wasn't able to work. Especially at my age. But it'll be easier with Father Kiely, with the help of God. He has a nice, comfortable house.'

As she handed him his glass and put down a jug of water on the table beside him her movements were brisk and practised; but her mind was elsewhere. She was suddenly visited by a return of the only nightmare she had ever experienced: a vision of women queueing for buses in Sheffield in the rain and cold; elderly women working in shops and offices; bright and chattering and effortful during working hours; sad figures with swollen legs, sheltering under umbrellas in the evening rush. Mrs Reid knew what ill-health and unemployment meant when you are coming up to fifty.

'Thank you, thank you, this is a lovely drop of Irish. I think I must have felt a chill in that graveyard. This will do me good.' He raised his glass in salute, and she nodded her head smilingly in reply.

'Graveyards are terrible places for that,' she said earnestly. 'It's all that long grass. It always seems to be wet. Although they do keep them a lot better here than at home.'

'Where would you like to be buried, Mrs Reid?' he asked pleasantly. 'Here, or at home?'

'Oh, at home, of course. I have the money left aside for it, the transport and all, you know. It's got awful expensive nowadays, but I keep in touch with the charges, and add a little out of my savings now and again.' She shuddered and shook her jowls. 'Oh, Lord, I'd hate to be buried here, in this unfriendly place. Besides, I have a nice plot at home.'

'So have I,' went on Pollard, as if he were talking of a holiday bungalow. 'I always go to have a look at it when I'm home. I pay to have it kept, of course, but if you don't follow these fellows they'd let the weeds grow all over it.'

'Isn't it a disgrace,' said Mrs Reid warmly. 'I had to kick up a terrible row about mine the last time I was home. I hauled him out of the house, and stood over him until he had it properly cleaned up. I was raging.'

'I don't blame you. You were quite right.' Pollard left down his glass and stood up. 'Can I go——' he enquired politely.

'Oh, of course, of course, it's just out there on the right.'

While he was away Mrs Reid stood up from her chair slowly, and repeated the exercise three times; sitting back at last with a contented expression. It was only when she moved unexpectedly and fast that the twinge troubled her. All the same, she murmured a silent prayer to the Sacred Heart on the wall above to spare her a recurrence.

'Do you know,' said Pollard coming back, 'I really ought to be going. I've taken up enough of your time as it is.' He picked up his glass, but did not sit down.

'Well, indeeden you haven't,' said Mrs Reid warmly. She was expecting Maggie to drop round later, and it would be quite pleasant to introduce her to the famous Mr Pollard. 'I have all the time in the world at present, until I go to Father Kiely. I suppose you know him, Mr Pollard?'

'Oh, yes, and his brothers in Tipperary. A fine family.'

Mrs Reid thought how different this was from his nephew, who did not seem to bother about important things like family backgrounds. She looked up at her guest with admiration. Putting down his glass, he turned to her, a thoughtful expression on his flushed face.

'I'm having a new headstone put over my old family plot at home; the old one is not nice, and some of the dates are incorrect. An architect I know has sent me a sketch of it.' He paused and cleared his throat. 'Would you like to look at it, and see what you think, Mrs Reid?'

She flushed with pleasure and rose carefully to her feet.

'Of course I would, Mr Pollard. But you know I'm not much of a judge of these things. I've only a little stone over my plot at home. It'd be nothing like yours.'

Pollard took down his mohair coat from the peg on the door, and got into it slowly, taking his gloves from the pocket and flapping them against his sleeve.

'What time are you always here at?' he enquired.

'Well, in the morning, of course, after Mass. Then from about eight on after I have my tea.'

'I'll call round some evening so, and bring the sketch with me. I don't want it too elaborate.'

Chatting amiably about crosses, edgings, gravel and slabs, they moved into the hall, and parted with elaborate expressions of mutual pleasure. It was the best funeral Mrs Reid had ever attended.

Part Three

XX

Nancy and Michael discovered that their childhoods had been spent in a very similar manner. Instead of avoiding him since she discovered that he knew about Hansen, she seemed to make a point of seeking him out. This did not surprise Michael: he realized that he had thrust himself forcibly into her life, and must therefore be an object of increased interest to her. He remembered a man many years before who had tackled him about a love affair he was having with a married woman which he thought was completely unobserved. He found himself seeking out the man in various bars which he frequented; and becoming quite intimate with him. It did not come as more than a mild shock to him when the lady eventually transferred her attentions to the informant. People who break into an enclosed atmosphere are often invited to stay and share the sense of claustrophobia, if only to afford the enclosed ones the relief of talking about themselves to a third person.

'I know you suspect that I'm two-timing Andy,' she said to him suddenly one day when Pollard had gone to Maiden Lane, and Rosamund was out with one of her gallery associates. 'But Johnny is just a friend. He's a great guy, and very funny, really gay in every sense of the word. Women like that sort of man, you know. But he is as queer as a coot, but really queer. I mean, some of the things he gets up to, you wouldn't believe, and I'm here to tell you. Funny, with all that, and the whole world knows it, he's a hundred per cent journalist. Very well thought of, and influential in Copenhagen.'

'I suppose it was he who gave the leak to the newspapers about your engagement,' said Michael quietly.

Nancy shot him a quick glance.

'I don't know,' she said quickly. 'Funny, I never asked him.'

Michael smiled to himself. She was really a very bad liar. But not, he thought, a habitual one. And she was very charming, with the greedy impulses of a spoilt child. No wonder Pollard found her irresistible. Most of the people he had spent his life with were shrewd, calculating, preoccupied with their plans. Nancy lived for the moment, holding it up before her face as if she were squeezing an orange into her mouth on a hot summer day.

'Did he read your palm?' she said, looking at his big, red hands which he had clasped before his chest, rather like the attitude of a priest in prayer. Dark hairs gleamed on his wrist, and more than once her glance had rested on them; a reaction he was familiar with in women. He opened his hands and held them out in front of him, palms down, fingers outspread.

'Yes, he did,' he admitted, turning down the corners of his mouth. 'He told me to be careful.'

'And are you?'

'I don't know. What do you think?'

For answer she sprang up from the sofa, and crouched down on her hunkers in front of him.

'Gimme,' she said, wriggling her fingers over his hand. He turned it round slowly and held it out to her. She placed it gently in hers, and he felt an unmistakable quiver of desire as he felt her fingers touch his wrist. This was better fun, and altogether more familiar than plotting for an inheritance.

'Ooh,' she murmured, 'it's awfully like mine. Johnny taught me a few things about palmistry, but I'm really only interested in the life-line.'

'How's that?'

'You're going to live to be at least eighty, and have nine children and three wives, and write poetry and breed dogs and win the sweep and travel all over the world. So there.' She sprang back

118

before he could reach out and clutch her by the neck. It would pass as a playful gesture, but he found he very much wanted to touch her, feel the pulse throbbing in her throat; something that always excited him in women.

'He told me I'd live as long as a Lesbian,' she said, sitting down again, and leaning forward with her hands clasped between her knees. She obviously felt the need to change the conversation.

'Do they live long?'

'Oh, yes. Didn't you know? They all live to about ninety. There used to be a colony of them in Eze in the South of France near Monte Carlo. They're still there, so far as I know. There was a story of a sailor who followed one of their girls up from the beach, and a few of the dykes beat him up.'

'You know Eze?'

'Not in that way, if that's what you mean. But I've been there. I used to spend summers on the coast when I was a kid. Winters too, often.'

'So did I.'

'You did.' Her eyes lighted up, and she bit her lip in surprise. 'Well, isn't that just grand. You liked it?'

'Yes, I liked it very much.' His gaze left her face, and he looked across the room vaguely, visited as he sometimes was by a whole series of complicated emotions and memories. Those years from his ninth to his sixteenth year. His bright, restless mother trailing him in her wake as she moved through a succession of small hotels and pensions in the South of France and Liguria: buried there now owing to that frantic misunderstanding. Looking back, it seemed to him that his childhood had been founded on fragments of ambiguity. He had once asked his mother, after playing in the garden with an English boy who had talked continually about his uncles and aunts, if all those people—the old ladies playing bridge in dusty public rooms, the old gentlemen in whites on verandahs, with hoarse, creaking voices—were relations. She had laughed, and whispered in his ear. 'Yes, quite close relations of ours, but they don't like you to mention it to them. Oh, yes, very much the same family as us. When you're older, I'll tell you.' She had not lived

119

long enough to tell him; but by then he knew. It was not the old expatriates that he came to think of as his close relations, but the young people, French, German, Scandinavian, who arrived on the Riviera in fast cars, and walked indolently down to the beaches, lean of frame, brown-skinned, with loose, agile limbs. The world was to be enjoyed as they enjoyed it; eating, drinking, making love far from offices, dull skies and belching factories. They changed, going and coming, constantly renewing themselves in others equally young, free and arrogant. One must never go away; one must remain constant among the magnolias and the flowering bougain-villaea. That had been his form of competition, when others were sweating over examination books, and learning the hard alphabet of the north. Walking along the red sanded paths, watching the white figures on tennis courts; saving up to sit among them on expensive hotel verandahs; following them with an envious eye as they strolled hand-in-hand along the Croisette, he had, almost unknown to himself, formulated a whole private philosophy of life. The fairest parts of the world were in the possession of the indolent. He closed his eyes and sighed as the vision blurred into a patch of glittering sea at the end of a speckled wood, and it was impossible to renew it except sometimes in the warmth of eager young arms, greedy young mouths and warm young bodies. He looked at Nancy with sad, heavy eyes.

'I suppose you were remembering it all,' she said in a low voice. 'I do too, often. Oh, God, how I wish I could go back there forever.'

'Perhaps you will,' he smiled crookedly, knowing now what he was going to do; aware as so often in the past that no sense of mundane duties was going to prevent him.

'I hope so, I certainly hope so. I get so cold here. Sometimes I feel I'm only warm in the bath.' She was silent for a few moments, and then chuckled and shook her head. 'Of course it's all a dream, really. It's supposed to be a very shallow life, or so people say, and I guess they're right. But somehow, it doesn't seem so to me.'

'Nor me. One can be just as shallow working in a factory. All those philosophies of the north, they're all really excuses for a damp climate and the building of more and more office blocks.'

'You know, I never thought of that. You could be right, you could be very right.' She caught his eye and held it for a moment, during which he felt sure she recognized exactly what his purpose was. 'What does Rosamund think of all this?'

'Oh, Rosie is happy anywhere. She can bring her easel along.'

'You're very close, aren't you?'

'Yes.' He did not feel it necessary to explain further; nor was it the time to do so. Nancy made no effort to probe further; she became suddenly brisk and practical again. Nostalgia was fun; but it had the unpleasant effect of rendering one incapable of making an effort to attain the very things one was most nostalgic about. One had to make very definite arrangements if one was to idle by sunlit coasts.

'Have you and she given any thought to that proposal I made? You know, making some sort of a settlement. After all Andy may live for a long time yet. It's better to have something now, something substantial. You can enjoy it now.'

It was worth investigating.

'What were you thinking of?' he said cautiously.

'Oh, some houses, two or three for you, the same for Rosamund. I know just how many he has, and he wouldn't miss half a dozen. They were all bought years ago, and just think of the value of them now. And, you know, even if Andy doesn't marry me, he could in time leave all he has to charity, or something. It would ease my conscience a lot, I can tell you, honest it would.' She was plainly sincere, and even if she had an ulterior motive, Michael could not but admit to himself the sense of her argument.

'Are you so sure you can get him to do it?'

'I think so.' She put her head to one side and made a monkey grimace, stretching her lips over her teeth without parting her lips. 'He has a bit of a bad conscience about me. Yes, I think he'll do it.' She looked at her watch. 'He should be home soon. Those funerals, one a week at least. It's just morbid. I wonder if he'll meet Madam Reid again this time. Funerals are just her cup of tea too.' Suddenly she drew in her breath sharply, drew up her shoulders and looked at

121

him with bright, open eyes. 'I am a fool. Why didn't I think of that before. Was it the Reid who told you about Johnny?'

'No, of course not,' Michael said with genuine emphasis. 'I never met her in my life until the other day. And that reminds me—why do you dislike her so much?'

'I can't stand the sight of her. She always seems to be watching me, the others too, in the house, sitting all evening at that fucking sewing-machine. She gives me the creeps.'

'Yes. She's never left whatever small town she comes from behind her. But I think she's harmless enough. Cute, of course, real peasant cunning, I know that type. She probably thinks we're all mad.' He drew his fingers over his mouth. 'And by her standards I suppose we are.'

Now that he had more or less accepted Nancy's offer of a settlement Michael felt immensely relieved. If the case had been a straightforward one of common deception which could be proven against Nancy he would not have hesitated. Somebody somewhere in the Irish community would surely have agreed to alert Pollard, leaving Michael and Rosamund with their hands clean. But the situation was too complicated; to make use of it now would have taken a great deal more energy and ruthlessness than he possessed. A couple of London houses at present-day prices would not be at all bad; and a compromise was safer than an all-out gamble that might not come off. It cleared his mind of several unpleasant ideas about Nancy, leaving him free to think of her in a way which was altogether more natural and a great deal more amusing for him. He had not forgotten Hansen's story about her and her supposed fear of adult, normal intercourse. If he had succeeded in discrediting her and had been sure of his case he would not have given it more than a passing thought, tempered with a certain pity. But now he was free to allow himself the full interest which the idea roused in him. Whenever important enterprises collapse they are always followed by a feeling of recklessness. He could now indicate to himself, if he cared to think of it, the exact moment that afternoon when he decided that the game was lost—and another commenced; an impulse entirely sensual, bringing him back on a tide of familiar sensations to a shore on which he felt himself at home. On the choppy sea of real financial piracy he had been swept to and fro at the mercy of currents he found himself incapable of controlling. But now with the clear knowledge of his own particular terrain he knew exactly what he wanted to do.

He looked at Nancy, a slow, infinitely patient smile breaking the set expression on his face; and was rewarded with a glance half fascinated, half anxious which he recognized and welcomed. It lasted no more than a few seconds, this exchange between two immemorial enmities, both perfectly aware of their inability to exist without the other; and was cut short by a sharp sound that caused them to draw apart and look away.

'That must be Andy now,' said Nancy in a slightly breathless voice. They listened to the steps in the hall above; but they did not come to the top of the stairs as they expected. Instead another door opened, closed. Nancy stood up, looking slightly puzzled.

'He must have remembered something he wants to do. He's gone into his office. I suppose I'd better go up. I want to get this thing settled as soon as possible. I hate letting things go from day to day. They grow.'

'Not yet.' Michael stood up and came close to her, keeping his hands close by his sides. He could smell the warm fragrance of her skin, and the fresh wood-shavings' tang of her hair. His own body was reacting in the familiar, pleasurable way; but he would not allow himself to touch her. That moment would come.

'I hope you're not going to double-cross me,' he said in a low voice.

'I hope you're not going to double-cross me,' she replied in the same tone.

He leaned his head towards her, and she closed her eyes and tilted her face up, like a small child waiting for a kiss. Gently his mouth touched hers, without any pressure or any effort to explore the warm moisture within. He felt her lips trembling under his, but gradually in the long moment that passed between them, as full of promise as a naked caress, she grew quieter under his steady, light engagement. At last, as carefully and steadily as a physician lifting

123

his hand from a nervous child, he drew his head away, and watched her eyelids tremble and open as if she were awaking from a deep sleep.

'Now, go,' he murmured, standing quite still as she stepped back and covered her cheeks with her hands, staring at his chest with a sort of blind intensity. Presently, after what seemed an age to both of them, she collected herself, dragged her hands from her face, and turned away. At the door she paused and looked back. He was still standing in the same place watching her. With a little rueful chuckle she shrugged her shoulders and went out.

Michael went over to the cabinet and poured himself a whiskey-and-soda which he drank standing up, supporting his elbow in his hand. Upstairs a door opened and closed again.

XXI

Pollard was sitting behind his desk scribbling on the back of an envelope when Nancy came in. He glanced up briefly, and turned the envelope over.

'Hullo. Did you meet a lot of people?' She leaned against the door with her hands behind her back.

'Yes.' He did not look at her, but opened a drawer, glanced inside and closed it again.

'Do you want me for anything?'

'Not just now. Did you finish the letters?'

'Most of them. Will I fix dinner?'

'If you like.' He patted one of his pockets, put a hand inside, felt around and withdrew it again. 'Are you going back to the flat tonight?'

'No, not until bedtime.'

'Ah, yes, bedtime.' He turned the envelope over again and stared down at it.

'I don't know about Rosamund, but I think Michael will be here for dinner. I've got some pork chops, enough to go around.'

'Where is Michael now?' He tapped the blotter with his fingers.

'Downstairs. He just came in before you.'

'Did he?' Pollard pushed his tie straight under his waistcoat.

'Yes. I think he expected Rosamund to be here. Will I ask him for dinner?'

'If you like.' He leaned forward and adjusted the calendar-clock at the side of his desk.

There was a pause, during which Nancy came forward a few steps and Pollard turned the envelope over again.

'I hope he leaves after dinner, because I want to have a little talk with you, Andy.' She was looking at him with a slightly puzzled frown.

He looked up, met her eye for a moment, then turned and glanced out the window. In the falling dusk the pillars opposite were honey-coloured and the doors behind them seemed to recede into the gathering darkness.

'There's no hurry about dinner,' he said. 'I had barm brack after the funeral.'

'Barm brack? What's that?'

'It's an Irish thing, a sort of currant loaf. It's dying out now, but some people still make it.' He took up a pencil and tapped the desk with it, a tiny, irritating sound that made her frown. 'What was it you wanted to talk to me about?'

'Oh, well, might as well get it over with.' She came to the end of the desk and leaned her thigh against it. Pollard thrust out his lower lip and put the pencil back in its tray. Then he leaned back in his chair and looked up at her with dull, weary eyes. But she knew better than to tell him that he looked tired.

'It's about Rosamund and Michael,' she began boldly. After all, she had encountered and smoothed over worse moods than this appeared to be.

'What about them?' he said sharply.

'Well, I've been thinking about them ever since they came. It must have been a shock to them to hear about me—about us. I think you ought to make some sort of settlement on them before, well, before we get married. Otherwise, I'd feel, well, I'd feel bad about it. After all they're the nearest relations you have.' She sat up on the desk and swung her leg, brushing the carpet silently with her flat-heeled shoes.

'What sort of settlement?' His face had grown darker, and the out-thrust lip was set into a rigid shape. But Nancy ploughed on, unaware that every word she uttered was damning her further in his mind.

'Oh, that's up to you, darling. A couple of houses each, say. It would make for good will all around, wouldn't it?'

'No doubt it would.' He clasped his mottled hands together and squeezed them tight. 'Who suggested this to you?'

'No one. I thought of it myself, before. Remember?'

'I see. You think two houses each would make them happy?'

'Well, it ought to. You haven't got any really small ones.' She paused and looked down at him with a smile. 'You know, dear, I'm not marrying you for your money. But we've been into all that before too.' She leaned forward and stared into his averted face. 'Will you think about it?'

'Oh, yes, I'll think about it all right. I'm glad you told me.'

'You are a funny man, you really are, Andy.' She brushed the side of his head with her fingers. He remained quite still until she withdrew her hand. Then he turned slowly towards her and inspected her with his tired, hostile eyes, allowing his gaze to rest on her small, plump breasts, then on to her thighs, tightly encased in faded jeans, and finally came to rest on the hand she supported herself with on the desk.

Nancy stood up abruptly. She had been looked at like that a few times in her life, always by men in bars or on public transport who were clearly transforming her in their minds into someone easily and readily available.

'What is the matter with you, Andy? Have I put my foot in it?' She sounded and felt like a small girl who had been rudely ignored by an adult relative. The curious nature of his inspection was something she was not prepared for; and certainly did not accept. Other men might look and feel like that; but the whole point about Pollard

126

was that his lechery never went beyond certain clearly defined and inevitable limits. But a woman who confines herself to preliminaries will often appear even more vicious than one who freely gives herself, especially to a man whose chief pleasure is confined to his imagination. Pollard was old-fashioned enough, and still near enough to his peasant ancestors, to regard Nancy's inhibitions as experiments in sensuality far more depraved than the simple coupling of two healthy bodies. It was a drug he had experimented with, found pleasureable, but ultimately noxious.

In answer to her question he held out his hands and beckoned her to come near. When she did slowly and unwillingly, he reached up and cupped her breast in his hand, moulding it gently beneath his grasp. Nancy drew in her breath sharply: there were certain things which were as necessary to her as the final throb to a more mature woman; and now in spite of herself she allowed her body to relax, moving slowly under the impulse of his touch. But when his pressure became insistent she broke loose and stepped back, shaking her head dumbly. Then with a little sigh she turned and hurried from the room.

For some time Pollard remained sitting looking down at his hands resting before him on the desk. He felt old and weary and surprisingly close to tears. He did not love Nancy; not for one moment had he deluded himself in that; but he was fond of her, finding consolation and a certain baffled excitement in her youth and slightly brash vitality. He had never imagined that he was the first man in her life, and he would not have cared to be; but he had believed her to be essentially honest. It never occurred to him that, like many Europeans brought up in ancient ways and accustomed to dealing with minds as devious as they were subtle, he confused transatlantic naïveté with honesty. The revulsion he often felt after his love-making had always until now given way to the certitude that a great deal of it was due to his own insistence: Nancy had never at any time taken the initiative. She had always appeared to him to be a fresh, open, impulsive girl; and the various suggestions she had made to him from time to time on business matters had merely served to convince him that she had little of the calculator in her nature.

But now, feeling suddenly older than he had ever felt, he realized that cold-blooded calculation was not necessary to make a creature so vibrant and young unfaithful; her very evident spontaneity would prompt her into the arms of a man her own age without her thinking too much about it. As he sat in the gathering darkness, with the headlamps of passing cars rippling along the row of pillars outside, he admitted to himself, fully now for the first time, that he had regarded her as a sort of mistress, and never really as an equal; and the idea of marriage was one of those gestures the old make in a desperate attempt to preserve the status quo. He wanted his concubine by his side always, and at all times, completely dedicated to him and him alone; and for that, and the sense of well-being he derived from her youth and vitality, he was prepared to legalize the rather uneasy relationship that had sprung into being on his own initiative.

But was she really making a fool of him? He leaned forward and rested his head in his hands. After all Mrs Reid could be mistaken; although in his heart he did not believe that she was. Then he sat back suddenly as if he had received a slight electric shock. It had just dawned on him that never once, on any occasion when he had met members of the Irish community since his engagement appeared in the paper, had one of them congratulated him. This new thought was alarming; and when he considered it, of immense importance. Were they all being tactful, in the devious way he understood only too well?

He would have spent quite a long time going over and over his relationship with her, probing a newly opened wound as men will when their vanity is slashed; but this new idea forced him into a slightly frenetic activity. He got up smartly from his chair, drew the curtains and went back to his desk. He opened one of the drawers which he always kept locked, and took out a small pocket diary dating back eight years. He ran down the tiny page with his finger and mouthed figures to himself. Then he took up the telephone and dialled a number. A voice answered; he asked for a name; there was a pause, and then another voice answered him. Quietly, without fuss, he gave his own name, exchanged compliments for a few moments, and got down to business: a name, an area, a description of a young woman's appearance. Thus briskly, with his usual business force and thoroughness, he set the machinery in motion that would rid him, he hoped, of the nightmare of doubt.

With renewed activity his old business cunning returned. He flicked through a desk diary and noted several names and addresses in Liverpool. For some time now Billy had been urging him to go and see some property he had in that area. It might be a good time to sell it and buy other property on the outskirts. He rose from his desk with a great deal of his confidence restored. He would go up to Liverpool tomorrow, and stay for three or four days. That would leave Nancy free to walk into the trap he had prepared for her.

He went down to wait for dinner, looking forward to a drink; and a hard searching look at his nephew. Suspicion is catching, and for those who feel that they have been cheated, the negative emotions are often as obsessive as the assumption of love.

XXII

On the third evening of his stay in Liverpool Pollard took a telephone call in his hotel bedroom. He listened for five minutes to the voice at the other end, and took some notes on the back of an envelope.

'Do you want me to enquire further?' the voice said. 'There has been only one visit by the young lady you described. It might be better to make absolutely sure.'

'Yes, I think so. Go ahead. And listen, give me a good time to ring you in London. I don't want you to ring me.'

'Eight in the morning is always the best. I'm usually here myself then. I'm not delegating any of this, as you asked me to.'

'No, better keep it to one, except when you want a witness. I'll wait for a week, then I'll ring you. All right?'

'All right. Good-bye.'

Pollard put down the receiver, and stared down at the scribbles he had made on the hotel envelope. The man he employed was well known to him, and had been very efficient in collecting information about certain individuals and firms in Pollard's active contracting days. On two occasions he had saved a great deal of money with his report on prospective partners who folded up a short time afterwards; and he had discovered four cases of embezzlement on the part of architects. He was a very useful man indeed; and not Irish. Pollard would never have employed one of his compatriots on business of this kind: they all knew one another too well. The voice on the telephone was British, ex-army, right wing and incorruptible: he had had him double-checked.

Presently, after washing his hands and brushing his hair in the bathroom, Pollard made another phone call. He had been meaning to do it since his arrival in Liverpool, but with typical caution waited for more details. Now the time had come to call in the experts.

'Is that the Cathedral presbytery?'

'Yes.' The voice was female, obviously the house-keeper.

'Is Father Illingworth there?'

'I'm afraid not. He's at a meeting.'

'Have you a priest on duty?'

'Yes, of course, but he's out on a sick call. Is it urgent? Can I get him to call you when he comes back?'

'I wonder if I know him?'

'Father Murphy.'

That was enough for Pollard. No Irish. He thanked the lady and put down the telephone. Priests were getting as difficult to contact as trade unionists. He looked at his watch and rang up the Archbishop's house. A male voice answered.

'Is his Grace at home?'

'I'm afraid not. He's blessing a new church in Garston.' Pollard knew all about that; in the old days he would probably have been building it. 'There's a meeting of parishioners.'

'I see. I'm a friend. Is his secretary with him?'

130

'No, he's on his day off. Can I help you at all? Father Mills here.'

Pollard had his story ready. One could never be too careful with priests: outside of confession they were as gossipy as old women were supposed to be.

'It's a difficult case. I have a friend here with me, a lapsed Catholic, Irish. I'm pretty certain he wants to see a priest, not necessarily for confession, but certainly with a view to it. But he still has some odd notions. He's Irish, and has a grudge against the Church in Ireland.' Pollard was gratified to hear a chuckle at the other end: Father Mills sounded English. 'So he wants to meet an English priest, and he won't go to a presbytery. I thought if you could get in touch with someone very unlike the usual Irish cleric, it might go a long way. Also a social occasion here would be the best way, I think. I can leave them together if things are going well.' Pollard warmed to his invention.

'I see. Where are you?'

'The Adelphi. My name is Pollard, by the way. I've had business dealings with the Archbishop.'

'Oh, of course, Mr Pollard. I've heard him speak of you.' Father Mills chuckled again. 'One of the things he said was that he wished you had been building this new church.' The voice was fuller now, open and friendly. The day was won.

'That's nice of him. I wish I were. But time marches on, you know.' Pollard felt pleased, and reassured. He was back among friends he understood. Why had he not thought of this before? But, of course, without the information he now had, they could not have been of much use.

'Now, let me see. I wish I could go myself, but I've got to stay here.' He chuckled again, this time with unconcealed merriment. 'But I think I know the right man. He's Scottish, by the way, and has spent most of his life in Africa. He's been on sick leave, and is staying with a parish priest, an old college chum. I'll tell you what, Mr Pollard, I'll ring him up, and then ring you back. Right?'

'That's very kind of you, Father.' Pollard put down the receiver, got up and began to walk about the warm, impersonal room. He

131

realized with something of a shock that this was the first time for a great many years that he had travelled alone. In Ita's time she had always accompanied him on private and holiday journeys; on business expeditions there had been Billy, or an architect, and always a cost clerk.

He sat down in an armchair, and tried to collect his thoughts. The information the investigator had given him was shocking, and as yet he was too preoccupied to be really angry; and in the past few days he had spent most of it, coming to the conclusion that he had made a proper fool of himself. He was not a man of violent emotions; and like most elderly people his moods fluctuated a great deal. Once or twice the memory of the intimacies he had indulged in with Nancy had struck him like a nightmare; but he had thrust it from him: the recollection of that naked body writhing under his lips was too much to be borne.

It had not occurred to him that his solitary days and nights in the warm, soundless hotel had provoked this revulsion as much as his suspicions, and the confirmation of them on the telephone; nor did he know that Nancy's proximity was as much the cause of his uncharacteristic behaviour as his own senile lust. Insulated in his anger and soothed by this unexpected solitude, he felt no desire at all. If he had been capable of analysing his emotional responses he would have realized that a genuine tie of love or affection is not so easily forgotten; but lust has no memory.

He took the envelope out of his pocket and tried to read it without his spectacles, which he had left on the night-table. The hasty scribbling swam in front of his eyes—not the first time this had happened to him recently; and in spite of his distress he made a mental note to visit his oculist soon. But he remembered what he had written down. An evening spent with Hansen from eight until two in the morning; another afternoon from lunch in a near-by pub to five o'clock in his flat. The most disturbing information of all he had not been able to bring himself to write down at all. 'Has a reputation for homosexuality and sexual perversion.' It was too awful to contemplate; especially as he had only a very hazy notion of what these activities meant.

132

Slowly he pulled himself to his feet again, and immediately felt light-headed. These hotel chairs were all too low, and the room was too hot. They catered for the young and agile. Old, he thought bitterly; old, and foolish. As he stood with eyes closed, trying to regain composure, another thought struck him like a blow. He grasped the edge of the table and leaned against it, and the giddiness left him as suddenly as it had come. Hansen was a journalist, the investigator had said. That was how the announcement of the engagement had appeared. It was an attempt to force his hand; and he remembered his anger. He had been thinking of a very private ceremony, preferably a secret one. He realized now that he had always shied away from committing himself. Perhaps in time there would have been no need for a marriage at all; he might have thought of something else that would bind that young body to him without the world being any the wiser. It was altogether immoral and completely against his deepest instincts; but he had never really faced that either.

And now, how many people knew? How many were sniggering over it? For a moment he felt that he was going to be sick; it was merely that the blood had rushed to his head, and slowly subsided again; but the hammering of his heart frightened him, and all thoughts of Nancy and her lover left him; he was immured in the prison-house of his own body. Thank God he had gone to the priests; it was something he ought to have done long ago.

The telephone rang; and bracing himself firmly, he walked carefully across the room to pick it up, lowering himself on to the bed with a sense of relief. Old: the unmistakable message drummed in his ears.

'Mills here. Father MacGregor will be there in about half an hour. I hope he can be of some help, he's a very interesting man.'

Pollard thanked him; and as he was putting down the receiver was visited by another unexpected thought, which made him jerk upwards as if he had suffered a heart spasm. Could further unsavoury publicity follow the announcement in the paper? Dismay made him forget the cold dampness of his body, the lightness in his head. He shut his eyes and waited, trying to gather his forces. Why had not somebody, Billy especially, warned him? Why did everybody seem to conspire against him?

He got slowly to his feet, went over to the refrigerator and took out a miniature bottle of brandy. After a few sips he felt better, and sighed with relief. Then he went back into the bathroom to wash his hands and brush his hair, forgetting that he had already done so. *I mustn't allow anything to upset me; I must keep calm,* he told his flushed face in the mirror, and nodded wisely to himself.

XXIII

Father MacGregor was small, rotund and sandy-haired. He was wearing a shabby black raincoat, with a thick woollen scarf wrapped twice round his neck, and he carried a pair of yellow knitted gloves under his arm.

'Where's the men's?' he enquired with a worried look as he unwrapped himself. Pollard indicated the way, and asked if he could order something in the lounge before dinner.

'Yes, please. A large, hot brandy with sugar. I'll tell you about it when I get back.' And he trotted off.

Pollard ordered the same for himself, and the drinks had just come when the priest arrived in the lounge. He looked about with the lost gaze of a stranger in a big railway station. His yellow gloves were stuffed in his jacket pocket. Pollard stood up and raised his hand. The little man smiled and nodded and proceeded to put on one of the gloves. They were new, and struck a glaring note against his clerical black.

'You can't take this as it ought to be taken with your bare hands,' he explained as he raised his glass. 'I have a terrible dose of diarrhoea. So you'll have to excuse me if I have to trot from time to time.' He closed his eyes and sipped. 'Where's your friend?' he said, opening his eyes again suddenly. They were pale blue, and round like a child's. Pollard coughed and shifted uneasily in his chair.

'I'm afraid there isn't any friend, Father.' Upstairs he had felt his age as never before; now he suddenly felt very young, guilty and not quite sure of what he ought to say.

'So that's the way it is.' The priest nodded and smiled. 'Well, I hope I'll be able to help you.'

'It's sort of hard to begin.' Pollard was feeling very much as he used to fifty-five years before, when the boys in his college were required during a Retreat to visit the missioner in his room for a 'little talk'. He had once wet his pants with fright.

'Take your time, there's no hurry. I'm unemployed.' Father MacGregor fumbled in his pocket with his bare hand and dug up a small phial containing a number of tiny white pills. 'I don't know the name of these, but would you believe it, they are supposed to paralyse the central nervous system. Down here.' He patted his stomach. 'I have a cold, but a lot of this comes from nerves. I have to see the Archbishop tomorrow, and I'm not looking forward to it.'

'He's a very nice man.'

'So I'm told.' The priest shook two pills on to his palm, threw them into his mouth and grasped his glass again. He swallowed his dose and grinned. 'I'm very far from paralysed yet. Are you having woman trouble?'

Pollard stared back into the round blue eyes which were regarding him with a curious, quizzical expression.

'How did you know that?'

'Well, it usually is. Somehow you don't look the type who's having doubts about your religion. Besides, people are never shy about that sort of thing. They write letters to the papers about it.' The gloved hand grasped the glass, and stayed there for a moment. 'Now brandy is the old cure, and nice to take too. Are you married?'

'My wife died a few years ago.'

'I'm sorry to hear that. And lemon too, it's a pleasant dose. Any children?'

'No. I'm afraid not.'

'That's always hard on a woman. Was your wife religious?'

'Oh, yes, very.' Pollard paused and tried to think of another word that would describe Ita; and failed. 'Yes, she was a very religious person, Lord have mercy on her.'

'Amen. Excuse me.' Father MacGregor got up hurriedly and made out of the lounge at a good pace, his yellow hand flapping at his side. Some of the men sitting round, leaning forward with briefcases on their knees, glanced after him. Clergymen were a rare sight in that place. But Pollard hardly noticed the executives; they were too familiar, and he had always been one of them before now. He was beginning to feel that all the tangled emotions of Queen's Gate Terrace were very far away; almost as if he were looking at actors in a play from a seat in the gallery.

'Nice attendant in the lavatory,' said Father MacGregor when he arrived back. 'Liverpool-Irish. Non-practising, I'd say from the way he spoke to me. Well, now, where were we? Oh, yes. I suppose you've got yourself involved with another woman. Are you thinking of marrying her, or is there an impediment?'

The priest's brisk manner was a great help; and the interruption had given Pollard time to collect his thoughts, and nourish the sense of grievance which had now almost entirely taken over from the anger he had felt previously. It encouraged the confessional mood. He saw himself now as a blameless older man who had been cruelly deceived. It was easy to paint a picture of Nancy as a heartless, calculating young woman who had returned ingratitude for kindness, and deception for honest affection. Even her age was no longer an embarrassment. But there are some things which even self-pity cannot turn to advantage. He did not refer to the now unthinkable love-making he had indulged in with Nancy; and the method used to discover the information he had received on the telephone did not appear to Pollard to be relevant.

Father MacGregor listened impassively, resting his chin on his hand, and looking past Pollard's shoulder. When he spoke, after taking another sip of brandy, he might have been discussing the weather.

'It's a very big gap in ages, although I've known it to work, especially when the man is vigorous.' He caught Pollard's eye, blinked and looked away.

136

The other looked down at his spotted hands, and shook his head. He had read the meaning in the priest's glance. Old, impotent, fearful and infatuated with youth. Something stirred in his consciousness; a realization of his own predicament; but it did not fit in with the role he had decided to play, and so it drifted away like a face glimpsed in a passing car. Something Nancy had done; something that might have committed him.

'Are you going to marry her?' Father MacGregor asked quietly.

Pollard looked at him with a startled expression.

'Of course not, Father. Why do you ask?'

'Well, you could still love her. In that case there is really nothing to be said, it's a matter for your own conscience. Human affection is a very private thing. It makes its own laws.' Slowly he peeled off his yellow glove and laid it down beside the empty glass.

'There's no question of that now, Father.' Pollard's voice was rough; the sort of tone he used in dismissing a worker who has been found wanting.

'You're probably wise. After all, at your age there is always the possibility of failing powers, and that, as you know is a cause for annulment.'

Pollard had not thought of this; if he had it might have revealed some of his own obscure motives, the fear of commitment that lay beneath his craving for warm young flesh. Now all he felt was a sense of disgust; and Nancy must be made to share in it.

'Yes, yes,' he replied, brushing the suggestion away, 'but this young man she has got herself involved with. He's a pervert, Father, a sexual pervert. I mean, well, I don't know—'

'I understand. It is a bit confusing.' Father MacGregor looked down at his empty glass as if he could have done with some replenishment. But Pollard was still nursing his own drink, and he was not in the mood for thinking of anyone else. 'But some men like that also like women, you know. And there are lots of women who like them.'

'You mean, she could be living with him, in the same way as she'd live with a normal man?' Pollard leaned forward eagerly. This was the whole point of the exercise.

'I don't see why not. It happens.'

Pollard leaned back with a sigh of relief, and wiped his forehead with the back of his hand. Already a reaction was setting in. He had discovered what he wanted to find out; and now he became aware again of his cold, clammy body, and the curious lightness in his head. He looked at the priest's glass, and held up his hand for a waiter.

'I think we both need another drink after all this,' he said, taking out his handkerchief and wiping his fingers. The waiter came and went with his order. Father MacGregor gave him a sharp glance. Like all priests, he had a keen eye for physical symptoms, and this man did not look at all well. No doubt he was under a heavy strain; but he had all the appearance of someone with a bad case of blood pressure.

Pollard was feeling drained and empty. He stared across the crowded lounge, and felt like a man alone on an empty platform, watching a group of people chatting happily across the tracks. He did not feel energetic enough to climb the footbridge. There was nothing for it but to go back down the entrance steps and walk home alone.

'Tell me, Mr Pollard,' he heard a voice say as if from a distance, 'have you any friends?'

He pulled himself together, gathering his forces to answer this attentive stranger.

'Oh, yes. Yes, I have a great many.' What had this got to do with what they had been discussing? He began to feel irritable.

'Are they business friends?' the quiet voice went on.

'Yes, they are, loyal good friends.' He thought of Billy, and then found himself searching in his mind.

'Would you for instance have discussed what we have been talking about with any of them?' Father MacGregor put on his yellow glove again, in preparation for his hot medicine.

'Oh, no, Father, of course not.' Pollard was quite emphatic, shaking his head and frowning. The priest looked at him closely, then leaned back as the waiter brought their drinks. Pollard was not aware of the long pauses that had fallen between them; almost ten minutes since Father MacGregor had given his final opinion on Nancy's possible connection with Hansen. 'I'll be as drunk as a lord,' the priest remarked presently when they were alone again, raising his glass in salute.

As he sipped his drink Pollard slowly and clumsily brought his thoughts back into some kind of order. That was an odd question to be asked. Billy was a good colleague and partner, absolutely loyal and honest; but an intimate friend to whom he could open his heart? To his great surprise he could not think of one; and again a wave of self-pity swept over him, leaving him cold and chilly. It was a moment as stark as the realization of a sudden death; when the head lolls, and the legs are twisted in an unnatural way, and the pulse fails to respond. He remembered one such frightening occasion, a moment of brutal truth when an old friend of Ita's had stood up after tea, and slowly without a sound crumpled and slid to the floor; a life cut off from its puppet-string by an invisible hand.

'I hope you don't mind me saying it,' he heard Father MacGregor go on in his brisk impersonal way, 'but I think you need friends, or a friend. People rarely have more than a few as they go through life. Business, no matter how successful, is never enough. Perhaps this young woman has done some good, after all.' He smiled and patted his stomach carefully, as if he were encouraging the pills and brandy to do their stuff. 'Did your wife have any friends who have kept up with you?'

'No, I'm afraid not. I was just thinking of one, she died before Ita. Strange that I should think of her now.' He had not thought of Nora Williams for years, and had not even been particularly fond of her. He felt the veins throbbing in his temples: no time, no time.

'I don't think it's strange. You've been used all your life to a woman's company, and that's a great blessing. You made a mistake with this young woman. It would be a good thing if you knew someone nearer your own age.'

Pollard shook his head; aware of a sense of desolation, now that this impossible business had been cleared up and explained. He looked across at the groups of business-men who were now beginning to break up and head for the dining-room. Without the brief-case, the column of figures, the blueprints, Pollard was as ignorant as a catechumen with some understanding and little knowledge.

'I'm afraid I never had time to make friends, Father. One is so busy—' He broke off, and tapped his forehead as if he were pointing to a source of power which had forgotten something important. In fact he was dabbing at his clammy skin, and blaming the central heating for the sweat he found himself in. Then, wrinkling his brow, he leaned forward and stared intently at his guest. He remembered now what Nancy had done.

'It's awful, but I nearly forgot. There's another thing I wanted to ask you. You see, this girl put an announcement in the paper. I didn't want it. I suppose now I never really wanted to go through with it at all.' His slightly dog-like expression of bewilderment misled the priest.

'I'm sure you'd never in the final analysis go against your Church,' he said, making his first and only miscalculation of the evening.

'Oh, no, no, of course not.' Pollard brushed this aside and went on with what was really worrying him. 'You see, I didn't deny it publicly at the time. Do you think she could follow me, I mean for damages?' His face bore an expression of anguish for the first time that evening.

Father MacGregor was taken aback. So far as he was concerned the interview had been a routine one; he could have coped with the problem almost without thinking. An ageing business-man, reared in the narrow ethic of Irish Catholicism, had developed a guilty craving for a young woman who was probably a pagan. The homosexual lover was unusual, but not unknown. There were far more involved cases than this in any study of pastoral theology.

Pollard was not the sort of man the priest would normally choose to spend an evening with outside of his duties. There had been few signs of a deeper emotion beyond self-pity; but the man looked ill, and was probably suffering according to his own lights. Once or twice in the last few minutes Father MacGregor had felt that some real communication had been established; he had felt that slight tingle of embarrassment and self-depreciation which always visited him when confronted with a genuine penitence. And now this elderly adolescent had suddenly reverted to type; if he had ever really stepped out of it. The priest was ashamed for him.

'I doubt it very much,' he replied coldly, 'if you have proof of misconduct.'

Pollard leaned back with a sigh of relief, his flushed and gleaming face relaxing in a contented smile.

'Well, do you know what, Father, but you're a marvel! Thank God that I asked for your advice. But, you see, God doesn't forsake His own. Imagine me not thinking of that! It'll give you an idea of how upset I was.'

'Yes,' said the priest quietly, 'I can see that—now.'

'You'll have to say a Mass for my intentions, you really must. But we'll have dinner first. And that reminds me of something else. You haven't a trace of a Scottish accent. How is that?'

'My father was working here in Liverpool when he married. He was a convert, my mother was English. I was brought up in England.'

'Imagine that now! And how many years have you spent in Africa?'

'Thirty-six.' Father MacGregor looked down at his gloved hand and slowly clenched it. 'I came back here last year for an operation. I'm quite better now, thank God, but the Archbishop wants me to stay here in this diocese. That's what I'm seeing him about in the morning.'

'Well, isn't that nice now. I'm sure you'll be delighted to be home after all those years.'

'I am by no means delighted,' said the priest with a glint in his eye and a note of suppressed passion in his voice. 'I hate the very thought of it. Africa is my home, my work is there, and I want to die there. If the Archbishop insists on keeping me here it'll break my heart. Everything I love is African, the country, the people and the deep faith that's in them. Oh, the first Christians must have been like that.' He stopped as abruptly as he had begun, and finished his cooling brandy with a hand that was trembling slightly. When he looked at Pollard again he had regained some of his composure. 'I'm afraid it would be unwise of me to take dinner.' He patted his stomach tenderly. 'I mustn't take anything solid, so I hope you'll excuse me.'

Pollard felt let down. He had been looking forward to a little celebration after this successful interview. And the company had been welcome after four days of solitude. He felt an overwhelming impulse to delay the departure of this odd little man with whom he was certain he had had one of the most intimate encounters of his life.

'Oh, you mustn't go yet, Father, really you mustn't. I don't feel like dinner myself. I'm not in form. I don't feel well at all, all this worry and strain, you know.' He looked at his guest appealingly, but Father MacGregor did not seem inclined to fall in with his wishes.

'That's very kind of you, Mr Pollard, but I'm afraid——'

'But, Father, I was going to ask you to hear my confession.' He leaned forward and gripped the arms of his chair. 'The heat is terrible here, I'm in a terrible sweat. I don't know what's come over me. But I'll tell them to turn it off in my room, and then we'll go up.'

'Are you quite sure?' the priest said doubtfully.

'Oh, yes, yes, I am, Father. Please. And have another brandy with me, it'll do you good.'

'If you insist,' said Father MacGregor with a patient sigh.

XXIV

'Why don't we all go to Johnny's?' said Nancy, jumping up and snapping her fingers. 'He's dying to meet you again, Michael, he thinks you're divine. Oh, don't worry, I'll be there to see that no harm comes to you, and Rosamund will too, if we go.' She looked at her watch. 'It's only half-seven now. I could give him a ring and tell him to fix dinner. He always has the most wonderful things in the fridge, and he's a fabulous cook.'

Michael and Rosamund, who were sitting together on the sofa in Pollard's sitting-room, looked at each other with raised eyebrows. For the past few days they had spent a lot of time with Nancy, who showed signs of recklessness; she rarely came in in the morning before eleven, spent several hours preparing and eating lunch and relaxing after it, and spoke very freely of all the things she wanted to do after her marriage. Morocco first, she declared with shining eyes and bated breath. She could not see why Michael and Rosamund could not join her; they must come, she insisted.

It was all very well building castles or mosques in the air; but Hansen was another matter. In the ordinary course Rosamund would have gone; she liked meeting new people, and her curiosity had been aroused by Michael's story. Now she shook her head, feeling certain that Nancy would not notice: recently she had been staring at Michael a great deal.

'I don't think, so, Nancy,' Michael replied. 'You see, I think he's far from divine, not my cup of tea at all. I know it's terribly old-fashioned, but there it is.'

Nancy made a face, and flapped a wrist; a gesture she made with full music-hall exaggeration, swaying her hips and rolling her eyes naughtily.

'Get you, dear. I bet you're scared out of your maidenly mind.' When this piece of clowning evoked no response from her listeners, she pouted, looked hurt for a moment, and then laughed rather too loudly.

'Well, that fell flat, didn't it? I'm sorry, I sometimes forget that there are people who just don't think it funny. So you won't come?'

Michael shook his head; and Nancy looked at him for a long moment, as if she wanted to say something and thought better of it. Rosamund glanced quickly from one to the other and frowned. They did not notice her, and she was about to get up and go upstairs to her room when the front-door bell rang.

'My goodness, who can that be?' said Nancy, clutching her neck, and opening her eyes wide. 'No one ever calls here at this time of evening. Do you think it might be Andy, come home unexpectedly, leaving his keys behind him? I'd better run up and see.'

When she was gone Michael hauled himself out of the sofa and poured himself a drink.

'What are you up to, Mike?' said Rosamund quietly.

'I'm fixing myself a drink, as Nancy would say.'

'That's not exactly what I meant.'

'Wasn't it? Can I get one for you?'

'Not at the moment. You know——' She broke off as they heard steps in the hall above, and then voices coming towards the stairs.

'That's not Nunky,' said Michael, putting down his drink and looking at the door. They remained quite still until Nancy appeared, flushed and laughing, followed by Hansen, smartly dressed in a black leather coat with fur collar and cuffs. He looked handsome, epicene and exotic; a peacock in a semi-detached. Rosamund, who often saw people in terms of colour, saw him at once in terms of yellow and blue of a particularly vivid and startling dye; his eyes were brighter, his hair more blond, his skin more golden than anyone else's; and he gave off that slightly phosphorescent glow, as if he were made to shine at night, which she had often observed in men in whom the sexes are mixed. It seemed to her that all of them appeared suddenly older, more ordinary, merging into the shaded light of the room which now more than ever struck her as half-submerged. It was an atmosphere in which Hansen was completely at home, lighting it up with his peculiar neon brilliance.

He took her hand in a warm, dry grasp, and gave her a long, smiling but searching appraisal when Nancy introduced him.

'I've been dying to meet you for so long. I've been to your exhibition. It isn't fair that you should live up to it.'

'It was brave of you to go,' was all that Rosamund could think of to say: she hated talking about her work.

'Yes, of course you don't want to discuss it, the good ones never do.' He turned around, leaving his sincere, artist's manner behind him like an invitation card, and directed a dazzling smile at Michael. 'But not nearly as brave as coming here tonight. Suppose the ogre of the house had returned, as bad fairies always do unexpectedly, and met me at the door? I would have had to summon up all my wicked spirits, to turn him into a pillar, of what? Uranium, I suppose. Salt has no value any more. And that kind of magic always leaves me prostrate. Mike here, always so thoughtful, would have had to revive me with a healing potion.'

'Will you have a drink?' said Michael stolidly. If he had changed the conversation it would have been less effective; he merely ignored Hansen's elaborate introduction.

'Oh, you are so formidable,' returned the Dane with a theatrical sigh, taking off his coat, swirling it on a finger, and draping it over a chair; a complicated series of expressions and gestures which he accomplished with the hair's-breadth precision of a skilled bull-fighter. Rosamund chuckled and shook her head. Hansen, resplendent in a tailored denim suit and yellow polo-necked sweater, caught her eye and crooked his forefinger over his mouth; a connoisseur appraising a rare object.

'Yes, you are elegant. Genuinely shabby jeans, and your hair pulled back anyway. I can't afford to do that, I'd look like a chorus girl who's been resting too long.' He turned to Michael and murmured in an aside: 'Gin and tonic, dear, lots of gin and just a pin-head of the other, enough to let the angels dance on.' He turned back to Rosamund. 'Yes, my instinct was right. Poor old Nancy, who hasn't the slightest chic, and looks like a colonel's daughter, a Yankee colonel's daughter, was trying to describe you to me. Of course she didn't succeed. She said you were kind of French-looking—why do all Americans imagine that the French have a fashion sense?—so of course that was no good. But I knew what she was trying to say, poor child.' He patted his flat stomach briskly. 'That's where the real elegance comes from, the guts. You can't buy it, and you can't put it on, even if it's by Pucci. The French, my dear, are so ungay, even poor, earnest Yves. I suppose you bought that style in a supermarket and just threw it on. My dear, it's so unfair.'

'Here,' said Michael, holding out his drink in a long, thrusting arm, as if he were practising a drill.

'Oh, thank you so much. How gracefully you could do it, if you

145

only worked in front of a mirror. Angels in your eyes.' He turned back to Rosamund who was fiddling with her belt. 'Kensington Market, I'd swear.'

'Yes, yesterday,' laughed Rosamund, who was enjoying herself. She could see why Nancy enjoyed his company; after all Pollard was not exactly light-hearted. 'I bought it from the most extraordinary young man—'

'Don't tell me,' cried Hansen, 'I know it only too well. By the way, isn't my English good? Young man, did you say. A hermaphrodite, my dear, and all women-mad. We are the only people who look like men nowadays. It's a queer world, my masters. Nancy, my dear, dull Plymouth sister, why so tongue-tied? Aren't you going to do the honours of the house? Which reminds me—I do so love to be inconsistent, don't you—I've come all the way here into darkest Kensington to sweep you all under my wings and take you out to dinner. How about that, eh?' He looked around from one to the other, and shook his head. 'You're all so terrified of Nancy's horrible old man. It's so craven. And Mike too. Are you all afraid he's going to cut you out of his will? Eh?' He threw back his head and allowed the gin to flow down his throat. 'Can you see it going down, my dears?' he said, straightening up and looking at Michael, who turned away and sat down in an armchair as if to indicate his distance from them.

'Like Catherine the Great?' laughed Rosamund.

'Ah, so you know. But of course you would. My favourite character in history. All those great big brutal men, eating out of her hand. And an intellectual too. I think she's divine. Well, now, about dinner, eh?'

'Do come,' said Nancy. She had been sitting on a low chair inside the door, watching Hansen as if she were a stage-manager. But before any of them could answer the telephone extension rang. Nancy got up and answered it.

'Yes. Oh, of course. Yes. Oh, no. Oh, my God, how awful. Wait a moment, I'll get Michael for you, he and Rosamund are here just now.' She looked round with a scared face, and held out the receiver. 'It's Billy. Someone has rung him up from Liverpool.

146

Andy's ill. Oh, God.' She returned to her seat and sat down abruptly, hugging herself with her arms and staring with frightened eyes at Rosamund.

'Hullo, Billy, what is it? A priest! Is it that bad? Yes, I see. Of course I'm ready. When will you be here? Right, I'll be waiting for you. Good-bye.' Michael turned from the telephone and spoke to Rosamund. She was standing quite still in the middle of the room, pale and calm; nobody thought it strange that she was the one they turned to. 'Some priest has rung Billy up from Nunky's hotel. Apparently he was spending the evening with Nunky when he became ill. Won't say what it is, just a bad turn. Anyway, Billy is driving up to Liverpool, and I'm going with him to drive Nunky back, or drive Billy's car, or whatever we think is best when we get there.'

Rosamund held out her hand and wriggled her fingers.

'Get me a drink, Mike. It can't be too bad or they'd have rushed him to hospital. Hotels don't keep sick people. Also, he wants to come home. How long will it take you?'

'Three hours at least, and then back.' Michael busied himself with the drinks. 'It's just after eight now, Billy is coming over, we should be there by midnight. I doubt if we'll come back tonight. That reminds me, I'd better pop round to the hotel and collect a toothbrush. Here, Rosie, I made it strong.'

'Could I have one, please?' said Nancy in a small voice. Hansen had gone to her and was standing beside her, patting her head as if she were a little girl. 'Why did he ring Billy? Why didn't he ring here? I can't understand that.'

Rosamund, who was taking her drink from Michael, looked at him questioningly. The same thought had struck her.

'I suppose it's the car,' Michael said levelly. 'Obviously, he can't drive back, so he wants someone to do it for him, and Billy is the obvious person to give me a lift.' Michael's face had that wooden expression which Rosamund recognized as one he adopted whenever he wanted to give the impression of meaning exactly what he said; usually something doggedly routine to ward off awkward questions.

147

Hansen picked up his coat and draped it over his shoulders like a cloak. With his quick instinct he had scented a subtle change in the atmosphere. Nancy had sat quietly, smiling a little, while he had made his entrance and gone through his little act. He was aware of her all the time; and he was sure that the other two were also. But now his impresario had suddenly crumpled. The tall, carelessly poised woman in her faded jeans and crumpled shirt-blouse in the centre of the room had suddenly and effortlessly taken charge. He was not quite sure why; but instinctively he folded his plumage and fell silent. The peacock had displayed his gorgeous train, and dazzled his audience for a while; but something quiet and dull and faintly menacing had disturbed the atmosphere; a change of wind, presaging the rain: time to take shelter.

'Oh, dear,' he murmured, dropping his voice into his chest from its high crowing call, 'I hope I'm not turning into one of those unlucky queens. I was always the reverse. Nancy, my dear, do you want to come out?'

She shook her head, and kept her eyes on Rosamund who stood quite still, holding her drink and looking from one face to another with a strange lack of curiosity. She might have been alone in the room. It was an attitude Hansen had often observed in people who are completely self-possessed; and he respected it.

'In that case I'll just fly away over the garden wall and into the barnyard. Shall we meet again?' he asked Rosamund.

'Of course,' she smiled with a polite nod of dismissal.

'Au revoir, tormentor,' he blew a kiss in Michael's direction, and turned to go. There was a swagger in his shoulders, like an actor making an exit after a scene which had not gone off well.

'Nancy, won't you see Mr Hansen upstairs?' said Rosamund gently. The girl jumped up, like a child in class, and hurried out after her guest. Michael and Rosamund stood quite still listening to the sounds of footsteps on the hall floor, and then the opening of the door.

'I hope they don't run into Billy, Mike.'

'So do I. It might be difficult to explain, while we're here. I'd better not have another, or should I? Billy will be driving up.' He sat on the arm of a chair and buried his hands in his pockets, as if he were cold.

'It's all very odd,' said Rosamund thoughtfully. 'I had noticed that he was becoming very unpredictable, very up and down, but I thought it was the general situation. Maybe it was blood pressure. Anyway, everything seems to be changed now, doesn't it?'

'Billy would know, I imagine. But we mustn't think too much about it, it's unlucky.' She shook the bracelet on her wrist, making a small clinking sound which she matched by shaking the ice-cubes in her drink, inclining her head to one side as if she were listening to something of great importance. Michael knew that the subject was closed. He felt dull and nervous as he always did when something happened over which he had no control. Rosamund, he knew, was different. She had a taste for the unpredictable. She had described it once as reminding her of a palette daubed with blobs of new, experimental colours, out of which she would in time fuse a design. This was for her a far more exciting moment than the completion of a canvas. And she never talked about that either. Footsteps sounded in the hall above and Rosamund sat down.

'I thought Hansen overacted a bit,' she said almost to herself.

Part Four

XXV

'You must be very tired, Mr Boyd,' said Miss Brooke anxiously as she put his cup of coffee and a fig-roll exactly in place on the little ring the warm saucer had made in the course of twenty years. She remembered well how upset she had been when she first noticed it: one of the few faults in a methodical manner. But Mr Boyd had merely said, 'Just put it down in the same place. At least we won't have more than one stain.' Now he hardly seemed to notice. His face was grey and tired; and Miss Brooke longed to smooth his sparse grey hair: an impulse she had restrained for as many years as she had been in the office.

'I think it's time for me to retire, Jenny,' he said heavily. 'I'm getting on, and a shock like this brings it home.' He stirred his cup slowly: three lumps; he had always had a sweet tooth.

'Oh, you mustn't think of it, really you mustn't,' Miss Brooke cried in alarm. If that happened she would retire too; and she knew, she was positive, that if she did she would die. Just like her father, after forty-five years of clerking for the London County Council. 'Besides, Mr Pollard isn't really bad, is he?'

'No, not at the moment.' Billy brought the spoon to his lips and tasted it. 'But there's no point in pretending that he'll ever be really active again. Thank goodness, it was very slight, as I told you, just a little paralysis in the left leg, and his speech is not affected. But he'll have to take great care of himself, especially during the coming months.' He lifted his cup and sipped a little more noisily than usual. Miss Brooke would have given anything to tuck a napkin under his chin. She wrung her hands tenderly in default.

'Oh, dearie me, you were very brave to bring him back from Liverpool. Suppose he had another stroke in the car.' Miss Brooke had gone over this journey twice a day for the past three days when she brought Billy his coffee. The notion of driving a sick man all the way from Liverpool fascinated her; and every time she got it wrong: in her dreams the unromantic Billy was always cast as the hero.

'I told you before it was Michael,' he said testily. 'I must say, he was a great help.'

'I'm sure.' Miss Brooke had long ago sensed that Billy had a poor opinion of Pollard's niece and nephew; and she liked to share his opinions. She thought of Michael as an idle young man who spent his time hanging round waiting for his uncle to die and leave him a fortune. His good looks made him even more of a wastrel in her opinion. As for Rosamund, she was an artist, and that was enough. 'I hope,' she went on, 'that Mr Pollard has a sensible will made.' Her fingers fluttered over her fluffy hair; a habit she had whenever she made an unusually daring observation.

Billy put down his cup and looked at her as if she really existed; an idea which had not struck him for many years. That she was absolutely discreet, he knew; but he was less sure of her good sense. Nevertheless, he had felt unusually perturbed during the last few days, and sometimes longed to share his troubles with someone. His sister was useless, being completely deaf. But his world was crumbling about him; and after all what he was going to say would not affect the price of property. So, putting down his fig-roll with an air of great solemnity, he took Miss Brooke into his confidence.

'As far as I know he has never made one.' He drew a deep breath and sighed. It was done, and he felt better already.

'No!' Miss Brooke drew out her vowels as lingeringly as any actress on television, and clutched her bosom in dramatic but genuine surprise. Indeed, she was deeply shocked. That such an important man of property should not take the administration of his worldly goods, even to the side of the grave, was a blasphemy she had never expected to hear. 'Noooo. It couldn't be.'

'Sit down, Miss Brooke,' said Billy, who was by now far gone in recklessness. This was the first time in his life that he had extended such an invitation; and the lady swayed on her heels with rapture. But she had enough strength to pull a chair forward and sit down nervelessly, without even flicking the seat with her handkerchief.

'Thank you, Mr Boyd,' she breathed, settling her skirt modestly over her plump knees. A ray of sunlight pierced the dusty window, and made her blink; but she hardly noticed it. Revelation was at hand.

'No,' went on Billy, shaking his head solemnly, 'I could never get him to do it. He always put it off. Mind you, I can understand it. I've known plenty of solid men in Belfast who just wouldn't think about it, with the result that all their property went to the lawyers in disputes. Terrible.' He scooped up a half-teaspoon of sugar and swallowed it. Miss Brooke, watching his jaws rippling, had never felt so domestic and abandoned in her life.

'Does that mean that all his money will go to the nephew when, if, I mean in case—' She broke off, overcome by delicacy; but trembling with emotion. In spite of the nearness of Billy and his significant confidences it was the thought of so much money so carelessly disposed that stirred her deepest feelings. Miss Brooke had not served the god humbly and faithfully for all of her adult life without becoming a firm adherent of the faith. No vestal virgin, forced to witness the pollution of the temple and the rape of her sisters by swilling barbarians, could have felt a deeper anguish.

'I suppose so.' Billy was gloomy. As a priest of the rites he found it deeply depressing to think that the result of years of patient, sober and dedicated labour should revert to a couple of people who had never, according to his lights, done a stroke of work in their lives. 'Mind you,' he went on, 'I like both of them, they have good manners, and after all they're his nearest relations. Better than—' He broke off and looked at Miss Brooke significantly.

She looked back with pursed lips, while a tremor of something like savage joy rent her bowels.

'Indeed, yes. And his illness explains a lot. I could never understand how a man with Mr Pollard's ability and acumen could ever have let himself down the way he did.' She paused, moistened her finger and applied it to a ladder in her nylons, which she was sure must be running amok in this moment of passion. 'Is she, er, still there?' she went on delicately.

'I'm afraid, yes,' went on Billy in a still gloomier voice. 'He has said nothing, and there was that unfortunate announcement in the paper.'

'You mean?' gasped Miss Brooke.

Billy nodded, and then shook his head. He did not quite know what to think; and even in his present mood he felt that it was not something that could be discussed with safety.

'Oh, dear. Oh dearie me, how dreadful. Can nothing be done?'

Michael had hinted at an impediment on their way to Liverpool; but Billy had not encouraged him. He wanted no hand, act or part in this distasteful business. So he merely pursed his lips and looked back blankly at Miss Brooke. She took the hint. Years of experience had taught her to sense the unspoken: Mr Boyd knew something, but it was still in the delicate stage, like a building site which awaits an adjoining plot to ripen and fall on to the market.

Billy sighed and looked at his empty cup. Miss Brooke made a decision: a big one, for it broke the routine of twenty years.

'Will I get you another cup, Mr Boyd?'

Billy nodded. What he really needed just then was a shot of Bushmills, but he thrust the thought from his mind hurriedly: drink in the office signified the end of the world. He watched Miss Brooke's ample bottom as she carried it briskly to the door; then began to open and close the drawers of his desk. His nerves were jingling; and he promised himself an early bedtime and a hot potation when he got home. Gertie could groom the dogs herself that night.

But he was not entirely lost to routine. All the while he had been talking to Miss Brooke something kept nagging at his mind. Now he suddenly remembered what it was; and taking out his wallet extracted two letters from it. They had been given to him to post

154

that morning when he visited Pollard. One was to the priest in Liverpool who had stayed in the hotel to meet Billy and Michael after their long drive; the other was for Mrs Reid at Cornwall Gardens. Billy wondered why Pollard was writing to her; but he knew that his partner often helped Irish people of good character privately: no doubt he had had some dealings of this kind with his tenant.

When Miss Brooke came back he gave her the letters at once to stamp and post in case he forgot them again. Then he addressed himself to his fig-roll while Miss Brooke stood with her legs pressed against the back of the chair, waiting to be asked to sit down again. But Billy had had enough of confidence for one morning; and sighing a little to herself she withdrew. But there was heresy in her mind. She was hoping that Mr Boyd would continue to be shaken by events. Clearly it was the only way in which he could be induced to have a nice, cosy chat again.

XXVI

Instinctively they kept their voices lowered. Although the walls were thick and one had to go out into the passage to get into their uncle's bedroom, the door of the sitting-room was kept open in case he should call. As they spoke, sometimes in whispers, Rosamund remembered those long summer evenings when she and Michael had walked together under the hushed twilit sky. To raise one's voice in that murmuring silence was unthinkable. As it was now.

Then, in the first ripening of their love, it had seemed to both of them necessary to keep it secret; why, they hardly would have been able to explain. Speak low if you speak love. Looking back in after years, Rosamund decided that even then, young, impulsive and obsessed though they were, some instinct had warned them off behaving as most other people did; their connection was not of the kind that proclaims itself aloud. Michael had had a horror of committing himself; and Rosamund unwillingly had taught herself to respect it.

That had been a period when time seemed to hang still from the sky, like a bird poised in mid-air: the illusion of a moment stretching out and containing them. They felt very much the same now, waiting in their uncle's basement sitting-room for something to happen. Nothing had been explained, nothing definite stated in the four days since Pollard came back from Liverpool, walking heavily on Michael's arm into his house, and carefully downstairs to bed. The doctor had come, recommended a nursing-home, and finding that this suggestion put his patient into a dangerously hostile mood, settled for a daily visit, blood-pressure tablets, and absolute rest for most of the day. The brain damage had been slight, and already the affected leg was responding well to treatment. So long as the patient avoided excitement, his recovery was almost certain. A warning was as good as a cure, said the doctor.

Rosamund and Michael were not unduly alarmed. As in the early days of their love, when the world was bright and there was every excuse for rejoicing, they displayed little sign of the good fortune which had so unexpectedly descended upon them. Billy had not denied the non-existence of a will when on their journey north Michael had bluntly asked him. His silence was an admittance; and since it was extremely unlikely that Pollard would have made any legal arrangements without consulting his partner, it was almost certain that Michael and Rosamund were still his heirs.

'Poor kid,' said Rosamund, looking steadily at Michael, who was sprawling in his uncle's armchair, his long legs loosely stretched, his hands behind his head. 'It's awful the way he treats her, avoiding her eye, and saying nothing. She must know he can speak perfectly well, and get about too.'

'I suppose it was that priest in Liverpool,' said Michael, lowering his chin on to his chest to answer her in an equally low tone. 'He said Nunky had made his confession just before he got this turn. I always thought that religion would hit him sooner or later.'

'Yes, but it would be so much kinder just to tell her to go. It's all very embarrassing. She sits in the office all day with nothing to do.

I suppose Billy is conducting all the business now.'

Michael put back his head and stared at the ceiling; and Rosamund watched him closely. For the past few days they had taken turns to visit Nancy in her office, bringing up drinks, and chatting to her about everything except the subject which was uppermost in all their minds. Nancy had made no attempt to talk to Pollard; she seemed to accept her dismissal philosophically; and never referred to it, although she made enquiries about the sick man every day. Rosamund did not quite know what to think of her; and Michael, although he spent as much time with her as his cousin, hardly ever spoke of her. Rosamund found this significant; but there was no point in talking about it: she knew Michael well enough for that. She had been the first to keep his secrets; in the savage way that life has of repeating itself when circumstances are different, she was forced to go on behaving in exactly the same way as she had when secrecy had been a joy.

But at the moment there were other things to occupy her mind; so many tangled threads binding them all together: in a way she was grateful for them.

'Have you noticed that everything seems to be in abeyance whenever someone is sick?' She looked at Michael's jaw-line, stretched taut under the firm skin as he sprawled with his head thrown back. How often had she drawn her finger along it in summer meadows long ago. Now it was as if she were an invisible body, perhaps even a ghost, forced to watch him going through the same motions without her. Hell must be a little like that. Yet she could not dislike Nancy.

'Yes, people just wait around.' Slowly, like a contortionist gathering his limbs together for another move, he raised himself into a sitting position, holding his knees tightly together as he sat up and looked at the empty fireplace. 'Waiting, I've always hated it.' He looked around sharply, and regarded her with cold, accusing eyes. 'You're rather good at it, aren't you?'

'I've had to be,' she replied simply, thinking of the long patient years she had worked at her painting, waiting for some degree of mastery, for a dealer who would take a risk on her, for the critics to

157

notice her work, and for the public to buy it.

'I've had to be,' she said, referring to that; but she knew that in other matters, above all in those which affected Michael, she was far from patient. Yet even here she had been forced to learn. 'Yes, I suppose I am by now. I suppose you're going out tonight?' They had taken turns to stay in with Pollard for the past two nights; last evening she had gone to a show.

He looked at his watch. Seven. Nancy had gone back to her flat two hours before. He would ring for Mrs Reid and tell her he wanted to see Nancy on business. It would serve a double purpose: making his call a perfectly innocent one; and ensuring that Nancy was at home. Mrs Reid would know.

In his bedroom, propped up with pillows, his mottled hands lying on the eiderdown beside a bundle of papers which Billy had brought him that morning, and which he had neatly divided into two, Pollard also lay waiting. The small travelling clock ticked faintly on the night-table, and every few minutes he turned his head and looked at it. He could hear footsteps clearly whenever anyone walked on the marble-tiled hall above. By now he knew the rhythm of them: Nancy's sharp, quick and decisive; Rosamund's slower, sometimes irregular; Michael's heavy, slow and slightly dragging. A few minutes before he had gone out closing the door gently behind him, almost as if he did not want to be heard. Pollard wondered what he was up to; some woman, perhaps; he had always been a tom-cat. Rosamund, he knew, was still in the room next door. Everything was working out nicely.

He remembered how Ita during her last illness had also got to know every footstep in the hall, and even on the stairs going up to the flats. He had thought about her a great deal in the last few days. He knew now with absolute certitude that it was her prayers which had saved him from a horrible godless entanglement; and the ridicule that would have followed. Last evening his investigator had rung up, and Michael tactfully left the room while he had taken the call on the extension. Thank God that he was able to walk quite well. A good rest and tranquillity of mind would do wonders for him; and now that he had made his peace with God all the old, time-honoured checks and balances of his Church had come back stronger and fresher than ever before; so that he knew exactly how he stood in relation to his conscience. He had no doubt at all that such an abundance of grace would speed his recovery.

He had been worried about that telephone call. But God had seen to that too: it had come at a convenient time. And the information given had merely confirmed the knowledge he had of a miraculous deliverance. Bringing her lover into his house while he was away! Before his confession and repentance such an event would have almost driven him out of his mind. But now all he felt was thankfulness. The girl was completely depraved. Yet in a curious way the more he was convinced of this the more reconciled he felt to the will of God. Prayer and the sacraments were surely a wonderful means of defence against all worldly ills. There were times during the past few days when he felt like thanking God for the slight cross He had sent him. It was a gentle reminder of the awful punishment he had been inviting. And the doctor, a good, God-fearing Catholic Irishman, had said that a warning was as good as a cure. Somebody's prayers again. From now on he would take great care of himself. He owed it to the Almighty.

It did not occur to him that his niece and nephew might have been in the house when Nancy had introduced Hansen to it. Showing him what she was soon going to possess, the greedy, sinful little pagan. The investigator had followed him from Russell Square, had seen him go in and come out alone. There had been no question of Michael or Rosamund; and his respect for them rose a little. They were too clever to get themselves mixed up in anything like that. When all was said and done, they were no friends of Nancy.

Another pair of feet clinked across the hall. It was one of the tenants from upstairs. Pollard had never noticed this before. They came and went at fairly regular intervals; so long as they paid their rents, and kept their flats in good order he did not think of them. Now they intruded as mere background noises. He turned his head and looked at the clock again. And almost immediately the front-door bell rang. He leaned forward, bracing his torso on his outspread hands, and listened. Rosamund ran upstairs to open the door; there was a sound of voices; and then a double pair of footsteps above, followed by a muffled sound of descent on the stairs.

He was resting against the pillows with his hands crossed over his stomach when Rosamund appeared at the door. She looked a trifle flustered, which was unusual for her. As he watched her slightly flushed face he experienced a curious sense of well-being; a feeling of potency, quite unconnected with what he now thought of as the lower instincts. It was very like the surge of triumph, always carefully suppressed, which he used to feel in the old days whenever he outdistanced one of his business rivals. During the episode with Nancy he had almost lost his sense of power. Now he experienced it again; and something dim, as yet unformed, stirred at the back of his mind.

'You have a visitor, Uncle Andy. Mrs Reid.'

'Oh, yes, Rosie. Show her in. It is very nice of her to come.'

Mrs Reid came in slowly, and a little awkwardly, he thought. She was wearing the same costume, hat and gloves which she wore for funerals. This did not strike him as in the least tactless; he knew she had put on her best outfit.

'How are you, Mr Pollard?' she said, standing just inside the door where Rosamund had left her, clutching her handbag against her skirt with her gloved hands.

'Come in, come in, Mrs Reid,' he said heartily. 'Sit down there.' He indicated a chair by the wall close to the end of the bed. Billy had pulled it out that morning, and it had been left where it stood. Mrs Reid sat down on the edge of it, and balanced her bag on her knees. She looked even more flustered than Rosamund, and fiddled nervously with the clasp of the bag. In a way he was a power in her life also; but this time the thought of it gave him an entirely different sort of pleasure. He felt nothing but gratitude towards her. She had shown that she had the courage of her convictions.

'I had a bit of a turn in Liverpool,' he went on, smiling at the thought of it. 'But I'm nearly all right now.'

'So your niece told me. And indeed you look fine, thanks be to

God.' She took a deep breath and hurried on, anxious to cover her awkwardness with words, now that she had broken the ice. 'She's a very nice girl, isn't she? And I met Mr Pollard in the street while I was coming up. He stopped and talked to me. He was going down to the Tube station. He said you were greatly improved too.'

'Indeed I am. I have to rest up for a bit. I was very lucky to have Father MacGregor with me when I got the turn.'

Mrs Reid raised her eyebrows. The mention of a priest immediately captured her interest. Pollard embarked on a long, rambling description of his meeting with the priest, leaving out every reference to the real purpose of their encounter. But there was plenty to say about the goodness of his companion, and his efficiency in dealing with an emergency. Gradually Mrs Reid's gloved hands quietened, as she listened intently to the recital. She had already heard of Pollard's illness from Maggie Harrington at Mass. Within twenty-four hours of his attack in Liverpool, all the Irish in London knew that one of their most prominent compatriots had had a stroke. First word had come from the staff of the hotel; and by the time Mrs Reid heard it he was supposed to be completely paralysed and on the brink of death. Being a woman who kept her own counsel, she did not tell Maggie that she had received a letter from him. Nevertheless, she had come prepared to find him a great deal worse than he was.

She opened her bag and brought out a small bottle, and a coloured card.

'This is a Mass bouquet I got for you. One of the Carmelites is saying it. And I thought I'd bring a little drop of Lourdes holy water, although I'm sure you have it in the house already. Still, it never does any harm to have more than you want. You can always give it away.' She left down her offerings on the night-table and resumed her seat.

Pollard was deeply moved, and slightly abashed. Ita had always kept Lourdes water in the house, dabbing it on her brow whenever she had a headache; or on any other part which was not functioning well; and she always claimed that it cured her. But after her death Pollard could not find the bottle; and had never bothered to have

161

another supply laid in.

'Well, I don't know what to say, Mrs Reid, really I don't. You're making me ashamed. All I can say is that I'm a lucky man to have such friends. Now I know I'll be completely better in a few days.' He opened the bottle, dipped his fingers in the water, flicked a few drops in Mrs Reid's direction; and they both blessed themselves in unison. Pollard had not been so moved in a genuinely happy way for a long time. He gazed at his visitor with tears in his eyes.

'Tell me,' he said when he had recovered himself, 'have you a devotion to the Little Flower?' He could not have hit upon a happier subject. Mrs Reid's face glowed; she settled down in her chair with relaxed shoulders and a glowing face; and assured him that the moment she got his letter she had gone straight to the Carmelite church to have his Mass said, and to light a candle before the statue of St Theresa.

When Rosamund knocked gently at the door half an hour afterwards they were prattling happily about miracles, novenas and all the Carmelite saints, like two happy people who had just won the Irish sweepstake. They looked at her with glazed eyes, as if she were a foreigner of uncertain origin and dubious beliefs come to remind them that the happy few are always surrounded in this world by the unblessed, the unhappy and the half lost. Pollard recovered himself first.

'Oh, Rosie, there you are. Well, now that you're here, would you be a good girl and make some tea for Mrs Reid?'

'Of course,' said Rosamund courteously. 'I was just about to make it. Or would you prefer coffee, Mrs Reid?'

'Oh, tea, please. But I'm putting you to a lot of trouble.'

Rosamund shook her head, smiled and withdrew; and Mrs Reid with a quick, furtive movement opened her bag and drew out some rosary beads which had a relic of the Little Flower, and which she was about to loan to Pollard until he was quite recovered. He kissed the cross gratefully, and hid the beads under his pillow. Rosamund was not worthy to partake of such mysteries; and out of a Christian respect for her ignorance and blindness, they changed the conversation to the neutral one of the proposed immigrants bill, which even she might be expected to understand.

162

XXVII

'Don't be frightened. I won't hurt you.'

'You promised. No, don't please.'

'Here?'

'Yes, yes, oh yes.'

Nancy held the dark head gently against her breast, and closed her eyes. But his arms tightened about her body and she grasped his hair, pulling his mouth back from her breast.

'You want to make me, don't you?'

He nodded, and his hand began to stroke her hips.

'It isn't any good, honestly it isn't. Oh, yes, it's wonderful, but it's no good for you.'

His fingers caressed her moist flesh, and again she closed her eyes and sighed, arching her back and stroking his damp shoulders. For a while he was content, pressing his lips to her breasts again. She felt his tongue, and knew that her control was weakening. His hard flesh was thrusting against her thigh, and she wanted to cry out as his fingers began to probe her secret wound slowly and skilfully. But she had to resist now; the familiar frenzy of terror was rising in her body like ice-cold water on fevered flesh. Her breasts were swollen with pleasure, but the terror was more immediate; and quickly, frantically she dragged his head away, and pressed her clenched fists against his damp chest. For a moment they stared blankly in each other's eyes; then with a harsh cry she lowered her head into his lap and buried her nails in his buttocks.

'No.' He grasped her head and attempted to pull her away, but she resisted, tearing at his hard, flexed muscles as they strained against her fingers.

'No, no.' But his grasp had already weakened a little, and submission came with silent greed.

Later when they were sitting facing each other like strangers in a waiting-room, Michael said quietly:

'I think I understand now, a little better anyway.'

'Do you?' Nancy's voice was dull, and the gleam of triumph,

which he surprised in her eyes when he had slumped back exhausted, was now hooded.

'Yes, you get your own back. It's a dangerous game, Nancy.' He felt the necessity. He did not know that he was defending himself.

'Perhaps.' She shrugged and stood up. 'Let's have a drink.' But before she could fetch them the door-bell rang. For a moment both of them were united in shock; mute, frozen, holding each other's gaze. Then Nancy, pointing to his coat which was thrown on the carpet, went to the door and opened it.

'I'll go down and see.'

'No,' he protested; but she had already gone out. He put on his coat, and stood in the centre of the room looking at the door. In his heart he knew who it was. When he heard the voices on the landing outside he went to the cabinet and began to pour out drinks.

'I think it's very unwise of you to come here,' said Rosamund immediately Nancy had closed the door behind them. The two women stood side by side looking at him accusingly. It was a situation he had experienced before. In moments of emotional deflation women tended to align themselves. 'Mrs Reid is with Nunky, and may come back at any time.'

'I know. I met her as I was coming here.' His voice was muffled, yet defiant, like a boy found raiding the larder.

'Are you mad?' Rosamund's voice was sharp. Only he detected the slight quaver in it. She was not good when she was angry: it was a physical reaction which seemed totally at variance with her character.

'You'd better go, Mike,' said Nancy in a small voice.

He put down the glass he was holding, and left the room with a quick angry glance at Rosamund. The two women stood still, waiting until they heard the front door bang behind him. Then Nancy went over to the drinks, took up one and handed another to Rosamund.

'I think we'd better get out of here too,' she said to Rosamund when they had finished their drinks. 'This is not a healthy place for anybody just now. I know how it is.'

She fetched a coat from the bedroom, and they went out

164

together, turning right on the Gloucester Road. They walked down to the Cromwell Road and went into a pub.

'I suppose you're in love with that guy,' said Nancy when they had seated themselves at a corner table with their backs to the wall; a refuge people instinctively seek when they are troubled.

'I love him,' said Rosamund flatly. It was, she knew, not the same thing.

'It was nothing, just nothing. Boredom and vanity. Would you accept that?'

Rosamund nodded.

'I know,' she said. 'I know. It was good of you to hurry me out also.'

'Well, I'm not a bad loser. No point in you fucking up things as well as me.'

'I suppose not.'

'I suppose you think I'm a slut. I am in a way, but I'd have played fair with Andy. I mean I'd have given him what he wanted. It wasn't altogether the money, you know. He made me feel kind of secure. Oh, hell, what does it matter now?' They leaned back as the drinks came, and felt a certain comfort in the contact of their arms. 'All the same, I'm going to stick around. He hasn't said a thing. I know what he's thinking. It's going to be kind of interesting to see what he's going to do.'

'That's what we're all waiting for,' said Rosamund, whose anger had gone. 'Not very glorious of us, I suppose.'

'I need the dough. Oh, if it hadn't been, I suppose I'd get along. But I just can't roll myself up in blankets now, and go to sleep and have no dreams. It's like that.'

'I know. It's an infection. I suffer from it myself.'

'Well, I guess you'll get it now.' She looked aimlessly round; then turned back with a sudden little gasp. 'The Reid woman. I forgot about her. Gee, she's weird. Do you know, she stopped me in the hall, oh months ago, when I first moved in, and lectured me on the dangers to a young girl in London? I never heard anything so batty in my life.'

'She probably meant well,' said Rosamund with a smile.

165

'She'd suit Andy, you know. He's got this religious mania too. It's kind of creepy, sometimes, you know what I mean?'

'Yes.' For a moment Rosamund had a vision of two opposing cultures; two very different ways of life: both forever thinking the other criminal, even evil. At one time the righteousness had all been exclusively on the side of the Mrs Reids of this world; but now the rights were divided, unevenly still, but sharply. It was something that had not occurred to her so forcefully before.

'I don't suppose it makes a lot of difference now,' went on Nancy, 'but she'll fill his mind with all kinds of dirt about me, I know she will. It's disgusting. Something ought to be done about people like that, they're poisonous. Don't tell me, I knew one in France. Of course Dad had his love-affairs. So what? But the way that old hag carried on about it! And she was a church-goer too. I mean, the whole set-up is crazy, isn't it? How can you be supposed to love your neighbour if you spend your time criticizing them? Oh, hell, let's have another drink.'

XXVIII

'I see Matt Harris's wife is dead,' said Mrs Reid comfortably, folding the *Irish Post* in order to study the death notice more thoroughly. She did everything neatly; putting things back exactly in their place; steaming off stamps for the foreign missions; regularly opening her purse and counting the loose change. Pollard was fascinated by the blue mittens she wore all day now. She always wore them when she was working, she explained, because of chilblains. It was one of her few vanities; and it did not impede her clever hands in any way.

'Do you know them?' said Pollard. For the past week he had been getting up in the mid-morning; taking his meals at the table; walking through the rooms in the basement without a stick; shaving with an electric razor. A masseur came in every morning to work on his leg; and the doctor had given him permission to go out for a drive and walk a little in the open air, if the weather was fine.

'Yes, I knew Matt years ago in Tullamore. A very decent man.' She lowered the paper, her fingers curiously bald-looking against the harsh blue of the mittens. Her spectacles glinted as she peered over them. 'I heard the wife was wild, but she settled down before she died. Cancer.' It sounded like a judgement of God.

'I think we ought to go. To the removal of the remains, anyway. Where is it going to?'

'St Mark's, Ealing. Seven o'clock.'

'Oh, I know Father Lacey there, a great Gaelic League man.'

'Who's going to drive the car?' Mrs Reid was always practical.

Pollard thought for a moment. The newspaper crackled; the bald fingers neatly folding it back the way she had bought it. She settled her spectacles firmly on her ears, and looked at him owlishly. They were for reading, and his face was a red blur to her.

'Micky, I suppose. He drove me down from Liverpool very well.'

Mrs Reid did not reply. Pollard had grown accustomed to these silences during the past ten days. He had first become aware of this reservation when, feeling particularly well after an encouraging session with the doctor and masseur, he had repeated a rather risqué story about a man of eighty-four whose wife had just had twins. Mrs Reid was not amused; and a slightly chilly silence had fallen between them. Pollard now knew exactly how she was likely to react to any given subject: it was easy for him, since Ita had had precisely the same outlook. But he was anxious to know why Mrs Reid disapproved of his nephew. He did not think that she would have known of Michael's amorous exploits, which Pollard himself half admired.

'Well, it might be a bit awkward at the church,' she said slowly, folding up the paper neatly and putting it down on the table beside her. 'I mean, he doesn't go to Mass, does he?'

'Oh. Oh, I see. Yes, I know what you mean.' Ita had complained more than once of Michael and Rosamund's apparent paganism. When he had protested once that that was their own business, Ita had replied that to close one's eyes was to do the devil's work; and that there was far too much so-called liberalism, paving the way for Communism. He had no doubt that Mrs Reid would give the same reason.

'He's a very nice-mannered young man,' she went on, taking off her spectacles and putting them back into their case. 'Quite a gentleman, but he that is not with me is against me.' She snapped the case shut; and that was that.

'Yes, quite. Well, I'll ring for a mini-cab.'

'Oh, no.' There was a note of genuine pain in her voice. 'That would be an awful expense. And they all cheat, I know that for a fact. Now let me see. Maggie Harrington, that's the lady I told you who goes to Mass every morning in the Carmelites. Well, she has a nephew who has a car. I'll ring her.' She looked round the room, and Pollard pointed to the extension. Since his illness it was always switched downstairs; Nancy took no incoming calls. Mrs Reid got through to Maggie, who said she would ring back as soon as she could.

While they were waiting Rosamund came down and looked in the door with a rather uncertain expression. Since he left his bed her uncle had taken possession of the sitting-room; and so for the past week had Mrs Reid also. It had seemed a convenient arrangement: Rosamund no longer had to prepare a tray for lunch and dinner; and for the past two days Mrs Reid had taken to coming in in the morning to get the breakfast also. Now Rosamund felt like an intruder whenever she came downstairs.

'Oh, hullo, Rosie,' said her uncle cheerfully. 'Are you off somewhere?' This was his usual greeting recently; rarely was she asked to come in and join them.

'Hullo, Mrs Reid, how are you? I suppose Michael didn't look in, did he?'

'No,' said Pollard, shaking his head. 'I haven't seem him for a couple of days. What's he up to? I was going to ring up the hotel. I thought I might need him this evening. But now it won't be necessary.'

Rosamund did not tell him that Michael had not come to the

house for nearly a week. There was no point with the living-room occupied; and Nancy sitting forlornly in her office upstairs reading detective stories.

'I saw him the other day in that café beside the bank down the road,' said Mrs Reid. She did not add that Nancy had been with him. Mrs Reid was not yet completely *au fait* with the situation; but her instinct told her that the less one had to do with the American girl the better. Besides, she understood from a remark Pollard had passed that it had always been understood that his niece and nephew were more or less engaged; and should have made a match of it long since.

'Oh, yes, of course,' said Rosamund brightly, 'I know. I met him there afterwards. I just wondered if he had come in here.' She looked at the two faces pointed towards her, both perfectly polite; but obviously anxious to see the last of her.

The telephone rang, and Mrs Reid got up to answer it. Rosamund backed out, feeling worried. Sensitive to atmosphere, she had become increasingly aware of an alien presence in the house: something far more impressive, and oppressive, than poor Nancy had ever been. At the top of the stairs she stood and closed her eyes: she was tired; tired of loving, tired of intriguing, tired of watching closed faces, tired of waiting. Then, shaking herself, and looking at her watch, she crossed the hall and went into Nancy's office.

Downstairs Mrs Reid put down the receiver after many expressions of thanks to Maggie, who was inclined to linger in search of news.

'Well now, that's settled. Tommy Harrington will be here at six. Plenty of time.'

'That's very nice of him,' said Pollard. He did not like to tell her that a taxi would have been cheaper in the long run. He would feel under an obligation to the man; and that usually meant a request for a job for some friend or relative. But he could not help admiring Mrs Reid's sentiments; she was a very sensible woman.

'Let me see,' she said, looking at her own cheap wrist-watch. 'It's nearly four now. Mr Boyd will be here in half an hour. You'll be able to rest for a while before we go to the funeral.' Since Pollard's partial recovery Billy had taken to coming in on his way home from the office; a visit that both of them thoroughly enjoyed.

'I thought you wouldn't like Billy much,' he said as Mrs Reid sat down again and retrieved her knitting from behind the cushion. She was never idle.

'Why?' she said, carefully unrolling her wool. It was a bright and hideous pink; a jumper she was knitting for the African Missions.

'Well, he's a real hard Protestant, a Presbyterian, and a roaring Orangeman. Not your cup of tea at all.' There were times when he could not resist teasing her. Although he subscribed to every one of her principles and prejudices, and thought them fundamentally right and God-fearing, he liked to think of himself as a man of the world, with a great deal more tolerance and sophistication than she might be expected to share. It was pleasant dealing on equal terms with Mammon; sure of returning to the one true faith afterwards.

'He's a decent, hard-working, honest man,' said Mrs Reid, pushing her spectacles into place with her needle. 'He told me all about himself, how he went out to work at fifteen, and how he supported his parents, and bought a house for his sister and himself. I think he's a very nice man.'

'He told you all that?' Pollard's mouth fell open in amazement. 'When?'

'One day he came when the doctor was in with you. So I made him tea in here, and we got talking.' She held out her wool and measured it with one eye closed. 'And I haven't anything against Protestants, even Northern ones. They can't help it if they were born that way. And they're usually very honest, a great deal more than some of our lot.'

She held her wool in rigid outstretched hands, and looked upwards with her head inclined. During the past few days she had learned to tell every footstep in the hall, even the tenants. Now a quadruple series of sharp pointed taps sounded through the silent house; signalling arrivals and departures, and sometimes the mood of the wearers, like a private Morse code.

'That's Miss Emerson,' said Mrs Reid quietly, resuming her own

170

little system of domestic clicks. 'And'—she paused and hovered over a stitch for a moment—'and, the girl in the office.'

XXIX

Whenever she looked back, after the events of that London sojourn and all that followed it, Rosamund dated the beginning of the end from those few moments she had stood at the top of her uncle's basement stairs weary and depressed, before going into Nancy. They had gone out together, as Mrs Reid had noted, and to cheer themselves up took a taxi to Harrods and went on a shopping spree. Two bottles of Givenchy scent from the ground-floor perfumery; and afterwards a slow progress through the food halls and the garden furniture departments which fascinated them both. Upstairs Rosamund fitted herself out with a woollen jacket to wear over her jeans and shirt-blouse; and Nancy, after much fitting and changes of mind, bought herself the same in a different colour. The whole expedition set them back seventy pounds each.

Afterwards, sated and feeling a trifle guilty, they went across the road to the Scotch House and ordered a couple of double whiskies.

'You know, I haven't got any real fashion sense,' said Nancy mournfully, as they both lit cigarettes and leaned back with the air of two prosperous but hard-worked housewives. 'I couldn't think of a single thing I wanted when I saw your jacket.'

'We'd better not wear them at the same time,' said Rosamund, 'or we'll look like a couple of girls out of an institution.'

'Sure, an institution for the bankrupt, as far as I'm concerned. That orgy left me ten pounds overdrawn.' She took out her cheque-book, and began to add up figures in the record slip, moving her lips and looking up at the ceiling like a schoolgirl adding sums. 'No, I'm wrong, it's seventeen quid. Gee, do I need dough just now. You know, Rosie, I'll really have to ask Andy for some money. He hasn't paid my salary for over a month. Oh, sure I know he's been

171

ill, but the cheque came from Maiden Lane. What do you think I've been going in everyday for?'

'Everything's weird at the moment,' said Rosamund, taking the bottle of scent out of her bag, and carefully undoing the wrapping. 'I'm thinking of going back to Dublin, although I had intended to stay on in London for this exhibition. I really don't know what to do.' She began to prise open the cording with her nail-file.

'How's that old bag Reid doing?' Nancy puffed at her cigarette in a curiously amateur way, blowing smoke into the air. Her plump fingers were slightly dirty.

'Very well.' Rosamund dabbed scent on her wrists and at the back of her ears. 'She certainly is a help about the house, and she's quite a nice woman really.'

'She's a bitch,' muttered Nancy, dilating her nostrils and sniffing the bright, spring-like scent. 'You know, it's people like her that cause all the trouble in the world. I'm certain it was her that put Andy off me. I can't think of anything else. Of course, that priest in Liverpool might have helped too.' She stubbed out her cigarette half smoked and took her glass from the barman. Rosamund paid, and they raised slightly weary glasses to each other. 'Do you think Andy will do anything about her? I mean, it looks kind of suspicious, doesn't it?'

'Oh, I've given up, Nancy. The whole thing is too messy, and humiliating. I'd be relieved if he married her in the morning.'

Nancy looked startled, and spilled a few drops of whisky on Harrods fancy wrapping.

'Who said anything about that? That old bag?'

'She's only about ten years older than I am.' Rosamund said with a smile.

'I didn't mean that, it's just that—well, you know.' Nancy dipped a finger in her glass and licked it. 'But that puts you and Mike up the spout also, doesn't it?'

'I suppose so.' Rosamund looked over at the bar counter: men standing with their backs to her staring at the row of bottles; in couples, leaning elbows on the counter, chatting earnestly; a few women, older than herself, sitting around with parcels, wearing a dazed look. It was the second time she had found herself in a pub with Nancy, chatting easily, and apparently with sincerity about deeply personal affairs. But she knew just how frank she was being; and supposed that was what being 'adult' and 'civilized' meant: keeping the social niceties, concealing one's real feelings. She wondered just now much Nancy was holding back.

'Have you been seeing Mike?' she said casually, up-ending her scent bottle on the back of her hand, and holding it out for Nancy to sniff. 'Divine, isn't it? Of course, it doesn't last nowadays.'

'I know.' Nancy inhaled deeply and closed her eyes. 'But what the hell. Mike? Oh, yes, I've seen him. There's no point in making an issue about it, is there? He's got a lech, that's all it amounts to. And I'm a born flirt. I shouldn't do it, it's too dangerous for me, but I can't resist it. He should have got that message by now.' She smiled her old-woman's grin. 'Me, I'm just a fag-hag.'

Rosamund smiled back. There was nothing she wanted to say. She had a curious feeling during the past few days that she had lived through this before. It was not an unfamiliar sensation; it went with a sense of detachment. She had lost the sensation of being at the centre of things; caught up in a situation she was too closely involved with to observe clearly. Now she felt herself to be diminished, like an actor withdrawing to the wings after his big scene, watching others move to the centre of the stage.

She had heard of actors who knew only their own parts; and had no idea of how the piece ended. She felt a little like that now; watching at the side, not quite sure how the play was going to end; but filled with a dim feeling of foreboding. This was the time to get out. Events were moving out of her control; the greed, which she was quite prepared to admit was the real motive behind all the moves she and Michael made, was less keen than it had been; but it had not disappeared. She had lived for so long with the assumption that her uncle's money, or part of it, was legally hers, that it was difficult to rid herself of it. It was a mean and ignoble ambition; not completely selfish, because of the natural impulse to keep a family fortune intact; but that was the most that could be said of it. Only the other evening when they had dined together at Bianchi's he insisted that there was now a greater possibility than ever that Pollard would make a will. Illness often encouraged people to settle their affairs. Rosamund thought that he was grasping at straws, but she had not argued with him. There was nothing to be done when he was conducting an affair, except to keep silent and wait. And after all, that was what they were all doing. She herself thought that Mrs Reid had come to stay; and that, more than any illness, would surely encourage Pollard to make some sort of settlement. But she had no intention of telling Nancy this.

'You know that one has a son,' Nancy said suddenly, holding her hand to her nose. 'He turned up at the door one day when she was out, and I was just coming in. A tall, fine-looking fellow, well dressed, not like her at all. Now, I wonder—' She looked closely at Rosamund, who merely smiled and shook her head. She would tell Michael, if he did not know already; but she was convinced now that all their parts were already written for them.

'Let's have one for the road,' she said sadly. She was possessed by a sense of failure.

'I got talking to him,' said Nancy. 'The son. He was very friendly, and I might as well admit it, very attractive. His mother wouldn't talk to him, he wanted to make it up. He asked me to tell her that he called, and the old bag didn't even answer. He's working in a hotel in Sheffield, left me the number and all. He was only in London for a few hours.'

'I feel like getting drunk.' Rosamund ordered the drinks and sat back feeling drained and empty. Michael would never change; she would always have to accept him on his own terms; they were making fools of themselves, hanging about waiting for an old man to hand them a fortune on a plate. All she could do now was what she had always done: soak up images which would come to half-forgotten life again in years to come, hardly recognizable after the long process of assimilation; but still rooted somewhere in the past, part of someone, somewhere.

She looked across at Nancy, and saw a pleasant pale face, wide eyes staring at her curiously, plump hands holding a glass of whiskey. It seemed to Rosamund to be the past already—an image of two women in a neutral place, outwardly placid and composed, sharing a table but little else. If she ever painted it she would call it *The Worldlings*.

XXX

Nancy did not turn up at Queen's Gate Terrace next day; and three days afterwards Billy received a letter from a solicitor, instructing him to forward her wages.

He brought it along with him that afternoon when he made his daily visit to Pollard; but made up his mind not to show it until he had made a little experiment.

His visit had already become a routine, which pleased him. Mrs Reid welcomed him warmly, which pleased him even more, since he had developed a healthy respect for her. This was a sensible woman, who had worked hard all her life, and clearly expected others to do the same. She might know little of the techniques of business and finance; but she had a great deal of common sense; and that in the end was the first quality necessary for success. Finally, she seemed, so far as Billy could make out—and he was not easily fooled—as honest a woman as one could hope to find: something rare in Southern R.Cs. He felt quite at home with her.

She chatted for a few minutes, and then went out. It was her habit to leave the men together for about three-quarters of an hour, and then look in to ask if they wanted tea. Usually their business was concluded in this time; but if it was not Pollard would ask for tea in twenty minutes, or whatever time he judged proper. This arrangement suited all of them perfectly. Mrs Reid liked to busy herself in the kitchen, humming tonelessly, and making egg sandwiches.

Today, however, Billy broke with routine, always a sign that he had important business on hand. To begin with he rang the bell, and when she opened the door remarked that he had left his key in the office. This was not a lie; but he judged it blameless if he did not add that he had deliberately left it there.

'Will you come in here for a few minutes?' he said, opening the door of Pollard's office. It was beginning to smell musty. He pulled out a chair for her to sit down, and went over to the window to look out. The line of pillars represented solidity to him; not quite the air of brash prosperity which the new buildings in the City gave him; but an indication that without these massive Victorian houses the City would never have existed. Billy did not believe all the woeful prophecies of doom which the economists were forever making about the British economy. He knew better.

'I hope you won't think I'm interfering, Mrs Reid,' he began, turning from the window; his chunky shoulders outlined against the off-white colonnade over the street. 'But I'm a blunt man, and I won't beat about the bush. Andy tells me that you're going to a Father Kiely.'

'Yes.' Mrs Reid looked down at her mittened hands, and twisted her wedding ring; the only ornament she wore. But Billy had seen her hands bared, and recognized the sign of work. It occurred to him that their backgrounds must be very similar: a poor home; work from the time they were able to dress themselves; and early acquaintance with the harshness of the world. 'I suppose I'll have to put him off for a week, I don't think he'll mind that.'

'That's what I was going to ask, Mrs Reid.' Billy stood by the end of Pollard's desk; to touch it while doing business with anyone would have struck him as disloyal. 'I was hoping that you'd stay on here. Andy is making a wonderful recovery, thank goodness, but he'll have to take care of himself. I wouldn't like to think of him being here on his own.' It did not occur to either of them to mention Rosamund's presence; neither thought of her as a serious person.

'Yes, I'd like to do whatever I can, Mr Boyd. It's a difficult case, he's not really in need of a hospital nurse, but it wouldn't be good for him to be in the house all day by himself.'

'Yes, that's what I mean. I was hoping that you might stay on, well, even permanently. I'm sure Father Kiely could be suited. We could all help to find him a suitable person.'

To Billy's surprise Mrs Reid's face grew red; and she appeared to be very confused. She twisted in her chair, took off a mitten and pulled it on again, and cleared her throat nervously.

'I don't know about that, Mrs Boyd. There's my—' She stopped and coughed again, covering her mouth with her mittened fist. 'Well,' she said in a breathless voice, 'what would people say?' She avoided Billy's eye and stared resolutely at his boots.

Billy's intuition was quick, and long years of financial negotiations had sharpened it even more; but he was not accustomed to dealing with domestic matters; and it took him a few minutes to grasp her meaning. Then it occurred to him that Andy must have been talked about quite a bit while the affair with Nancy was going on. To people in Mrs Reid's circle the set-up must have seemed highly scandalous. To take up residence as his housekeeper now might very easily expose a woman to gossip. Billy was well aware how self-sufficient church-going circles were in London, and how censorious they could be: it was a way of life very little known by outsiders; but the cells knew one another, and what was going on. He had heard his sister say that church-going communities in London were a bit like the early Christians in Rome; or the Communist groups. As a church-goer himself, he saw exactly what she meant.

'I can see what you mean,' he said bluntly. 'Yes. But surely you could ask Father Kiely for more than a week.'

Mrs Reid frowned; and gave Billy a sharp, suspicious look.

'It's a good position,' she said in a querulous voice. 'I don't want to turn it down. It mightn't be so easy to get another one.'

Billy saw the force of this argument, and the doubt that lay behind it. It was something he could share with her: the fear of losing a good job. Even Andy could not follow them here: he had inherited an assured position; had never really experienced insecurity.

'Oh, well, we'll leave it for the moment, Mrs Reid. We'll think of something.'

She stood up, and looked at him mildly: an interview was over; and she waited silently for him to dismiss her.

177

XXXI

'I can see it all now,' said Michael, stirring his lead-coloured coffee with distaste. 'She's sly, and dishonest as well as bigoted. That time I went to see her—she denied knowing anything. Oh, she was very clever about it, made out to be shocked by the idea of anyone expecting her to interfere. Yet who else could have told him about Hansen? I suspect he knew before he went to Liverpool. Remember those funerals they were always going to? He changed after that. Yes, she's playing her cards very cleverly.'

'I suppose so,' said Rosamund. They were seated in a sad little café near Foyles, where they had both been stocking up with books; a biography of Braque for her; half a dozen Agatha Christies for him.

'And how long is she going to stay?' he went on, opening a packet of sugar cubes, crushing the paper in his fist, and arranging the cubes on top of one another. It was the third packet he had opened. 'She told me she was off to be a priest's housekeeper—very apt, I must say. But did she mean it? She hasn't gone yet. How do you find her?' Michael rarely came to his uncle's house, since Mrs Reid's advent; he complained that there was no place to sit. But Rosamund suspected another reason.

'Oh, I find her all right. She does all the work, cooking, cleaning, everything. She's even hoovered out my room.'

'I hope you didn't leave anything important lying around.'

'I haven't anything important, except letters about exhibitions, that's all.' The coffee was foul; and they had come in here chiefly to sit down. The Charing Cross Road was, next to the unspeakable Oxford Street, the most tiring thoroughfare in London; she supposed it was the long treks she had always made there from book-shop to book-shop. The few other people looked equally dispirited, dotted among the dilapidated tables like flotsam on a beach; a middle-aged woman in a crumpled raincoat whose face might have been carved out of soaked wood; an elderly man with skin the colour of rusted iron; a young woman with wild dyed hair

178

like seaweed, and a pair of vague, jellied eyes. Rosamund had always found cafés like this, with poor service and poorer food, infinitely more depressing than the seediest pub. Here people crouched over cups of slops, hardly touching them, staring out at the relentless traffic and the slow, drifting, vague-eyed passers-by. It was a place without much hope. The waitresses were young, pallid and apathetic; there was a smell of rancid oil from the kitchen; and all of the tables were encumbered with bottles of sauce: symbols of inadequacy and dejection. To Rosamund the place was a series of disconnected blobs of greyish-brown.

'I bet she has a method in her madness,' Michael was saying, looking with distaste at a plate of fusty, crumbling cakes which had been set down between them. 'If Nunky wants a woman about the house she'll make her own terms, see if she won't. Those holy-maries always have their eyes on number one.'

'You think he might marry her?'

'I think she might marry him. He's not well, she's making herself indispensable. Another few weeks and he won't be able to bear the thought of doing without her. And as she's so "respectable"—' He broke off and turned down the corners of his mouth.

Rosamund said nothing. Privately she thought that if Uncle Andy wanted to remarry, Mrs Reid was far more suitable than Nancy had been. But she was tired of the whole business; and she would have agreed enthusiastically if Michael had thrown in the towel also, and suggested that they go back to Dublin. It was not like him to display such perseverance; usually he tired of things more quickly than she did.

'You know she has a son, don't you?' he went on, looking over her shoulder.

'Yes.' She did not explain. Already she knew that he was still seeing Nancy, simply because he never mentioned her. Neither of them had made any reference to the scene in the flat when she had come to warn him: both of them knew that her motives were mixed. Rosamund supposed that Nancy intrigued him more than others, because she was not willing to have the usual casual affair with him. Perhaps he did not believe in the fear she claimed to have of sex.

And he was not prepared to admit failure: his women were always submissive.

'Apparently they're not on good terms. Now, I wonder what would happen if he turned up on Nunky's doorstep, demanding money? It might take the gilt off the ginger-bread.'

'Perhaps.' She was bored and disgusted with these intrigues; especially since no one seemed to have the energy to carry them through. 'No doubt he'll hear about it.'

Michael was wearing a polo-necked pullover; the high neck made his face appear slightly bloated, and emphasized his double chin. He plucked at it, as if he were conscious of her thoughts.

'I think somebody ought to tell him,' he murmured, raising his cup to his lips, and putting it down again with a grimace.

'Why don't you?' Rosamund's voice was dry and sharp.

'I couldn't, he'd know who I am. And the anonymous letter is not in my line. But I know a fellow in Sheffield.' He looked at her with a curiously sly expression. 'Let's get out of here, this place is hellish. Where are you going?'

'Grafton Street. There's an exhibition there I want to see.'

'OK. I'll walk as far as Piccadilly with you.'

In Bond Street she ran into Hansen outside Cartier's. London was like that, Rosamund had often observed. People moved in a series of loosely connected circles which were constantly touching. The musical were forever running into one another in the opera houses and the concert halls; those interested in sport had their own venues, pitches and pubs; actors gravitated to a few well-known bars; the press met in Fleet Street; and those who did not have a strict working schedule and liked to stroll often ran into one another in Mayfair. London was not as easy to get lost in as was supposed; unless one had already led a solitary life.

'Darling,' exclaimed Hansen with a brilliant smile. 'How lovely to see you. Please don't think that I'm toying with the idea of investing in one of those little baubles. But, look at that.' He took her arm and pointed to a dangerous-looking emerald bracelet in the jeweller's window. 'Isn't it heaven? Emeralds, not diamonds, are a girl's best friend. Now, let me see. Are you off to Sam Snodgrass's exhibition—wouldn't you think he'd change his name, the silly cow?—but I assure you he's clever, oh so clever. All that fashionable dowdy chic. You won't like it. But the public will. They think he's significant.'

'You like pictures?' Rosamund said stupidly. She had been thinking of a project of her own: vague-coloured, half-human patches of colour were whirling about in her mind, awaiting the moment of acceptance, when she released them into some kind of pattern.

'Oh, come now,' he said gravely, looking at her sharply. 'You're not quite all here yet, are you? Of course I'm interested. Apart from anything else, I write up all the fashionable shows for my paper. They pant after culture in Copenhagen.' He looked at his watch. 'Come and have a drink, we've got nearly an hour. By the way, have you had lunch?'

'Yes, in a pub in Piccadilly.'

'There's a pub in Stafford Street, what is it, the Cock or the Goat? I can never remember.' As they walked across Rosamund found herself observing him. With his bright yellow hair, bronzed skin, and electric blue eyes, he looked very much the picture of a well-to-do Scandinavian out for a stroll; and his expensive camel coat, blue Nehru shirt and gleaming shoes added to the picture.

The Goat Tavern in Stafford Street was packed to the door, so they went around to Brown's Hotel, and ordered a couple of gin slings in the St George bar. In that quietly expensive atmosphere, with its glowing panelled walls, deep carpet, blue-suited men and a few haggardly elegant American women, Hansen seemed to blend with the background. He was wearing a well-cut grey tweed jacket under his coat; and the bright hair, the aggressive tan, the general gleam and glitter were muted here; as were his gestures. A chameleon, she thought; thinking of his appearance in her uncle's sitting-room. That had been overdone; or perhaps he had been nervous.

'I suppose you'll want to know about Nancy,' he said when their drinks had arrived. 'Well, she's moved in with me. Now don't jump to conclusions; I have a spare room. Did you hear that she sent a solicitor's letter to your uncle?' He looked at her keenly; a flash of a light-bulb.

'No, I didn't.' She was adrift in earnest now; hearing her uncle's business from a stranger. Irrationally, she felt hurt. After all, Pollard was now her closest relative, nearer in blood even than Michael; and she had always been fond of him. 'I can't see him discussing that until it's settled.' Her voice was unconvincing.

'Not even with Mrs R?'

'I doubt it.'

'And not with Mike. He'd have told Nancy.'

He was looking at her now with a frankly malicious gleam in his eyes. He had sensed her apathy, and was hurt by it. Now he was, like a conductor drawing sounds out of a band, making sure that she reacted. Rosamund looked at him blankly for a moment, stiff and antagonistic. Then she relaxed, helped herself to an almond, and shrugged.

'OK.' He put down his drink and held up his hands, palms out like a Javanese dancer. 'I think I know how you feel. I'm a bit worried myself. Nancy is such a little idiot in many ways. Does she think she can act the Victorian maiden with him? It's obscene. You know what I mean. She has this frantic fear of sex, and an equally frantic obsession with it.'

'I wouldn't call it an obsession.' Rosamund was aware of his skill in adjusting the delicate balance of the passing mood. But she could not pretend to be uninterested now. 'It's more like an adolescent crush, like we had at school for one of the nuns.'

'And me for the great big butch drill-master.' He rolled his eyes and grimaced. A tall young man with American skin and shoulders passed by on his way to the bar. He was as handsome as a tailor's dummy; and dressed on the whole like one. Hansen looked after him, and turned back with a sigh. 'So terribly trite and boring, so obvious and empty. But when you're young it can be devastating. People say these things leave no scars, but they do, oh yes, they do. Sometimes far more than the adult experience. I worry about Nancy.'

'Yes, I believe that. Why don't you do something about it?'

He fell silent; age falling on his face like a passing shadow, as he sat with his head down, his chin pressed to his chest. When he looked up his mouth was hard, and tiny muscles rippled above his jaw.

'What can I do? Besides, I'm a fatalist. It's a new experience for him, and he's letting go, letting go. He should be with you, working on the old man, doing something about Mrs R. She has a son, you know. They're not on good terms. Perhaps something could be made of that.'

They were clutching at straws now, Rosamund thought. She did not think that Mrs Reid's son, however ill-disposed, would make much difference. The day was won and lost, not by intrigue, or shrewd planning, but by something in the character of all of them.

'What will Nancy do, if she gets money?' she asked, fingering the top of her glass as if it were a bowl she had just cast.

'Go off, travel, have a good time, on half of it. She believes in enjoying herself now.'

'Will you go with her?'

'Ah.' He laid a finger on his cheek and closed his eyes. 'That's what I'd like to do, yes. But, now, I'm not so sure.' He opened troubled eyes, and shook his head. Rosamund was curiously touched. Perhaps there was something honest and even pure in the relationship of those two; both in many ways adolescent; finding something restful in an affection free of normal tensions. Hansen possessed a certain worldly sophistication; a quick wit; and a great deal of nervous courage. But essentially he had remained a child; with a child's greedy candour, and a child's sudden blind cruelty. And his charm, as it waxed and waned, had all the pouting brightness of adolescence; and a great deal of its vulnerable grace. What hope had he and Nancy against the hard, shrewd wisdom of Pollard and the associates he could summon to his aid? What hope had any of them, creatures of sensations and images and flashes of colour? They all grew bored too easily, especially with the things that most people regarded with serious awe.

'Have you ever felt like throwing everything there, and making off?' he said suddenly. 'I mean, just walking out on Mike?'

'Yes, frequently.'

He leaned forward and brought his face close to hers; his eyes were as hard and glittering as a cat's at night.

'Well, do it now, before you get really hurt. Nancy will survive. She'll always come back to me. He's exciting, he's charming, but he's not the boy you were once in love with. I've seen your work, my dear. There are places he can never go with you, and you wouldn't want him to. Would you still love him if he were an artist too? Ah, ha. You've made something out of your life. He hasn't. Oh, I know, he's an intensely private person, he will never belong to anyone, he has a solitary soul. But, my dear he's absolutely no fucking good. He's never had to work for anything. Never. That can rot you inside. As if you didn't know.'

Rosamund recoiled from him as sharply as if he had clawed her face. She looked around helplessly for her gloves; Hansen rescued them from the floor beside her chair; anticipating a barman who smiled and turned away. She rose awkwardly to her feet and hurried out of the bar, her eyes wet with tears.

It was a long time afterwards before she realized that, by another of those London coincidences, her experience of that city with Michael had begun and ended in the same hotel.

XXXII

Pollard took off his spectacles and handed the letter to Billy. He tapped his teeth gently with the tortoiseshell frame and watched the other's face for reaction. Billy looked up presently with a smile.

'Wilkins. What a man for them to go to!'

'They're amateurs. I suppose they heard he takes borderline cases.'

'And sells them down the river. Do you remember that case of Dillon who broke his leg at the races and swore he was driving one of our trucks?'

'Yes, and two witnesses prepared to swear a hole in a pot.' He folded his glasses and held them on his knee, tapping the hinge against his bad leg. He felt a dull prick and nodded to himself. Now that he knew that breach of promise was no longer a legal matter, Pollard was disposed to be generous. It was a game. Wilkins knew that Pollard wanted no publicity. He was being asked to pay for silence—an expensive commodity.

'Well, what'll we offer him?'

'This letter is three days old,' said Billy, with a question in his voice.

'Yes, I know. I had other things to think about. Mrs Reid is worried about Father Kiely. She told me you were speaking to her about it. I thought you were talking about my health.'

Billy smiled. His old friend missed nothing. And he was getting his priorities right once again.

'We were in a way. I hope she'll stay.'

'I think so.' Pollard had a good-humoured air about him; things were going well, but not settled yet. Billy thought he could tell how things were going to end. In the meantime there was work to do; not very serious, but necessary. 'What do you think—about Wilkins, I mean?'

'Oh, I imagine a thousand for himself, four or five for her. Of course I'll tell Ted to start with five hundred and two thousand. How about that?'

'It seems all right.' His voice was casual but Billy suspected that he wanted to be fairly generous. Pat Cooney had handled most of Pollard's private business for several years, and could be relied on to strike exactly the right note. They were settling out of goodwill: nothing else.

'There isn't much of a case. But we don't want any further publicity. I think Wilkins, with the thousand in his pocket, will point out to them that they're lucky to get anything at all in open court. Now is there anything else?'

'I don't think so, Billy. You have it all there. Now, about that Chiswick property—should we accept that offer?'

The two men, falling gratefully back into the habit of years, leaned forward, putting on and taking off spectacles, and fingering sheets of estimates which Billy took from his brief-case. Nancy, and her dreams, were disposed of neatly, finally and without fuss. Hansen was not even mentioned: he was not important.

In the kitchen Mrs Reid sat down to rest and survey her work. Over the past few weeks she had scoured, scrubbed and polished the place until it looked like an advertisement for a modern cooking alcove. Nancy had been an enthusiastic cook; but she was less interested in cleaning up. Mrs Reid had found the oven of the cooker thickly coated with congealed grease; it had taken three applications of Force to render it efficient again. And the presses had been full of half-used packets of flour, soup powder, and sugar; all well on the way to decomposition. Mrs Reid had had to buy four mousetraps and a tin of rat poison, which fortunately was not taken; but mice had been executed in considerable numbers.

Now everything was in order; and she slowly peeled off her rubber gloves and looked sadly at her hands. She had three ambitions in life: to bring her son back to the faith of his fathers; to live in a flat or house with a smokeless coal-fired range, and finally to find a cream or ointment to make her rough hands smooth and white again. She had spent, according to her own computation, a fortune on Boot's and Dorothy Gray's hand creams, and looked up dozens of others advertised on television and in the papers and magazines; all to little avail. She supposed that if she could afford it she could go to a skin specialist and get special treatment.

She took up her mittens from the press behind her and put them on. Then she looked round the small wedge-shaped kitchen again. It was at the back of the basement, with a side window taking light from the surprisingly tiny yard behind. But between the small room which was used for dining and the kitchen one had to pass through a large room which housed the central heating plant, and looked like the bottom of a big ship with all the pipes running under the ceiling. But Mrs Reid had surveyed it with a fairly expert eye, and she reckoned that part of it could be let into the kitchen to provide space for a range. One had to have a doctor's certificate to install a smokeless range in London; and she had no doubt that Pollard would be able to get one easily.

She glanced at the tray, neatly covered with a white cloth, which lay in readiness for the tea which she would shortly bring into the sitting-room for the two men. They always asked her to join them, although she was careful to bring in only two cups.

It was pleasant to sit talking with them; and as yet she had not quite got used to it. Mr Boyd was a great help; chatty, good-humoured and friendly: quite the opposite of what she had expected him to be. If she had been more experienced in the ways of a world very different from her own, she would have recognized Billy's friendliness and obvious approval as a very important factor in the curious change which had come upon her way of life. She had almost forgotten that he was an Orangeman, and regarded him as a sensible, honest man whose outlook on most things was exactly the same as her own. For some time she had been troubled about the possibility of his being a Freemason—something which in Mrs Reid's book was infinitely worse than leprosy—but she had been reassured by her confessor in the Carmelites that such an idea was now out of date, and that Freemasons were no longer condemned by the Church. While this did not altogether convince her, it did put her mind at rest. She was glad for Billy's sake: it would have been distressing to think of him as a lost soul.

About Pollard, she did not know what to think. Mrs Reid was almost completely unacquainted with romance, and would not have recognized it if she encountered its spirit in another. What little she did know of it was confined to television plays, and serials in women's magazines: and it struck her as silly, immoral and stupid. She had married because she had been brought up to regard this as the fulfilment of every woman's life. Her husband had been vetted by her parents and his family pronounced decent. That he turned out to be an alcoholic was an occupational hazard; and it was far less shameful than adultery or a loss of faith. Indeed, drunkenness was looked upon as a little male weakness, which might put a family out on the road without a roof over their heads; but it brought sympathy, not real moral disapproval.

If Pollard had made even the slightest attempt to approach her in an unseemly manner she would have put on her hat and coat and left the house forever. But he had not. This, in spite of his illness, was to be accounted in his favour. Mrs Reid in her peasant wisdom knew that women of fifty odd, and a great deal older, were just as likely to stir the viler passions in men as girls of sixteen; especially if the women and girls encouraged such approaches. In her philosophy, most of the evils of the flesh were brought about by the behaviour of her own sex. If women did not respect themselves what could be expected from men? She had no doubt at all that Pollard's deplorable affair with the American girl was entirely due to Nancy's forwardness and lack of Christian morality. She was an abandoned slut who had deliberately encouraged the baser instincts of an old man who should have been occupied in making up his soul.

That he was now contrite and in a state of grace was obvious and reasonably certain: he was going to Mass and communion on Sundays and Church holy days; and he often spoke respectfully and sadly of his dead wife—always a good sign, especially when the late Mrs Pollard was well known to have been a deeply religious woman.

Nevertheless, Mrs Reid was not altogether easy in her mind. She had not, according to her own conscience, done anything wrong. It was mere good sense to keep her counsel when young Pollard came to her, making enquiries. He was a pleasant gentleman; but he was not the sort of person she would trust in such a delicate affair; too irresponsible, a man without weight who had done nothing but enjoy himself all his life. She rather liked him; but she did not approve of him.

She was also puzzled by the disappearance of Nancy. When she had time to think about it, Pollard's story of her having a no-good brother was not very convincing; the sort of thing a shrewd man of business would invent to cover himself. But he must have found out something about the girl; and Mrs Reid had a stubborn opinion of what it was. Of course, he might have repented when he was taken ill in Liverpool; and she would like to think that this was so. Not that it was important now; the important thing was that the girl was out of his life.

All this was satisfactory; and she could find nothing to reproach herself with. But she was uneasy about her own position, which was uncertain and left her open to gossip. Only the other morning Maggie Harrington had tackled her about it.

'Now listen to me here, Annie Reid. What are you doing keeping house for old Andy Pollard? I know he's a fine man in many ways, and his poor wife, God rest her, was a walking saint. But wasn't he living with that American one he was supposed to be getting married to? At his age! What have you to say about that, that's what I want to know?'

Maggie had stopped outside St Mary Abbots and laid a heavy hand on her friend's wrist.

'Well, I told you how decent he was to me about the flat, didn't I? And when he got that stroke, God bless us, I only called to see how he was. But the poor man hasn't one belonging to him to make him a cup of tea. His niece is one of them artists, and you know what they're like. Although she's a very nice person, I must say, but useless.' Mrs Reid felt an ice-cold breeze sweeping down Kensington Church Street, and piercing the marrow of her bones. But she could not brush Maggie off; that would be fatal.

'Well, God knows he has enough money to pay for a nurse,' exclaimed Maggie hotly. 'Don't tell me he's mean! So why should you be working yourself to the bone looking after him? Now tell me that, Annie Reid?'

'It just happened,' was all that Mrs Reid was able to mumble in reply; and she knew that was an explanation that would not satisfy Maggie for long.

She was roused from her thoughts by the sound of Billy Boyd coming through the boiler room.

'Will I carry in the tray for you, Mrs Reid?' he said heartily.

'Not at all.' She sprang to her feet and went over to plug in the kettle. Ordinarily Billy would have gone back, having made his diplomatic offer. But today he lingered, clearing his throat, and planting his sturdy feet wide apart on her polished floor.

'I wonder if I could ask you to do something,' he began.

Mrs Reid turned back, took the cloth from the tray, and held it in her hand to indicate that she was listening.

'It may come as a surprise to you, but Andy, who is the best business brain I have ever known, has never made a will. Isn't that odd?' He took a handkerchief from his breast pocket and moistened his lips. Mrs Reid made no comment. She was very much surprised. 'So,' went on Billy quickly, 'if he ever mentions anything like that to you—I mean, like providing for charity and things like that, maybe you'd ask him if he has it down on paper. That's all.' And he turned and marched out, leaving the kettle to bubble under its lid, before Mrs Reid, who was left speechless, could attend to it.

XXXIII

After tea Mrs Reid brought the things back to the kitchen to wash up. Something Billy had said while they were chatting in the living-room had made her thoughtful. His sister Gertie had to go into hospital for a few days soon for a small operation, the nature of which he did not specify, but which Mrs Reid, an expert in such matters, assumed to be what she herself always termed 'a woman's complaint'.

'How are you going to manage?' Pollard had asked.

'Well, I'll have to stay away from the office for a few days, on account of the dogs. Can't leave them to strangers.'

'Yes, I know. But how are you going to manage for meals?'

'There's a nice hotel along the line in Wimbledon. I had my lunch and dinner there before, when Gertie had flu.'

'Is it the Tilden?' said Pollard eagerly, looking at Mrs Reid.

'Yes, did I tell you about it? They give a very good meal for two quid.' Billy looked very serious: money was money.

'We were there for Peter Leech's funeral,' put in Mrs Reid eagerly. It was nice to be able to exchange experiences. 'It's a very good place, indeeden it is.' She exchanged a smile with Pollard; and felt very pleased with herself. The corporal works of mercy often brought their own reward.

'Well,' said Billy presently, slapping his knees. 'I must be

190

pushing off. Thank you for the lovely tea, Mrs Reid. I wish I could make scones like that. I had an uncle that worked in the Ormeau Bakery in Belfast, and 'pon my word he never did better.'

Mrs Reid went back to the kitchen flushed with pleasure. She took off her mittens and washed the tea things, humming tonelessly to herself. Then she took a tube from her large plastic shopping bag and sat down to rub cream into the backs of her hands: a new preparation from Boot's. It had a pleasantly clean perfume, a little reminiscent of old-style carbolic soap, which was her favourite scent. It always seemed clean; and the kitchen now had a decent antiseptic air: polish on the rubber-tiled floor. Jeyes fluid from the refuse bin, which had had to be scrubbed out three times; detergent from the vessels; and the fresh tang of newly cleaned wood from the cupboards and presses along the wall. If there had been a coal-fired range, warm and shining, it would have been an ideal kitchen.

As she rubbed her chapped hands Mrs Reid had an idea. She had been much taken aback by the domestic arrangements in Pollard's house. Like most people, she had imagined that the homes of the prosperous were as well-managed and carefully disposed as their investments; everything running as smoothly and effortlessly as an expensive motor-car. But such was not the case with Pollard. From several remarks he had made, she gathered that after his wife's death he had gone out for most of his meals, either to one of the restaurants round the corner on Gloucester Road, or near to the office in Maiden Lane. A daily woman who came in in his wife's time had retired; and the replacement who now came at irregular intervals was in Mrs Reid's opinion no better than a tinker. It was amazing that a man with so much money should be content to live in this way. But Mrs Reid was not stupid, although her mind was narrow and rigid. She was beginning to learn about the rich.

The maternal instinct was strong in her; the only real intimate human passion which she understood; and it had been frustrated in her relations with her son. In spite of the fact that they were both many years older, she regarded Pollard and Billy in this spirit; neither obviously had the faintest idea of how to look after himself. She had expected more from Billy, on account of his hard Northern horse-sense; but now it was clear that he was just as helpless as his partner. And Rosamund, of course, was no help at all; Mrs Reid strongly suspected her of having no honest instincts of any kind.

So, while she waited for her hands to dry, she decided that she would put it to Pollard that Billy should come here for his meals, while his sister was sick.

In the living-room Pollard was also thinking. He felt well and in fine spirits, and had taken the risk of lighting a cigar; soon the room was filled with the rich, monied aroma of fine Havana. Pollard rested his head on the back of his chair and looked up at the ceiling through the coiling smoke.

Billy's visits always made him feel better. At first he had put this down to pleasure at seeing his old friend so obviously concerned about him. But now it occurred to him that there was more in it than that. For a long time past, the best part of a year, his relationship with Billy had become less and less intimate. And with that had come also a situation which he now looked back on with horror. All his life he had made decisions, judgements, assessments; he had been a man of influence whose findings had often affected the lives of a large number of people: he possessed power. But for the last year he had been the one who had been disabled and defenceless, attending on the every word and mood of another. As he thought about it now, he grew cold in spite of his comfortable chair and expensive cigar.

Billy had brought him back to life again—his life. Like an athlete flexing his muscles after an accident, this sense of power had come back gradually. The making of decisions, the disposition of money and property, the consideration of great affairs, and the potent satisfaction of influencing the lives of others: all these were far more important to him than any other human activity.

With the return of normality, he began to think of those immediately dependent upon him. In spite of their private means, he thought of Rosamund and Michael in this way. Certainly they had obvious expectations; and they were 'family': Michael the only one now who bore his name. With renewed energy, and the sense of power which he had temporarily laid aside, he decided that he

192

would do something for them. But there would be conditions, especially for his nephew. He gave himself up to this pleasing thought and sighed happily. And Billy's suggestion of a tax-free foundation was a good one. He would think about that too; especially since he suspected there was more behind it than his partner had revealed. He knew how Billy's mind worked: a subtle operator, in spite of his bluntness.

He closed his eyes, and almost dozed off in his happy, optimistic state; but he was awakened by a slight cough. Mrs Reid was looking down at him with an anxious look on her face.

'Oh, oh,' he mumbled, sitting up, and spilling ash on his waistcoat, 'I nearly dozed off. You feed us too well.'

She sat down on the edge of the sofa, neat and tidy in her working clothes—a dark tweed skirt, and a navy-blue twin-set. But her mittened hands were coiling restlessly on her lap.

'I wonder,' she began haltingly, pausing to clear her throat again, 'if you would like to ask Mr Boyd here for his meals, while his sister is sick. It's no trouble for me, and I'm sure it would be nice for both of you.'

Pollard looked down at his waistcoat and decided to brush it later. Such a thought had never entered his mind; and now he could not understand why. A woman's intuition was a marvellous thing.

'Well, indeed I would not mind,' he declared heartily. 'I think it's a great idea. I'll give him time to get home and then I'll ring him.' He looked at her admiringly. 'It's very kind of you indeed to suggest it. Billy is a favourite of yours, isn't he?'

She nodded and smiled. Who would have thought it only a few weeks ago? She was certainly learning more and more about the habits of the well-to-do.

'He's a remarkable man,' Pollard went on happily. 'He's just advised me to make a will, and do you know, he made it sound exciting? Not the best time to suggest it to a man who's just recovered from an illness. But that's Billy's way. All the years I was as strong as a horse—not that I'm all that weaker now, I can tell you—he never brought it up. But really the tax situation is so bad now that one has to make provisions for the future.'

Mrs Reid looked at him perplexedly. She was a little out of her depth. She had still to learn a few things about the rich.

'You mean he was talking to you about, ah, settling your affairs now?'

'Yes, he was. Oh, I must explain, you don't know Billy as well as I do. He didn't mention a will as such. He was talking of bringing his own arrangements up to date—he's very warm, you know—and he mentioned that it might be a good thing if I looked into mine also, tax-free foundations and that sort of thing. But I knew what he meant.'

Mrs Reid had now got the message, and she found herself getting very red in the face.

'I think it's a very wise thing for a man in your position to have his affairs settled,' she said slowly. 'To tell you the truth, I was going to mention it to you, not that it's any business of mine.'

'You were?' For a moment an expression of anxiety, almost of fear, flashed across his eyes. 'Did the doctor tell you something?'

'He told me that if you took your pills, and took reasonable care, you would make a complete recovery, and probably see him down, with all he has to do.' She tilted her head and stared at him unblinkingly. 'And you ought to know that yourself. No matter what people say, a patient always knows whether he's getting better or not. I'm perfectly sure that if he thought you were not really well Mr Boyd would never mention such a thing. Besides, a man in your position should have made all arrangements years ago. You don't want to hand everything you have over to the Government, do you?'

Pollard looked at her for a few moments. He did not know that Billy Boyd had just brought off a double coup. But he had the reassuring feeling that he was firmly back among friends. The thought gave him encouragement. Surely now, with the tide high, was the proper time to make all possible arrangements. His possessions, his near relations, his business associates were all taken care of in his mind. He still had to think of himself.

'Talking of arrangements,' he began, having put out his cigar in respect for the solemnity of the moment, 'I was thinking of going over to Ireland when I'm really up and about again. I have interests there too. But there's something else. Do you remember me talking about the plot I had at home?'

'Of course.' Mrs Reid became herself again: this was her territory. 'I hope you haven't had bad news of it. With the way times are going, they're even desecrating graves now, the Lord between us and all harm.'

'No, no, it's nothing like that. It's just that I've been thinking of buying a new one.'

Mrs Reid's eyes opened wide, and her firm jaw dropped a little; then she pulled herself together. The obvious explanation was ready at hand.

'I didn't know it was full up. Of course, that often happens with family plots. Mine is a new one, of course, just room for my poor husband and myself, nothing fancy.'

'Mine is not exactly full,' went on Pollard, looking at her significantly. 'It's just that with the plans I have I thought of getting another plot. The old graveyard is full now, but they were lucky to be able to buy the adjoining field, and it has a lovely view over the river.' He stopped and gave Mrs Reid a quick, enquiring look. 'What do you think of burial arrangements for second marriages?'

Mrs Reid wished that she had brought her knitting with her: she felt naked to the world, and woefully in need of something to hold on to.

'Well,' she said in a muffled voice, 'I was always told that there were no marriages in heaven. So, I suppose, all three go in together.' She pulled at the end of her mitten, and flexed her fingers.

'And when there's a remarriage between two people who have been married already?' Pollard said redundantly. 'An uncle of mine, a widower, married a widow, and they got a new plot between them. I always thought it was a good compromise.'

'Well, I don't know,' said Mrs Reid helplessly. 'I'd have to ask the priests.'

'I don't think they'd have any objection.' In his present mood Pollard was prepared to take even the Church on. It was a wonderful thing to recover from a distant brush with death. It made a man ponder on first causes. 'Anyway, I hope to be going over in a month or two.' He paused and looked at his extinguished cigar. 'I was hoping that you might be able to come with me.'

Mrs Reid grew very red and clasped her hands fiercely together. She could not but approve of the tactful way in which he had broached his subject; but a proposal was still a proposal, and had to be carefully considered. In spite of her confusion she felt an upsurge of excitement. What was being suggested to her, over the last resting places of the anointed dead, was something which a few short weeks ago she would have dismissed as shortly as she did all those romantic tales in coloured magazines. But a short sojourn in Pollard and Boyd territory had accustomed her to the very real benefits of being able to buy three fillet steaks every day, without having to worry about the rent at the end of the week. And she was not unaware of the effect this miraculous change in her life would have on several of her compatriots who had short-changed her in the course of her life.

'I'd love to see the new graveyard,' she said, after a suitable interval, and in deep measured tones as befitted the solemnity of the occasion. 'It sounds grand, thanks be to God. A stake in the old country. But I'll have to think about it.'

Pollard sighed contentedly. He knew the day was won, and with it the promise of comfortable days ahead. Mrs Reid had not called him Mister, a very significant matter; it was early days yet for them to slip into the habit of Christian names. He took up his cigar and prepared to relight it.

Annie Reid, her future assured, proposed another cup of tea to help them to keep calm on this congenial occasion. As she rose to go back into the kitchen she thought happily of a splendid, glowing range, and the very newest in sewing-machines. God was good.

XXXIV

'Oh, Miss Emerson!'

Rosamund turned back from the door to find Mrs Reid hurrying up the hall, breathless and red in the face. 'I heard you coming in, but I didn't think you'd be going out so soon again. Your uncle is looking for you.'

'Is he?' said Rosamund listlessly. Since Billy had taken to coming for lunch and dinner, she had been dining out more often; and always alone. She had called at Michael's hotel that morning; but he was out. The clerk had looked at her closely, and remarked that as far as he knew he had not slept in his room last night. Rosamund came away with her mind made up to go back to Dublin within the next few days.

She followed Mrs Reid down the stairs, and found her uncle walking about the sitting-room, dressed in a grey pin-striped suit, with his hair newly cut, and a red carnation in his buttonhole. He looked bright, shining and remarkably healthy. Mrs Reid went down the passage to the kitchen.

'Sit down, Rosie, sit down. You haven't been favouring us with your company lately.'

'Well, I didn't want to give Mrs Reid too much to do.'

'Nonsense. Ann wouldn't mind in the least, she's missed you.' Rosamund looked up sharply. So it was Christian names now. She felt mildly interested; but at the moment the thing she most wanted in the world was to get back to her studio in Dublin and plunge into work. She had wasted a lot of time.

'Oh, well, that's very nice of her, and very kind. But I've been around the shops buying painting material and so on. I think I'll go home at the end of the week.'

Pollard stood in front of the fireplace, and looked at her keenly for the first time in weeks. She looked pale and peaked, and untidy, and he noticed that her fingers were slightly dirty. But he was pleased with her general appearance; at the moment he was enthusiastic about his relations, and in spite of her unkempt look Rosamund was still a handsome and well-bred woman. If only she would dress herself properly.

'What's Micky been up to? I haven't seen him for ages!'

'Neither have I.' Rosamund shrugged her shoulders, and avoided his eyes.

'It's time he married,' said Pollard heartily. Never a particularly sensitive man, his own satisfaction at the way his affairs were prospering had made him even less so. These young people were so stupid. Not enough to do.

'What?' said Rosamund sharply. She was attending now; and Pollard felt gratified. He had been too negligent of his duty lately. It was time to get these youngsters moving. He repeated what he had said, and added:

'Why didn't he marry you? What age are you now, Rosie, thirty-eight? Don't you realize that time is passing?'

'What's all this about?' Rosamund took a packet of cigarettes out of her bag, and flicked her lighter.

'I've been looking into my affairs—not before time, I may say— but I'd like Micky married, or at least intending to be, before I make final arrangements.'

'Surely that's something you'll have to see him about,' said Rosamund coolly. A month ago this announcement would have startled her; certainly it would have roused her interest. Now it seemed merely silly. She looked at her uncle through a light haze of cigarette smoke; and thought—not for the first time—how independent of surroundings he was. Michael, Nancy and Hansen seemed to blend into their backgrounds, like most people of ambiguous or uncertain temperament; but Pollard always dominated his, so that one forgot the place one was meeting him. She had almost completed a painting in Dublin before she came away on a recurring theme: a series of faces, blurring one into the other, all with a tiny characteristic of its own, yet all essentially the same. Pollard would not have fitted into that; or would he?

'Michael is really a quiet, sensible fellow, and a great deal more dependable than people think. He has a good head on his shoulders, and all he needs is some responsibility. That would make a real man of him. Now, if he had married ten years ago, when he ought to have done, he would have had something to show for his life, instead of drifting about as he is.' Pollard's voice seemed to come from a distance to Rosamund, as she sat preoccupied with her own thoughts; but she caught the general meaning of it, and asked herself in amazement: is he talking about the same person? A vision of drifting faces, all different, all the same, passed before her mind's eye. Was Pollard talking about the Michael he wanted him to be, or is everyone different in other eyes?

'It's ridiculous the way you and he have been hanging about each other all these years,' her uncle was saying in an aggrieved voice; looking at her with an accusing eye. 'If you couldn't get him to marry you, you should have broken with him, and let him make his own life.'

So that was it, thought Rosamund angrily. Essentially, she was at fault. A man who has done nothing with his life can sometimes be saved; brought back within the fold of the bourgeois world he has neglected; but an artist is a complete outsider: his work can never be understood, even when he makes money out of it.

'I can see that you have a lot to discuss with Mike,' she said with a bitter little laugh. 'Have you anyone in mind—anyone really suitable—to make him respectable?'

Pollard glared at her; and she could almost read the words that were formed in his mind: 'Not you, anyway.' Instead he turned away, and lowered himself carefully on to the arm of his chair. She realized that in spite of his healthy appearance he was a little shaky yet; but at the moment she could feel no sympathy for him. He was just an old man who wanted his own way, and expected others to fall in with it.

While they were sitting in angry silence Mrs Reid came back into the room. She too was always herself; neat, compact, resolute, sure of her own opinions: Rosamund suddenly realized where her uncle had got his new slant on Michael. Mrs Reid would naturally blame the woman. Rosamund should have married her man, and made a home for him; seen that he made a 'success' of his life; and if she dabbled in a little 'art' in her spare time that would be forgiven.

'Now, Andrew, it's time for your rest. You mustn't get yourself too excited over business.' Her voice was low but determined. Rosamund had a feeling that her uncle had met his match. And that mention of 'business': she knows what we were talking about; and of course she would be likely to believe that men's lives were made

199

or undone by women.

Pollard rose to his feet, giving himself a little shove with his arms, and looked at Mrs Reid with a smile.

'You're a terrible bully, that's what you are, Ann.' They stood for a moment smiling benignly at each other; then Pollard turned to Rosamund.

'If you can get hold of Micky, tell him I'd like to see him tomorrow, if possible. To his own advantage, you might add.' He took Mrs Reid's arm and went slowly out.

Rosamund got up quickly and poured herself a drink, feeling shaken and very much alone. As always in moments like this, she thought of her paintings; that canvas in Dublin needed a good week's work to finish it. But she could not concentrate on the details; and she began to walk restlessly about the room, feeling a little as she always felt here, like a fish in a tank. A dull grey light petered down from the area, itself damp and streaked with greenish stains. The furniture looked like lumps of cleverly designed tufa, shaped to look like ocean rocks.

As Rosamund was standing in the middle of the room, holding her whiskey in her two hands, staring dully about her, Mrs Reid came back. She looked at the glass with a gaze that lingered just a moment long enough to express disapproval. She sat on the arm of Pollard's chair, and looked steadily at Rosamund, who stared back at her as if she were seeing her for the first time; as in a sense she was. Mrs Reid's eyes were brighter and bluer than she had remembered; her mouth a trifle thinner; her hair thicker and coarser; and her hands in their ridiculous mittens larger and more capable. I'm seeing her at home, thought Rosamund. Street clothes are a fine mask.

'Andrew is worried about his family,' Mrs Reid began, dispensing with small talk. 'He would like to see them settled, naturally. After all, you and your cousin are the nearest relatives he has. He's settling his affairs. Of course, he's almost fully recovered, and with God's help can look forward to many years of good health. But he's had a warning. I hope you'll be able to get your cousin to fall in with his plans.'

Rosamund looked at her silently, and made no reply. But Mrs Reid showed no sign of embarrassment. She cleared her throat, holding her fingers in front of her mouth, and went on:

'Has he told you our news?' she enquired mildly. There was no change of voice, no hint of triumph in her manner. Rosamund shook her head, and swirled the whiskey in her glass. The tang of it was a certain comfort.

'Your uncle has asked me to marry him.'

'Congratulations.' Rosamund did not think it necessary to ask if she had accepted the offer. The fact that she had seen it coming; had even predicted that if it came about Pollard would finally settle his property did not occur to her then. She wanted to get away from all that London meant, now, as quickly as possible. Later, she supposed Michael would show up again; and she would be grateful and glad to see him; and they would fall into the same old routine. Or would they? This time she had an uneasy feeling that it might not happen like that.

'Is your cousin still seeing Miss Cook?' Mrs Reid asked in the same flat tone. Rosamund was aware that a truce was being offered; but she was not in the mood to accept it. Clearly Pollard knew nothing of this; and Mrs Reid intended her to know that.

'I haven't the faintest idea. Why should he?'

The two women looked at each other for a short, hostile moment. Then with a slight smile Mrs Reid got up and walked slowly out of the room. Rosamund sat down to finish her drink.

XXXV

The spring sunshine, filtered through the yellow Venetian blinds, filled the room with a soft, mellow light. The blue carpet, the daffodil silk curtains had a deeper surface tint; the silver snuff-boxes glimmered on their polished table; and the framed photographs were milk-white behind their kindling glass. Dust motes, caught in the slanting rays from the blinds, sparkled like tiny cells on the face of the ocean. And on the high, chalk-white ceiling faint shadows lingered in the corners like fading summer clouds.

Nancy was taking a telephone call in the tiny hallway. It was from Hansen in Copenhagen. He was on one of his regular trips back to base, and had been delayed because of a change of personnel in the office.

'Of course it's all right, darling. Yes, I have seen him. No, not here, you silly. Just lunch and a few drinks one evening in the Minster. Wilkins? Yes, I did. I rang him, and told him to accept, as you said. It's not great, but I think he's right when he says we would probably get nothing in open court. I suppose I'll get the cheque in a few days. You will? Yes, I think that's best. When you come back. I know solicitors are hell about hanging on to money. All right, I'll wait. Hurry home, darling. Bye.'

She came back into the room and leaned against the wall, closing her eyes and inhaling deeply. There was something about the smell of this room which always soothed her; the rich, mellow scent of books in their leather bindings; the hyacinths growing in oblong tubs under the windows; the bowls of pot-pourri on the mantel and the tables, and in the bedroom beyond: it was a combination that suggested leisure, opulence and an awareness of living. Today she had added some personal indications of her own presence: the bunches of daffodils and tulips scattered about the room; they were city flowers, not cut at dawn, and had no smell of sap, but they were patches of garish natural colours that stood out in the exquisitely blended décor of the room. And from the bathroom came the fresh tang of Floris verbena essence, still lingering after a late bath just before midday. She had had to get out then while pleasurably soaking herself, and answer the telephone. It was Rosamund looking for Michael. She had left a note in his hotel; but it had not been collected. Would Nancy please tell him that his uncle wanted to see him. Nancy replied that she would if she saw him, giving the caller to understand that she was equally unfamiliar with his movements: at that moment he was out buying the newspapers. She told him when he came back; he made no comment; but went to Queen's Gate Terrace at two. It was now four, and he had not returned.

Nancy opened her eyes and looked at the window. A sudden gust of wind rattled the Venetian blinds and stirred the curtains lazily. She remembered that she had had no coffee after lunch, and went into the kitchen to make it. Soon that pervasive aroma, the smell of summer cafés and rich lingering meals, filled the rooms with its nostalgic fragrance. Only freshly ground coffee smelled like that, Nancy noticed: one had no memory of office cups made with boiling water and brown powder in sad utility mugs. She came back into the living-room with a silver pot and a tiny Moroccan cup on a brass tray; sat down on the sofa, lit a cigarette and picked up yesterday's *Financial Times* which Michael had left in a heap on the floor. She read the theatre reviews while sipping her coffee; and then allowed the pages to slip from her knees on to the floor again. She was asleep when Michael came back; curled up like a child in the corner of the sofa with a hand under her cheek. The enclosed peace of the past few days had induced in both of them a mood of animal indolence.

He sat down quietly at the end of the sofa, placing his hand gently beside her stockinged foot; warmth mounted through his fingers like a coiling thread of smoke. She stirred, yawned, and sat up with a jerk, rubbing her eyes with her knuckles.

'How long have you been there?' she said in a furred voice.

'About three minutes. Let's have a drink. I think I've earned one.' He was looking at her with a sidelong smile, a thin blob of dried saliva lodged at the corner of his mouth. She knelt up, leaned forward and licked it away; a swift, impersonal movement, like a dog welcoming his master back from a five-minute absence in another room.

'Get me a Martini, please. I'm too dozy.' She curled her legs under her, punched a cushion under her arm, and shook a lock of hair back from her forehead. Her eyes followed him lazily as he went to get the drinks: an expression, also a little canine, giving her eyes an appearance of patient, watchful attention. 'How did it go? Has he heard about us?' Neither of them had really believed that the summons had come because of that. Michael had been very careful; leaving the address of a friend in Bristol with the reception in his hotel. It had been mislaid as messages of that sort usually are; but he did not know that. And if Rosamund knew, she was not the sort to tell their uncle.

'No, no, nothing like that. It was most extraordinary. He offered me a third of his property.' He turned round with a bottle in his hand, and squinted through it.

'You've got to be joking.' She jumped up and raised herself on her toes, peering at him with quivering nostrils.

'Not a bit of it. He was in a rare good mood. What's a third worth? You ought to know.' Liquid splashed into glasses, as she went down on her heels, frowning and biting her lips in concentration.

'I'm not going to tell you, until you give me that drink.' She threw herself forward and leaned over the top of the sofa; tousled, and bright-eyed and eager; a bone in sight.

'I was taken by surprise,' Michael went on, leaving down the drinks, and coming to the sofa where he bent down and kissed the top of her nose. She wrinkled up her face, and put out her tongue; but he had turned back. 'He's all full of the future, making plans, making wills, laying down the law. I must say if this is the effect Mrs Reid is having on him, it's better than I expected.' He handed Nancy her drink and she sat back on her haunches and pressed it against her breast.

'Was she there?'

'No. But he's marrying her.'

'Christ!' Nancy spilled a few drops on her sweater, and wiped them carelessly with her thumb. 'Then there's something behind all this. There always is with women like her, their smug little brains never stop ticking. Mike, be careful. She'll do you in, I know she will, I just know it.'

'It looks as if she'll have the two-thirds. She can afford to be generous. Perhaps this is the only way she could get him to make a settlement. Oh, and there are two houses for Rosie. That was thrown in, like a bone, at the end. Poor Rosie.'

'Poor Rosie.' She sipped her drink, and looked at him from under her lashes. 'Well? Go on.'

Michael leaned against the back of the sofa and crossed his arms over his chest; it was an attitude he often adopted while drinking.

'There's a catch, of course.'

'Of course. I knew there would be. Did you expect anything honest with that one at the back of it?'

'I doubt if she suggested that I should get married.' Michael's voice was low and amused; his change of fortune had put him in high good humour; and the condition was intriguing to say the least.

Nancy looked closely at him, and said nothing. This interlude had been pleasant and even exciting, with Michael behaving himself well; sleeping alone in the spare room, falling with apparent good will into the only intimacies that she allowed. The crudeness of his first assault had not been repeated; but she was aware of his watchfulness; the restrained ardour of a man who was deliberately suppressing his natural impulses in the hope of future gratification. She was well aware that the refined and dangerous sensuality to which she responded was a new experience for him; with a man less knowledgeable it would have been impossible. But her experiments, which she knew struck him as depraved, were as natural to her as quick, easy copulation to others. Both of them were playing with knife-edges; and she was skilled at the game. All her life she had responded to the threat of a blatant male sexuality; and been equally terrified of it. She had explained this to Michael; and he had appeared to be sympathetic. He had put her at ease with firm but delicate hands; soothing her in a low patient voice.

'Who knows?' she murmured. 'Did he suggest you marry Rosamund?' In a life lived in shadows, committed to evasions and flight, she had learned to hate the crude, battering glare of common day, with its unambiguous demands and rites; its clear, primitive dictates for survival; its coarse breath and impatient gestures. All her life she had remained timidly in the overheated intimacy of the girls' dormitory, with its quivering sensibility, prurient curiosity and feverish isolation; a world of fears and sighs, familiar sobs and furtive caresses; a world of affecting surfaces, and deep, half-drugged narcissism. Beyond lay the terror and fascination of alien images, commitment, pain and submission. She did not know that she was far from unique in her little cocooned cell; she had merely preserved the neophyte's hidden piety in a world of men where she walked with the quivering courage of a nervous puppy.

'He mentioned it. But I got the impression that he was thinking of something younger.' He leaned forward and stroked her head, lightly and lingeringly, in a way she liked. But now she twisted herself loose, kneeling back on the sofa, dull-faced and solemn.

'Well, I'm not on the list anyway.'

He did not draw back, but continued looking at her, hunched forward with the blood mounting in his face. She had already noticed the broken veins, the shadows about the eyes, the pad of flesh under the chin; the wrinkles spreading out from the corners of his mouth. She had a blurred and far from clear impression of a man who was running to seed; with no ambition beyond the nursing of his own pleasures and interests; but with the faint traces of something deeply experienced and explored, once only perhaps and long ago; the tell-tale signs of human passion and involvement. And she found herself as always shrinking from it, and attracted to it; the furtive obsession of a woman who flees and looks over her shoulder. She could smell the faint tang of perspiration that he exuded in his excitement; it mingled with the sharp fume of the drinks, like an aphrodisiac; sweet, cloying and disgusting. This was the world of men and their heavy, brutal passions; the world sanctified by custom and usage; a place where she walked warily, bearing her shameful secret like a birthmark concealed by a lock of hair.

'No, not on his list.' He did not take his eyes from her face, and giving him a swift sidelong glance, she caught him moistening his lips, and was reminded of a rutting dog, tongue lolling, back arched, loins quivering. She eased herself on to the edge of the sofa and stood up.

'Have you anyone in mind?'

'No. Naturally, I asked for time.'

'Naturally.' She put her drink on the fireplace, and leaned her shoulder against the mantel. It was here, sitting on the rug, that she

206

had told Hansen about the man who had attempted to rape her. It was the sort of thing he found it easy to believe. But there had been no attempt, nothing; and there were times when she thought Michael instinctively knew it: it was the sort of condition that would appeal to a man like him—as cancer fascinates the specialist; and as men fascinated her.

When she turned back to him, taking her glass from the mantel-piece like a dreaded responsibility, she knew exactly what she was going to do; and how he would respond.

'Andy has paid for my holiday. I've decided what to do with the money. I have to pay the solicitor two hundred pounds—a bit stiff for one letter, but of course without him I would probably have got less, or nothing. Well, that leaves eight hundred to spend, and a nest-egg of four thousand, that I'm going to put in the bank for a rainy day.' She gulped her drink, and coughed, beating her breast. 'So I'm going to Cannes. Morocco can wait; I want to soak at the moment. I'll hire a car, and run up to Pop every so often; but mostly I'm just going to laze about, until the money is gone. I'll take a room, and buy my own food, it's not so prohibitive if you do that. Yes, I'm going to have me a ball.'

'Would you care to run into a friend while you're there?' said Michael, feeling that she was waiting for this. 'I think I can afford a month or two.'

'Breakfast at the Blue Bar,' she smiled.

'A picnic on Saint-Honorat. Those little chapels in the long grass.'

'The old men playing *boules* in the harbour.'

'Looking up through the magnolia trees.'

'Sitting outside the Carlton, across the road, watching the world go by.'

'It's terribly vulgar, but I used to do it when I was a boy.'

'Didn't we all,' Nancy said with a laugh, coming round from her side of the sofa, and handing him her glass. 'More, please.'

As he refilled their drinks Michael thought of all the years he had waited for this sudden change of fortune. Real independence at last; not the sort that depended on the complaints of tenants and the repairs to roofs. There were so many ways in which this honeymoon period of anticipation could be extended: he could not be expected to settle down immediately. In the meantime there were six months, a year perhaps, in which he could really enjoy himself. It was not much to ask of life; but it was terribly difficult to achieve. He did not want to marry Nancy; even apart from his uncle's reaction to the idea, she was too brittle, too superficial, too indeterminate for that. But she was perfect as a companion for a pleasant and restful interlude; and her slightly forced air of childish perversity pleased him. That would add sauce to the meal. He knew that love was an illusion; a fire that flared up like a chemical substance and left a taste of acid on the mouth. An arrangement was so much easier to make, and so much more sensible; and that was what he intended to settle for; but not just yet. In the meantime there was this passing accommodation; something which Nancy with her fund of spurious wisdom would fully understand. Attraction did not last; pleasure demanded a change of scene; only the stupid expected constancy. Those who lived by practical standards like these could manage together very well. Chance was the ultimate deity; and like the outworn gods of sacrifice and propitiatory gifts, It always looked after Its own.

The man with the flushed face and happy eyes, who turned about to toast his latest victim, had no dark secrets, no hellish ambitions in his heart, no smudge of ashes from a forgotten love on his cheek, no greater and more tormented knowledge at all than she. Love was a convenient illusion in another's eyes; something to keep on a lead for fear of lost property; an undemanding presence by a warm fire on a winter's day; a welcoming sound behind a closed door after an absence. Nancy, he thought gratefully, could easily be trained to provide all this. For the ultimate needs of the reasonably sensual man that he imagined himself to be, she would never be completely suitable; especially now that his horizons had widened. But for a while at least she would be a warm and faithful presence.

The late afternoon sun flooded the room with a honey-coloured glow, and warmed the back of his neck as he sat on the sofa, drinking to their future. Nancy curled up on the carpet and rested her head against his knees. He stroked her soft golden hair gently, until the shadows began to steal out from the corners, and the curtains stirred like evening sails. Presently his fingers, slipping down on to her warm neck, slackened and grew heavy; and from the regular pulse of his relaxed body Nancy sensed that he had dozed off. She drew away, crept silently on her hands and knees across the rug, hopped up on the cushions at the end of the sofa, bedded them down, and curled up drowsily with her head touching her knees, watching him contentedly with heavy eyes. She sighed and nuzzled her head against the cushion. She was fed, watered and gently consoled; after all, the most she had ever hoped for in life was affection.

XXXVI

Annie Pollard looked down at her hands, folded quietly on her lap. They were neither very white nor very smooth; but they were no longer rough and chapped. The week before her marriage she had embarked on an expensive course with a skin specialist in Knightsbridge, and five months later was pleased if not overjoyed with the result. Ten pounds a week out of the household money, and ten more from her own allowance, was an expenditure which she sometimes thought was matter for the confessional; but the ambition of many years was too strong; and she was moreover a patient and determined woman. At least she no longer felt the necessity for mittens, which was a blessing, especially with the magnificent sapphire engagement ring which Pollard had given her. She held up her hand with fingers outstretched and looked at it thoughtfully.

'It's a fine investment,' said Billy with a smile. They were both sitting in the living-room waiting for Andy to make his appearance. Both were dressed in their church best; a charcoal-grey costume, and a net black beret with a diamond pin for her; a pin-striped blue suit for Billy, with a black tie out of respect for the occasion. He had left his bowler hat in the hall.

'Less would have done me,' said Annie comfortably. 'After all it was a bit silly at my age, but Andy just arrived back with it, and what could I do? What's that you were saying about the yard in Camberwell?'

Pollard had interrupted them a few minutes before, looking for his black tie; and his wife had had to help him also with the back buckle of his new waistcoat, which was stuck.

'Well, these people say that they have two other offers for it, both a great deal more than ours.'

'In that case it's a wonder they haven't closed with one of them. It's adjoining our present yard, isn't it? I think they're trying to put the price up. What does Andy say?'

'He's inclined to think that any property bought now is an investment in the future, with prices going up all the time. And of course he's right.'

Annie looked down at her ring and twisted it slowly. Her black crocodile bag was wedged in the chair beside her, with her black suede gloves neatly folded on top of it. She thought of the cotton gloves she had to buy for her first husband's funeral, and the grey overcoat which a neighbour had lent her; but there was no point in dwelling on that now. She looked up at Billy with a frown.

'That may be all right, but I don't see any point in paying more for anything than you have to. Do you know who these other offers are from?'

Billy shook his head, and waited. In the four months since his partner had come back from Ireland with his new wife, Billy had developed an increasing respect for her judgement in business matters, which was shrewd, conservative and cautious. When Andy had wanted to buy a large house with a hundred acres in Kildare as an Irish residence, she had dissuaded him; and they were now negotiating for a smaller place in Wicklow. 'Where can you get gardeners now?' she had asked. 'And the heating costs!' Andy was disappointed; but agreed.

'No, I don't,' Billy admitted. It was a point about the Camberwell business that puzzled him.

'Shouldn't you?' she asked pointedly. 'I mean, in the property

210

world, surely you have a fair idea of what's going on? This piece of yard is really no good to anyone else. At least, that's what I think. I'd say there are no other offers.'

'Yes, I believe you're right. I think we should wait.'

'And in the meantime, surely you can make enquiries? I bet you can find out.'

Billy looked at her admiringly and smiled briefly. Then he assumed his mourning face again.

'How is he?' he said in a low voice, nodding his head in the direction of the bedroom.

Mrs Pollard shook her head and lifted her handbag on to her knee. It had cost a hundred and twenty pounds in Kensington High Street; another investment, but one which, although appalled at the price, she approved: no married woman was respectably turned out without a decent bag.

'He's taking it very badly, Billy. Of course, it was a terrible shock. I nearly fell dead myself when I heard it. Such an awful way to die, and so sudden without a priest or anything. But Andy is inclined to brood about it. Says Michael was the only one of his name left and all that. It's true, I know, and I suppose if the poor man hadn't been killed like that, he might have pulled himself together, and made a decent life for himself. Although, I'm not so sure—' She broke off, and exchanged a meaning look with Billy, who leaned forward with a secretive air.

'I suppose there's no way he'll ever find out about the details, the background and all that?' His voice was hardly above a whisper.

'I don't see how he can. I rang the Guards back and told them about his illness and all, and asked them to deal only with me. But there was little else to do except arrange for the funeral. She's in hospital still in that place in France, and I don't suppose we'll ever hear from her again. It was a good thing she was driving the car, or she might have followed poor Michael's solicitors for compensation. Andy gets all the property, doesn't he?'

'Yes, there was no will, and he's the nearest relative. Queer, isn't it?'

Annie Pollard shook her head and sighed. It certainly was a very queer world. She thanked God that it was she who answered the telephone that morning a fortnight ago. What would Andy have said if he had heard that his nephew had been killed in a car accident in the South of France with Nancy Cook at the wheel? She had rung back and asked the Irish police to release no information to the newspapers. Later Billy contacted an associate in Dublin who got in touch with some Irish journalists: nothing appeared except that Mr Michael Pollard, nephew of Mr Andrew Pollard and cousin of Miss Rosamund Emerson, the well-known artist, had been killed in a motoring accident near Cannes in the South of France. It all seemed curiously unreal; far away and inflexibly private, like most of Michael's life.

'Any word from Rosamund?' said Billy in the same tone.

'No. We rang her up when we went over for the funeral, but there was no reply. A friend of hers came to the Mass and said she was in Greece and had left no address. That upset Andy even more. Here he is now.'

Pollard came slowly into the room, perfectly dressed as befitted a man of property on his way to a Memorial Service; but he looked drawn and weary. He sat down on the sofa beside Billy and looked at his watch.

'Twenty past ten. We have plenty of time. I don't suppose there will be much traffic on a Saturday morning.' His voice was weak and querulous. Although he had suffered no relapse since his slight stroke in March, the events of the past two weeks had aged and upset him deeply; and after his trip to Ireland for the funeral, Annie had tried to persuade him to put off his plans for a Mass in London for the time being; but he insisted. It was to be said in St Patrick's, Soho Square, the unofficial centre for all Irish religious and patriotic activities in London.

'There's no hurry,' said his wife soothingly. 'We'll get there in plenty of time. Billy has the car outside the door.'

Pollard took out his handkerchief and blew his nose. His eyes were moist and rheumy, and he wiped them carefully, shaking his head and sighing deeply.

'Poor Micky, poor boy,' he muttered. 'Just when he was going to settle down and make something out of his life. He told me he was off there. I told him that was no place to look for a sensible wife, but he said he hadn't had a real holiday for ten years, and I hadn't the heart to stop him.'

'Now, you mustn't upset yourself, Andy. It's God's holy will.'

'His mother took him off there when he was a boy,' Pollard went on, paying her no attention. 'She's buried there, you know, in Italy, in San Remo, not far from where poor Micky was killed. Left that instruction in her will. We couldn't believe it at the time. Strange, isn't it?' He stopped and looked at his wife with tearful eyes. 'Maybe we should have buried him there with her, but I thought I was doing the best thing.'

Annie stirred uneasily in her chair and darted a quick look at Billy. There had been trouble already about the burial. Pollard had suggested that Michael should be buried in the new plot he had purchased; but his wife had objected. The idea of sharing her eternal rest with a man who did not practise his religion, and who had been killed in the company of a girl whom Mrs Pollard assumed to be his mistress, was more than she could stomach. She told her husband that she would not go into the grave if Michael was buried in it; and he had had to give way. But he had not forgotten it.

'The last of us,' he muttered brokenly. 'It's awful, awful. I can't believe it. God can't be so cruel.' He turned round heavily and confronted Billy, who was looking extremely embarrassed. It was bad enough for him to have to drive up to a Roman Catholic church that morning for the first time in his life; but getting involved in a squabble about superstitious Romish burial rites was altogether outrageous. Billy intended to be cremated, and had left instructions for his ashes to be strewn on Belfast Lough; and that was that.

'Billy, do you think Micky might have had a child somewhere? Would Rosie know? I bet they'd know in Dublin. Do you think there's a chance of it? He was a bit of a womanizer, God help him, a bit of a devil, and I wouldn't be a bit surprised if he had got someone in the family way. Maybe we'll hear later. I mean if he was paying anybody and the money stops.' There was something pitiful in the old man's clinging to this frail hope of his family's continuance; and for a moment Billy and Mrs Pollard were too stunned to reply. Then, gathering up her bag and gloves, his wife stood up and looked down at him with angry disapproval.

'Andrew Pollard, how could you think of such a thing! On your way to Mass and Communion! I never heard anything so awful in my whole life. May God forgive you.'

'And buried in a strange grave,' he went on, fumbling with his handkerchief which he had spread out on his knee. 'Not even let into his own family plot. I should have buried him in Italy with his mother, that's what I should have done. One of the last things he said to me before he went off was that he was going to visit it, and see that it was kept up. Oh, the poor lad. When I think of all that's gone.'

'That's enough of that, Andrew,' said his wife in a hard voice. 'Stop it now. What Michael wants is your prayers, not this kind of nonsense. It's going on for eleven. Come on now, give me your arm. We don't want to be late.'

Slowly, mumbling and muttering to himself, Pollard allowed his wife and Billy to assist him out of the room. At the door of his house he stood waiting while Billy went to fetch the car from Gore Street; the splendid new bottle-green Rover which Pollard had bought after his wedding for his first trip to Ireland. He looked down the street at the line of pillars, mellow and gleaming in the October sunlight; monuments to former grandeur and the sense of continuity; survivors now in a strange new era which did not plan or build for the day after tomorrow.

The journey to the church was accomplished in silence; neither Billy nor Annie Pollard quite knowing what to say. If the old man continued acting in this manner, his wife was determined to send for the priest; always more effective to her way of thinking than the doctor. She was thankful now that she had asked Father Kiely to attend the Mass; she would have a word with him afterwards. He and Father MacGregor, still awaiting his African visa from the Archbishop, were both assisting the local clergy in the concelebrated Mass.

Soho Square on a Saturday morning was a little less crowded

with traffic than usual; and all the vacant parking places were taken by the cars belonging to the more prosperous members of the Irish community. Those who regarded themselves as more or less integrated favoured British cars, with the Rover as the ultimate manifestation of success. Mercedes were favoured by the junta who retained strong Republican sentiments; a dwindling minority. They stood about in little groups on the pavement outside the church, the sober colours of the men brightened here and there by a wife who was determined to make her entry by her husband's side; a custom picked up in England, and generally regarded as very *avant-garde*.

None of the mourners, with the exception of Larry Daly, had ever met Michael. They were there to pay tribute and to express their sympathy with his uncle, who remained a leading member of their ranks, a man well thought of by Church and State. Michael had become an abstraction; someone whose sad fate touched their hearts in a general way, well tuned as all of them were to the reverberating chords of tragedy. Life, they knew, with the accumulated experience of their race, was brief and uncertain; full of pain, sorrow and loss; and this was an opportunity to express their understanding and their solidarity. Tragedy could strike any of them at any time, they knew, with sad, fatalistic wisdom. A young man with fair prospects had just been cut off in the prime of life; an incident both unremarkable and inevitable: such was life. They did not know the details of his short existence; but they could all identify with his end. They knew nothing of the thoughts and feelings of a girl in a hospital in Nice, who was weeping for a lover whose life had been snuffed out in a mess of blood and crushed bones at her side; a man who she now believed had brought her into the ranks of sorrowing and fulfilled womankind; and whose child she was carrying in her womb. She did not now think of him as a slow and patient voluptuary; but as one whose gentleness had made her whole. The memory of his sensuality was blotted out in the ultimate orgasm of death.

Nor did the congregation at St Patrick's think of the woman who had loved him all her life; who had not yet heard of his death; and whose trial of loneliness and grief was yet to come. Tragedy had touched them all equally; and life was a brief flirtation with illusion.

Mrs Daly, wearing her mink coat for the first time that autumn, was chatting with two other women; both fretting in Canadian squirrel, and furious with their husbands for exposing them to the condescension of Daly's wife.

'My husband knew him quite well,' she was saying in a soft, television Irish voice. 'A nice, well-mannered fellow, I've heard him say.'

'I heard he was a bit of a no-good,' said one of her listeners tartly. Really, Mrs Daly was an awful pain in the neck; well used she was to mink.

'What was he doing in the South of France?' said the other plaintively, for that was her style. 'Roaring along in a fast car, God bless us. All the same, I pity him.'

'So do we all,' replied Mrs Daly sharply; and for a moment something like peace filled their troubled hearts as she went on: 'A lonely death, far from home with not a friend near him, poor boy. I can't help thinking of my own brother, killed in a car accident in Cork, God rest him, but it's a cruel world.'

The two other women murmured agreement with this; their enmities stilled for the moment in that curious truce between the immemorial and the petty which the prospect of death and grief always induces. Mrs Daly's eyes were dark, huge and swimming; and the three overdressed women were for an instant insulated in an attitude of sadness, and silent, mysterious fatalism. It did not last long.

'Is it true that old Andy was taking him into the business?' said one of the women.

'Yes, it is,' said Mrs Daly, briskly emerging from her grief: she was the one in the know. 'Sad, isn't it? And I hear the poor fellow was going to get married and carry on the name.'

'Well,' said the other coarsely, 'sure as God made little apples Annie Pollard isn't going to do it.'

'She's a very fine woman,' said Mrs Daly sharply. 'Of course, she's a bit backward. Knows nothing about art. Not what you'd call cultured.'

The two women exchanged glances, and one of them coughed significantly. They had heard Mrs Daly on art before.

'Hasn't Andy a niece who's an artist?'

'Oh, yes, a brilliant one. I have several of her pictures. I wonder if she'll come with him. They do say that she and her cousin—oh, but I mustn't give scandal. Father Tommy would kill me.'

Her two companions exchanged another glance. They had heard of Mrs Daly's priest son before also, many a time.

'Did you hear that Father Willie Wright—you know, Jimmy Wright's son—has left the Church? Gone off with a nun, I hear.'

Mrs Daly pulled up the collar of her coat and moved away in dignified reproof. Really, these two were as common as cow-dung. She had timed her move well, for at that moment Pollard's car drew up, and the small crowd of men on the pavement moved aside, leaving a lane into the church, as if they were receiving royalty. Pollard got slowly out and stood for a moment leaning on his umbrella, while Annie descended from the back seat. Mrs Daly stepped into the empty lane and came forward, her eyes moist, her hands held out expansively before her. She kissed the two mourners, murmuring soft, wordless cadences of grief. Then slowly, with his wife on one side and the triumphant Mrs Daly on the other, Pollard went from group to group, shaking hands, nodding and inclining his head gravely. He knew he had been right in arranging for a memorial Mass in London; all his friends and neighbours were grateful for this opportunity to return the sympathy he had extended to so many of them in their own bereavements over the years: it would have been churlish to cheat them of the friendly satisfaction of making a return. And so, surrounded by the dark phalanx of mourners—not one of whom was at that moment thinking of the dead man—Pollard passed slowly into the church.

Billy parked the Rover in a space thoughtfully left vacant by the waiting men, and closely guarded by them until the chief mourner arrived. He got out, and walked round to Frith Street in search of a drink. The service would be over in about thirty-five minutes; and he intended to go back in good time and wait in the car. In the interval he wanted to think about the Camberwell property. He had spotted a man in the crowd outside the church who lived in the area, and who had got his first job from Pollard in the days of the construction company. It seemed to Billy that he would be an ideal fellow to sound out the ground.